S0-AKK-133

# A RUIN OF ROSES

# Also by K.F. Breene

**DARK BEAUTY AND THE BEAST RETELLING**
A Ruin of Roses
A Throne of Ruin
A Ruined Kingdom

**DEMIGODS OF SAN FRANCISCO**
Sin & Chocolate
Sin & Magic
Sin & Salvation
Sin & Spirit
Sin & Lightning
Sin & Surrender

**LEVELING UP**
Magical Midlife Madness
Magical Midlife Dating
Magical Midlife Invasion
Magical Midlife Love
Magical Midlife Meeting

**DEMON DAYS VAMPIRE NIGHTS WORLD**
Born in Fire
Raised in Fire
Fused in Fire
Natural Witch
Natural Mage
Natural Dual-Mage
Warrior Fae Trapped
Warrior Fae Princess
Revealed in Fire
Mentored in Fire
Battle with Fire (coming soon)

# A RUIN OF ROSES

## BY K.F. BREENE

Copyright © 2021 by K.F. Breene

All rights reserved. The people, places, situations and craziness contained in this book are figments of the author's imagination and in no way reflect real or true events.

Contact info:
www.kfbreene.com
books@kfbreene.com

Acknowledgments:
This book is for the readers.

You wanted more spice. You wanted crass. You
wanted me to go wild. You got it.

A special thanks to Amber Hyde and Heather
Rainwater-Alvarado for the titles that everyone
picked to go forward.

I couldn't do this without all of you in my
corner. I'm forever thankful.

# PROLOGUE

A LOW GROWL rumbled through the Forbidden Wood. My heart jumped into my throat.

The beast!

I darted behind the nearest tree and flattened my back against the rough bark. My tweed bag hung across my torso, filled with the precious cargo I'd stolen from the everlass field. If the beast found me with this—if it found me in the Forbidden Wood at all—I was done for. It would kill me as it had done countless others, regardless of the fact I was only fourteen.

It didn't matter that I was too young to shift, if shifting were still possible for us after the curse. If I was old enough to steal, I was old enough to die for my sins.

A tree branch cracked. What sounded like a large foot crunched brittle grass. Another touched down, the creature slowing. It either sensed someone close or had caught my scent.

I sucked in a breath and squeezed my eyes shut, my hands shaking. Loud snuffling filled the silence. The beast sniffing out its prey.

My parents didn't even know I'd come. Nana had fallen ill, the effects of the curse that had damned our kingdom. Everyone said there was no cure. But I'd found a way. I could slow the effects, at least. I needed the everlass plant, though, and we hardly had any. I was still learning how to properly grow it. No one else in the village could do much with it at all. Something about it spoke to me, though. I would figure it out eventually, I knew I could—but right now, I was out of time.

My lungs burned. I was afraid to breathe.

More grass crunched under the beast's enormous feet. It was moving in my direction!

A whimper escaped my lips. I slapped a hand over my mouth, but it was too late. The footsteps ceased. It had heard.

The darkness lay thick around me. Silence.

The beast roared, making me jump half out of my skin. Fear doused me in adrenaline, and then I was running. Sprinting as fast as I could go. I crashed through the brush. Rounded a tree.

Its footsteps gained. It was coming so fast! How could I possibly escape?

Loud grunts sounded way above me, its breath puffing out as it moved. If its head was that high off the ground, it was much bigger than the rumors had said.

A wall of brush waited up ahead. Two trees crossed within it, creating a narrow opening between the thorns. I took a chance and dashed between them.

Sliding sounded behind me, and I glanced back to see two enormous feet ending in long, sharp claws churn the dirt. They stopped just before the opening.

Crying now, unable to help it, I kept going, getting onto my hands and knees and crawling. Dense foliage covered me overhead. Thorns ripped at my flesh. I continued to crawl, now on elbows and knees.

Breath blew out behind me. It was tracking my scent.

The dark hollow up ahead announced the end of this natural tunnel. Blood trickled down my cheek from where a thorn had ripped through. The bag of everlass crunched under my body. I knew that would be bad for the elixir, but I didn't have much choice.

I needed to get it out of here. Nana's life depended on it. Her cough was really bad, and her breathing was shallow. She needed help.

Summoning my courage, I pushed up to a crouch in the darkness, looking out at the starless night. Trees rose all around, and the ground was a tangle of weeds and brambles. Nothing moved. Could the beast have moved on?

In my heart of hearts, I knew the answer, but my fear was out of control.

I thought about staying put, but it could wait me out. Or come in after me. It had an armored face, everyone said. A few vines and thorns wouldn't trouble it.

I sprinted forward, sobs choking me.

Its roar followed me, ever closer. My breathing came in harried, haggard gasps. I pumped at the air with my fists and rounded a tree. The edge of the wood was just up ahead. Although other horrors could cross that line, the beast, the guardian of the Forbidden Wood, could not.

Lights in the village jiggled in the wet haze of my vision. Candles in windows. Fires in yards. They awaited me. They were right up ahead!

The roar rattled my bones, much too close.

The end was near.

# CHAPTER I

G LOWING GOLDEN EYES tore me out of sleep. I sucked in a terrified breath and sat up in a rush. My hair was plastered to my face with sweat. My shirt clung to my back. A nightmare.

No, worse than a nightmare. A memory.

I still remembered busting through that tree line at fourteen and catching my foot on a rock. Falling and skidding on my face. When I'd stopped rolling, I lay sprawled out, facing the wood.

Those glowing golden eyes had glared at me through the darkness. The beast's head had been impossibly high, among the tree branches. I'd never seen its body. The night had consumed it.

That image still played on a loop in my nightmares all these long years later. Nine years of replays.

A ragged, wet cough brought me out of my panic. I

pulled in a deep breath to ground myself in the moment. The hack sounded again. Father. He was getting worse.

I sighed wearily, pushing back my hair and then the covers.

My sister, Sable, jerked awake in the narrow bed beside mine in our tiny room. We didn't have much, but at least we had a roof over our heads. For now, anyway.

Muted moonlight filtered through the threadbare curtains, and I could just make out her face turning to me, her eyes large with fear. She knew what that cough meant.

"It's okay," I told her, swinging my legs over the edge of the bed. "It's fine. I have more of the nulling elixir. We haven't run out yet."

She nodded, sitting up and bunching the sheets near her chest.

She was just fourteen, the age I'd been when I narrowly survived the beast only to lose Nana anyway.

It was different now, though. Since then, I'd worked diligently with the special everlass elixir I devised. It still didn't cure the curse's sickness, but it drastically slowed it down and nulled most of the effects. Because of it, and because I'd given the recipe to the village and helped them learn to make it, we'd only lost one person so far this year. If the winter would just let up already, spring would help us revitalize our gardens. The plants mostly went dormant in the winter, not growing many new leaves. The gardens in our small yards weren't big enough to sustain us if we had someone on the brink. There were many on the brink.

My older brother, Hannon, pushed open the door and stuck his head in the room. His red hair swirled around his head like a tornado. A splash of freckles darkened his pale face. Unlike me, the guy didn't tan for nothing. He came in two colors: white and red.

"Finley," he said before realizing I was already up. He left the door open but stepped out, waiting for me.

"He's deteriorating," Hannon said softly when I was in the hall. "He doesn't have long."

"He's lasted longer with the sickness than anyone else. And he'll continue to last. I've made some recent improvements. It'll be okay."

I took a step toward Father's room, just next to mine, but my brother stopped me with a hand to my arm. "He's on borrowed time, Finley. How long can this go on? He's suffering. The kids are watching him suffer."

"That's only because we're down to the weak ever-lass leaves. As soon as the spring comes it'll be better, Hannon, you'll see. I'll find a cure for him. He won't join Nana and Mommy in the beyond. He won't. I *will* find a cure. It must exist."

"The only cure is breaking the curse, and no one knows how to do that."

"Someone knows," I said softly, opening Father's door. "Someone in this goddess-ruined kingdom knows how to break that curse. I will find that person, and I will wring the truth out of them."

A candle in a holder flickered on the table by the door. I picked it up and shielded the flame from the air as I hurried to Father's side. Two chairs bracketed each side of the bed, always present. Sometimes we used them to gather around him when he was lucid. Lately, though, they were used for vigils, so we could watch with trepidation as he clung to life.

My father's lined face was ashen within the candlelight. His eyelids trembled as though he were trapped in a nightmare.

He was, I supposed. We all were. The whole kingdom. Our mad king had used the demon king's sly magic to settle a personal grudge, and we were all suffering the consequences. Actually, *he* wasn't. He'd died and left us to rot. What a peach. They hadn't said what he'd died from, but I hoped it was gangrene of the dick.

I set the candle on the bedside table before checking

the fireplace at the other end of the room. The coals throbbed crimson then black, giving off enough heat to warm the kettle of water above it. We never knew when we'd need hot water. Given the curse had wiped out modern-day conveniences like electricity and running water, almost plunging us back into the Dark Ages, we needed to make do with what we had.

"Dash says we hardly have any usable leaves left, and the crop you planted isn't ready yet," Hannon said.

"I didn't plant—Never mind." I didn't bother explaining that the everlass would spring up naturally every year if you coaxed it with good soil and rigorous maintenance. Hannon wasn't much of a gardener. "Dash shouldn't be telling stories."

Dash was the youngest, a boy of eleven who moved more than he listened...except when he was listening to me mutter to myself, it seemed. I hadn't realized he'd overheard me.

"I'm good with plants and gardening, but I'm not a stem witch, Hannon. It's a hobby, not magic. It might not get ball-chillingly cold here, but it's cold enough to stunt plant growth. I just need a little sun. I keep asking the goddess, but she clearly does not give a crap about us. Divine, my arse. Maybe we should go back to the old ways of our ancestors. They worshipped a bunch of gods sitting on a mountain or whatever. Maybe one of them would listen."

"You read too much."

"Is there such a thing?"

"You daydream too much, then."

I shrugged. "That is probably true."

My medicinal station waited in the corner, herbs and a mortar and pestle set on a wooden tray. The two measly leaves in the ceramic bowl had already been dried in the dying light of the evening sun.

Very poetic, this particular healing recipe. Bone-chillingly poetic. It had taken a lot of reading and trial and error to figure out what worked best, and I wasn't finished. I was sure the demon king was laughing at me somewhere. At all of us. He was the bastard who'd taken the king's gold and worked up the bullshit curse that currently plagued our land, after all. His minions had been stationed in the kingdom to watch us struggle. Too bad they weren't rotting beneath the ground with the late king. They deserved to be.

"What was that?" Hannon asked, his temperament far sweeter than mine, though that wasn't much of an accomplishment. I'd set the bar pretty low.

"Nothing," I murmured. It wasn't ladylike to swear, or so the people of our antiquated village always reminded me. It was equally unladylike to flip them off after they scowled at me. Very uptight, this village, and without two coppers to rub together, the lot of us.

My father convulsed, spasming with each wet cough.

Hands shaking, fighting to remain calm, I crushed the leaves with the pestle. A pungent aroma, like ripe cheese mixed with garlic, blasted my senses. They might be small leaves, but they were full of healing magic.

My father lunged toward the side of the bed.

Hannon was there in a moment, sitting beside him and bringing up the bucket from the floor. He helped Father lean over the lip and retch. There'd be blood in that throw-up, I well knew.

"Focus," I told myself softly, shaking two drops of rainwater off my fingertip and onto the crushed leaves. I'd collected those in the dead of night. That seemed to work best.

That done, I sprinkled in the other herbs, which were much easier to come by—a sprig of rosemary, one leaf of dill, a splash of cinnamon. And, finally, the ingredient that was almost as important as the ever-lass—the full, healthy petal of one red rose.

It had to be red, too. The others didn't work nearly so well. I had no idea what red roses had to do with this curse or the demons, but the effects of that ingredient increased the potency of the elixir tenfold. It made me think there were one or two more ingredients out there that I hadn't tried yet that would act as a cure. A long-term cure where we didn't need more and more draught just to see the same effects. Something that would null the sickness altogether. If it was out there, I'd find it. Hopefully in time to save Father.

Father's groan spurred me on. A rattled breath struggled through his tightened throat. At least he had a strong heart. A heart attack had taken Mother a year ago. Her body had been under too much pressure, and her heart gave up the fight. I hadn't been as good at the nulling elixir then. Father had more time.

*He has to have more time.*

"Honestly, Dash is right. We need more supplies," I said, working the pestle. "Our plants aren't enough."

"I thought you said yesterday that no one else had any left either?"

"Not that they are willing to spare, no."

Everyone had ailing parents and *maybe* one or two ailing grandparents, if they were lucky. Our resources were tapped.

"Well then, where are you…" He let the words drift away. "No."

"I don't have much choice, Hannon. Besides, I've been in and out of that field a bunch of times over the last few years with no problems. At night, even. The beast probably doesn't patrol the Forbidden Wood anymore."

My hands started to shake, and I stopped for a moment and took a deep breath. Lying to Hannon was one thing—he was a trusting soul and wanted to believe me—but I wasn't foolish enough to believe my own lies. Just because I hadn't seen the beast in any visits since the first, that did not mean he'd given up hunting trespassers. Our village was at the edge of the kingdom, and I was sneaky. I took great pains to ensure I wasn't seen. I heard the roars, though. He was out there, waiting. Watching. The ultimate predator.

The beast wasn't the only danger in the wood, either. Terrible creatures had been set loose by the curse, and unlike the beast, they didn't seem to be hindered by the tree line. They used to burst out of the Forbidden Wood and eat any villagers out after dark. Occasionally they'd barge through a front door as well, and eat villagers out of their homes.

It hadn't happened in a long time. None of us understood why they'd left us be, but they were still in the wood. I'd heard their roars, too. That place was a clusterfuck of danger.

"It's fine," I reaffirmed, even though he hadn't rebuffed me vocally. "The everlass field is close. I'll just nip in really quickly, grab what I need, and get out. I have a great sense of direction in that place. In and out."

"Except it is two days until the full moon."

"That'll just help me see better."

"It'll also increase the beast's power. He'll smell better. Run faster. Chomp harder."

"I don't think a soft chomp would be any better than a hard one, but it doesn't matter. I'll be quick. I know the way."

"You shouldn't know the way."

But from the way he said it, I knew Hannon was giving up the fight. He didn't have any more steam to talk me out of going. I kind of hoped he'd try harder.

I grimaced when I'd meant to smile, and my stomach started to churn. I did need to go. And I *had* gone a bunch these last few years and come back safely.

I'd hated it every time.

"When?" Hannon asked somberly.

"The leaves are the most potent when harvested at night," I said, "and we are on borrowed time, like you said. No time like the present."

"Are you absolutely sure you need to go?"

I let my shoulders sag for a moment. "Yes."

An hour later, I stood in the front room with a tweed crossbody bag draped across my sternum. The plant seemed to respond best when carried in this type of bag. I'd gotten the tip from a book and proven the theory with trial and error.

My brothers and sister stood with me.

"Be careful." Hannon squeezed my shoulders, looking down into my eyes.

Standing about three inches taller than my six feet, he was the tallest man in our village. One of the strongest, too, with large arms and a thick frame. Most would assume he would be the one risking his life in the beast's haunt. Or the one hunting for our dinner in the safer forest to the east. But no, Hannon was the guy who wrung his hands and waited at home to patch me up when I came bleeding through the door. Good thing, too, because I'd limped in on more than one occasion. Those damned wild boars in the east forest made an art of mauling. Vicious fuckers.

The beast was another situation altogether.

*Courage.*

A night bird cried a warning in the distance. The cottages around us on the dirt lane squatted in silence, their inhabitants asleep at this time of night. Asleep, or sitting quietly in their darkened homes, not wanting to draw the notice of anything that might've slunk through the tree line. It might not have happened in years, but people around here had long memories.

"Don't take any chances," Hannon said. "If you see the beast, get out of there."

"If I see the beast, I'll probably piss myself."

"Fine. But do it as you're running."

Sage advice.

"It's fine, Hannon. I took the smell-masking elixir. That usually works when I'm hunting. It'll help."

He nodded, but the pep talk apparently wasn't done. "There is only one beast," he said. "That's the main concern. You've confronted the other creatures in that wood and come out swinging."

Not exactly, but as I said, Hannon was a trusting soul. He didn't seem to know when I was lying. If he thought I was tougher than I was, he'd worry less. Who was that hurting?

I turned and gave Sable a fierce hug, kissing her on the head. Dash was next, and then I had to peel him away.

"Let me go, too," Dash begged. "I know where it is. I can help collect more. I can fight off the monsters!"

"How…" I stopped myself. Now was not the time to shout at my younger brother. I pointed at Hannon instead. "While I'm gone, find out how he knows where the field is. Wait to punish him until I get back. I want to be in on it."

I gave Hannon one last hug and quickly set off. I

could do this. I *had* to do this.

My bow had been broken last week by one of those bastard boars, so I was going in with nothing but the dagger and the pocketknife tucked into my trousers. Neither weapon would do a whole helluva lot against the beast. Then again, if the beast really *did* have scaled armor, the ten arrows I owned wouldn't do much to protect me, either.

I cut through the back gardens of two cottages, scaling the fences, and approached the edge of the Forbidden Wood. A patch of goat-trimmed land was all that separated me from it. Weeds crawled toward the perimeter...and then wilted and died. Ghostly trunks rose on the edge, twisted branches reaching for the village. Beyond lay shadowy depths, sliced through with moonlight under the star-flecked sky.

I cleared my mind of the stakes. Pushed away the image of Father's sickbed. Tossed aside the worry in Hannon's eyes and the feel of Sable and Dash clinging to me when I hugged them goodbye, hopefully not for the last time. Right now, it was just me and these woods. Me and the creatures that lurked within their deteriorating depths. Me and the beast, if it came to it.

I would not let my father down. I would not fail him.

The edge of my dagger slid against the hard leather

of its sheath hanging from my hip. I stepped lightly and carefully, aiming for springing ground and avoiding anything that might snap or crinkle. It was easy now, still in the village. Once I passed that tree line, it would be a whole lot harder. A whole lot deadlier.

Not a sound vibrated through the air. No wind stirred the frostbitten branches or boughs. My breath puffed white. I noticed every little detail of my surroundings. I was the prey, and I did not want to tango with the hunter.

The air cooled as I crossed the threshold. I stilled and took a deep breath. Panic would get me dead. I needed to keep a level head.

Onward I went with watchful eyes. I needed to pay attention to any movement. Any change in scent or sound.

I remembered a time, before the curse, when the Forbidden Wood had been lovely. Green and lush. Now, though, the brittle grasses crackled under my worn boots. The bark felt flaky under my fingers. No leaves graced the branches, even of the evergreen trees, and no flowers adorned the winter budding plants.

Up ahead, around a large pine scantily clad with needles, I spotted it—a birch that didn't seem to fit in with its peers. Just behind it was my destination.

The everlass field had been less than half its current

size when I first found it. It had grown over the years, not that it really mattered. I could only use what I could steal, and I didn't dare do that often.

*Crack.*

Adrenaline dumped into my bloodstream. I froze with my hands out like an idiot, as though ready for actual flight. I might have courage, but I clearly wasn't cool when handling danger.

That had sounded like a twig snapping.

With bated breath, I waited for something to happen. Then waited some more—watching for movement, listening for sounds. Nothing.

Letting out a shaky breath, I continued on. The shapes of trees shifted around me, crawling across the star-speckled blackness above. A creature shrieked distantly on my left. The sound spread through the air before trailing away, like ripples in a pond. My heart sped up, but the sound was too far away to worry me at the moment. Hopefully the creature would keep screeching so I could track its travel route.

A horrible scream rent the air, also distant. It sounded like a human in peril, being eaten alive or gruesomely tortured, or a man with a paper cut on his finger. It was intense distress, in other words, needing help immediately, or death might ensue.

*Nice try, fucker.*

I'd heard that creature before. I'd actually even seen it as I was panic-sprinting home one time. Its goal was to lure do-gooders. People came to help, and it killed them.

Or that was how it clearly thought its ruse would go. Except all knew that in the Forbidden Wood, it was everyone for themselves. There were no do-gooders here. That thing could go on screaming for all I cared. That would at least prevent it from sneaking up on me.

The birch was close now, rising stoically.

Its branches shivered dramatically, as though it were cold.

I froze again, and suddenly wondered why I always shoved my arms out like some sort of confused dancer when I freaked out…

But seriously, why in the goddess's secret cupboard was the tree shivering? That hadn't happened before. I'd passed this tree every time I came to this field, and it had never moved because of anything but the wind.

*This is a shit time for a tree to be doing the jig, folks,* I thought to the invisible audience watching my adventure. It was something I'd been doing since I was little, and I hadn't given up the habit at twenty-three. Back in the day I'd done it because I was pretending to be a jester or a queen, but now I did it out of comfort. And eccentricity, I supposed.

*Let's keep our heads here, everybody. Things are getting a bit strange.*

I gave the shivering birch a wider berth, thankful when it stopped moving. The night fell quiet once again, the screaming imposter taking a break for a moment. The field lay before me, coated in moonlight.

I scanned the area beyond the clearing. Nothing moved. No other trees shivered.

A backward glance—with narrowed eyes at that birch—and all was equally clear. No bodily warnings of danger approaching, no feeling of eyes on me. It was now or never.

Dagger back in its holster and pocketknife at the ready, I scanned the plants as I carefully made my way through them. Most herbalists would call them weeds. But most herbalists were faeries, and they stuck their noses up at plants they couldn't grow. Or so people said. No one in the village had seen one for sixteen years.

Of course, that didn't stop the faeries from seeking them out. Everlass was *the* most potent healer in all the kingdoms. And guess what? It only grew in lands ruled or maintained by dragon shifters. Suck on that, faeries.

Even though this kingdom was basically in stewardship of the demon king because of the curse, it still had the magic of the dragons. Most of the nobility had been killed soon after the mad king perished, but the everlass remained unscathed. All we had to do was learn to work with it.

I'd always thought it was romantic. Without the presence of dragons, the everlass wouldn't sprout from the soil. It was like the protective dragon magic infused the very fibers of the ground we walked on and gave the everlass courage to take the leap.

This plant was regal. Regal meaning incredibly fussy and hard to work with. If you were too rough or hasty in your ministrations, it would shrivel and reduce in potency. It demanded focused and careful attention, if not love.

And I did love it. Why wouldn't I? It was saving my village.

I freed only the largest and healthiest of the leaves, being careful not to upset the seed pods that would ensure new life when the time came. As I went, I pruned any dead or dying leaves, of which there were very few.

I tucked the leaves into my sack, allowing them room. It wasn't good to bunch them together so soon after harvesting. They worked better when they had a little space to breathe, like the plants themselves. If I didn't have to worry about being chased, attacked, and eaten, I'd carry the leaves home in a big tray, none of them touching their neighbor.

When my bag was full, I straightened up and swept

my gaze over the field. I wondered how many other people snuck into this place to use it. I'd never seen anyone else, but the plants were properly pruned and managed. That spoke of a group of caring, knowledgeable people, probably from the other villages. I'd seen what happened to the plants of my neighbors who didn't do their due diligence. They grew wild and unruly.

I wasn't the only one who showered these plants with love. Not surprising, but still, it warmed my heart. I hoped the other villages were at least faring as well as we were.

A whinnying owl call startled me out of my reverie. I pinched my face, listening. It was off to the side, decently close. That wasn't startling in itself—it sounded pissed off, but it could just be mad at its mate or another bird. Maybe it had noticed a little critter making its way across the ground or something, I didn't know. I wasn't an owl behavioral expert. No, what was startling was that it was the first time I'd heard that sort of owl in the Forbidden Wood.

A shivering birch, and now an owl. What was going on tonight?

Whatever it was, I didn't like it.

*Be quiet now, everyone. If we're sneaky-sneaky, no one will bother us.*

I pivoted where I stood and put on a burst of speed, still picking my way through the plants with care but doing it as fast as I possibly could.

A soft *chuff* caught my attention and flooded me with a fearful chill. My flight reflex very nearly had me hiking up my pants and sprinting through the wood like some sort of hobgoblin.

Was it the beast? Something else? Maybe it didn't matter. The sound had come from a larger animal, and anything that large in this wood was a predator of some kind.

I let my breath out very slowly. The animal was southwest of me, in the same direction as the owl's outburst, but closer.

I looked down at the pocketknife clutched in my shaking hand. That weapon was not going to cut it.

Damn it, now I was thinking in dad jokes.

Straining my eyes, I watched for movement as I grabbed the blade to fold it away. Watched to see if anything interrupted the shards of soft moonlight piercing the shadows. The still night didn't reveal its secrets.

*Courage now, folks. Everyone remain calm.*

I turned slowly toward home, carefully lowering my feet one at a time. I didn't want my feet to slide on the crusty dirt. Breathing slowly helped, too. I needed air to fuel my brain and my muscles. I needed to think or run, or both simultaneously. Blind terror never helped anyone.

My pocketknife made a *snick* sound as I closed it and the blade lodged home. I paused, gritting my teeth. Silence reverberated around me...until a wail rang out, like an old woman grieving over the lost. Loud and low and full of bitter agony.

I jumped. My pocketknife tumbled from my fingers.

*Fuck! I dropped the fucking knife. Hold on to your dicks, folks, this is about to get hairy.*

Another cry, this time like an infant. It rattled my senses as the knife hit the ground in multiple thumps.

This new creature's sounds came from the north. Directly north. Fifty yards, maybe, possibly a bit more.

Loud grunts followed. *Hunka, hunka, hunka.*

Same direction, similar distance. It was obviously the creature from a moment ago, some sort of mockingbird of terror. What the grunts were supposed to attract, I did not know or care.

I bent in a rush, trying to peer through the deep shadows to find my knife, and then ran my fingers against the ground, searching. Dried grasses brushed my palm.

Another owl blasted its warning—or maybe the same owl? I didn't know. Were they tenacious fuckers who followed trespassers like grumpy old men? I needed to look that up. Regardless, its call was much closer this time. Thirty yards, maybe less. Southwest, in the direction of the large predator.

Fuck the pocketknife.

I straightened up swiftly, adjusted the sack of leaves, and put on a burst of speed around the birch. It shivered like it had on the way in. This time, though, the movement seemed more intense. The leaves clattered together like dancing skeletons. Branches creaked, waving in the absence of wind.

What in the double fuck was up with that tree? Had I cut down its cousin or something?

The mockingbird of terror abruptly stopped its grunting. It had heard me. It *knew* something was here.

That goddess-damned birch would join its cousin if I had any say. I'd dance naked around the flames.

Swallowing a swear, I hurried forward to put some distance between me and the freaking-out flora. A patch of brittle grass between two thick trunks awaited me ahead, and I slowed. My vision had narrowed to directly in front of me, and my heart pounded adrenaline through my body, signs of the flight reflex. I slowed further and sucked in a breath. I could not blindly run. I *could not.* I had to think this through. I had to be smart.

The falling knife hadn't been that loud. The creatures in the area didn't know I was here. They only knew that the birch was a diva cuntface looking for attention. And even if they *did* know there was a trespasser in their midst, they wouldn't be able to track me. My scent was hidden due to the hand-crafted herbal brew I'd drunk before leaving the house, and the ground was too hard for my feet to make distinct tracks in the darkness. Right now, I was still an unknown.

I eyed the grass ahead while listening. The birch finally settled down, leaving a gaping absence of sound in its wake. No movement caught my ear. No screeches.

My chest felt tight, strained with the pressure of staying calm. I focused on my breathing and started moving slowly forward again, easing the dagger from its sheath as I did so. The grass issued some light crackles before I met hard dirt again, only cut through with patches of dead grass. I barely stopped myself from heaving a loud sigh.

An owl screeched overhead.

I jerked and jumped at the same time. The blade of my dagger thudded uselessly off the tree trunk to my left. The owl called its warning again, and I wished I had my bow so I could shut that thing up right now. *Get off my lawn, owl!*

The old woman's wail sounded again, slicing through me. Northeast, tracking me.

I moved faster now, careful with my footfalls. I had about a hundred yards to go to get out of this place. Maybe a bit more. Not very far in the scheme of things, but how fast could that creature run? I was fast, but it was almost certainly faster. And the village border only meant something to the beast. Crossing the boundary line wouldn't be enough to escape this creature. I'd need to get inside my house and lock the door. That was plenty of distance for it to catch me.

Walking would be a lot slower and not much quieter. The alternative to walking was to stand my ground with a half-starved body from years of barely getting by and a medium-sized, somewhat dull dagger. Nice odds.

A strange feeling rolled through my chest, like a heavy weight turning over. Shortly afterward, a shock of fire coursed through me, and I couldn't help sucking in a startled breath.

It felt…wonderful. Fucking amazing, actually. The heat, the power, and the…*desire*?

Oh shit. Incubus. I hadn't taken the draught to stop a demon's lust magic because I hadn't thought there'd be any in the Forbidden Wood. But why wouldn't there be? They got a free pass all over the kingdom. My not having seen them in here before meant very little.

Thankfully, they weren't dangerous enough to give me pause.

Grip tight on the dagger handle, I pushed through the pounding in my core and kept moving. Ignored the sudden explosion of wetness between my thighs, sending shooting sparks of delight every time my upper legs gave even a glimmer of friction. And what was that smell? Balmy and spicy and delicious. Fuck, that smelled good.

The sound of a wailing baby tore through the night air, desperately close, twenty yards or so to my left. The mockingbird of terror had moved in my direction on a diagonal. Somehow it was tracking me without being able to smell or see me.

Or maybe my smell-blindness elixir didn't work as well as I'd thought…

I looked upward, thinking about climbing. It would be a struggle to reach the nearest branches. I doubted I could do it quickly or quietly, and even if I managed it, what if the creature could fly? It would be on me in a heartbeat.

Running might be my only option.

Before I could, the strange weight in my chest lurched. Lava spilled out and dripped down to my sodden core. I couldn't stop a moan as an intimate presence feathered across my skin, as though someone were physically touching me with silky fingers.

My breathing turned ragged as I desperately tried to

29

shut the feeling out.

It was…incredible, though. The best fucking thing I'd ever felt. Primal, almost, reaching down into the very center of me and pulling out a raw hunger I didn't want to shy away from. Desperate desires flitted through my head, of touching, of tangled bodies, of the taste of a hard cock sliding into my mouth.

Fuck me, this incubus was strong. I'd never felt something like this before.

I had to push past it. I had to ignore the sudden, brain-fogging desire to drop down right now and spread my legs, begging to be taken. To be dominated.

When the hell did a girl like me want to be dominated?

Right fucking now, that was when.

This was not how I got out of this wood alive. This was not real.

It certainly felt fucking real, though. This wasn't like the demons in the village, who had a sort of oily presence in their lustful magic. This felt like a piece of me…a secret piece of me…exposed.

Shit. Not good. I *had* to shut it out!

*Keep moving*, I urged myself. *Keep going. You're stronger than this.* Resist!

I pushed forward again, stumbling like a drunk. How was I going to fight the mockingbird of terror in this state? Was the incubus working with it? If not, it needed to show itself so I could kill it really quickly and move on.

The seam of my pants rubbing against my slick sex nearly undid me. My hard nipples rubbed against the coarse binding surrounding them, which was suddenly not nearly tight enough. My quickened breath was not because of my fast walk.

This was so fucked up. I could barely focus on my extreme panic.

A low growl sliced through every band of pleasure wrapping around my body, and the desire fell away like cut ribbons. In its place, cold terror once again reigned.

I jerked to a stop, dagger up, eyes as big as the moon. The baritone rumbling continued, freezing my blood.

I turned my head slowly toward the sound on my right.

Shadow lined the rough grooves of bark on the large tree. Moonlight carved through the darkness beside it. I didn't hear or see a damn thing. For a few solid moments, nothing in the whole wood seemed to move.

A shape popped out from the left, the opposite direction from where I'd been looking. The leathery body was bent over on two stout legs, its head still cresting mine by about four feet. Small arms and little hands reached forward as its huge mouth gaped open. I'd half expected something like a bird. Not the case. Two rows of teeth dripped with saliva.

It lunged at me, intent on snapping my face between its jaws.

# CHAPTER 2

I DODGED AND prepared to strike, but I didn't get the chance.

A huge form blasted out from the space between the two trunks to my right.

I cried out and fell backward, my dagger falling uselessly from my hand. The form moved so fast that it was nearly a blur. I barely saw the hulking frame, its shoulders well above my head, and the enormous legs ending in six-inch claws. Darkness slid across it as though they were old friends.

A picture out of my nightmares.

The beast.

A fierce growl was all the warning the mockingbird of terror got before the beast plowed into it and took it back the way it had come. I didn't get a chance to see the beast's head. I did watch its tail slide across the ground, though, the spikes on the end whipping in the opposite direction.

A high-pitched squeal of agony accompanied the wet, gloppy sounds of teeth tearing through flesh. Fire raged through my body, but thankfully, the desire was long gone.

Not one to waste good fortune, I grabbed my dagger and jumped up. A moment later, I was running with everything I had. Ripping through bushes and ducking under branches, I didn't stick to any kind of path. I didn't care if I could be tracked or heard. I doubted anyone would chase a scrappy little shifter who couldn't shift, not with the monstrous melee going on behind me.

I burst out across the Forbidden Wood's boundary and raced around the village the long way to my house. It would be faster if I didn't have to worry about jumping fences.

I stomped up my steps and barged through the door. Before I could catch my breath, I turned and slammed the door shut behind me. I yanked the heavy timber at the side in place across the door, securing us in.

Hannon pushed up from the couch, his eyes anxious. Seeing me with my back against the door, panting, he hurried to the little window overlooking the porch, grabbing the interior wood shutters to block it off.

"No," I panted, my chest still heaving. I unslung the pack with everlass and straightened it out. I didn't want my nearly deadly trip to have been in vain. "Leave it."

He paused with the shutters halfway closed. Without a word, he slowly pushed them back before peering out into the night.

"You saw it," he said softly.

Straightening up, I gulped air and shook my head. "No. I mean…" I licked my lips, utterly parched.

Without a word, he moved toward the kitchen. After years of nursing our parents, he didn't need to be told what a person needed.

"Kinda. I saw a huge shape. A body. And a tail. And the foot. *The* foot. It had to have been the beast."

"How close was it?"

He shouldn't be asking that. He never asked how close my close calls were. That kept me from having to lie.

This time, though, I didn't feel like covering up what had happened.

I told him everything, from the shaking birch, to the weird, territorial owl, to the strong incubus that never materialized, to the strange escape.

"I don't think it was coming after me," I finally said, having moved to the couch and finished two cups of water. "I mean…at first it obviously was. It stalked me. So did that other creature—"

"How?" Hannon asked, sitting in the wooden chair opposite me. He'd made it.

"All the noise around me, I guess, I don't know. The birch and then the owl. Or maybe the draught to deaden smell didn't work? It's not like I have ever properly tested it in the Forbidden Wood. I've only ever tested it in the forests to the south and east, on real animals in natural habitats, not on demon creatures in an evil ecosystem. The magic in the Forbidden Wood is twisted."

"Well." Hannon rubbed his face. "I'm going to bed. Father is sleeping peacefully right now. The elixir earlier really helped. Maybe he'll be lucid tomorrow."

I nodded and stayed put for a moment. I'd need to dote on the everlass leaves tonight if they were going to work for me. I had to nestle them into their drying tray and sprinkle them with water to keep them fresh until they could be dried in tomorrow's dying sun. Very high-maintenance, those leaves. But if you treated them well, they kept your loved ones alive.

For a moment, though, I just wanted to sit and unwind. There were still so many questions to ponder, like what was up with that birch tree? And where had that owl come from and what was its problem?

Most importantly, though, what had happened with the incubus? I highly doubted the mockingbird of terror could turn a person on. It had its thing, and sexy-time was not it. Neither did I think the beast moonlighted as a sex god. I would've heard about that. So what was affecting me like a filthy good time, and was it still out there? Because incubi had no problem wandering into the village and taking what they wanted. Sure, they might usually be easy to ignore, but this one was something else.

LATE THE NEXT morning, I held out my mug for a specially made tea in our homely kitchen. Coffee was a thing of the past, new supplies lost to us when the curse went into effect. Coffee beans were grown in a few kingdoms, not to mention the human realm beyond the magical veil, but we weren't one of them. When my parents had been plagued with headaches after the supply ran out, I devised a mixture to calm the ache and still give a little kick to start the morning. It had done the trick, and now I looked forward to it.

Hannon pulled the pot off the hook hanging over the fire and tilted it. A tiny bit of life-saving draught filled my mug.

"Try again," I said with a yawn, keeping my mug in the air.

"We're out. I indulged a little too much last night when you were getting chased by beasts around the wood. I still slept like a baby when you got back, though." He grinned at me.

I scowled, took a sip, and leaned against the clean but chipped stone countertop. "Whose turn is it to go to the marketplace today?"

"Yours, thank the lovely goddess."

"What's up with you?" I looked at him over the lip of my mug as he went about kneading bread. He was the useful one in our family. He'd essentially taken over for Mom, cooking and sewing and woodworking and doing all kinds of other handy stuff—he was the master of all trades. My abilities were limited to healing, hunting, fishing, gardening, and narrowly escaping the beast of the Forbidden Wood. It was partially why I needed to take all the risks. This family could not survive without Hannon. Not even for a little while.

He rolled his eyes and stopped his kneading for a moment. "Daphne."

I felt a grin creep up my tired face. "We all need admirers."

"Yeah, well..." He shook his head and went back to his task. After a moment, he spilled his guts. "She knows

I had my twenty-fifth birthday last month."

My grin widened. "Prime mating age, yes. Go on."

"She has something she wants to ask me."

"No…" I pushed forward gleefully. "Is she going to propose?"

"Women don't propose, Finley. I think she wants to ask me to propose to her, though. She's not been subtle about her…desires."

I could feel my toothy grin. Hannon was not like most guys in our spit-wad of a village. He didn't chase skirts and visit the pubs after dark to fornicate with succubi. He liked to get to know a lady before progressing to the next level. Because of that and his stout frame and gingerific good looks, he did seem to get to the next level (banging) every time he put the effort in. He just didn't put the effort in very much.

And that drove the ladies wild.

"Women aren't supposed to hunt, either. Or wear ill-fitting men's trousers. Yet here I am…"

"You're different."

"You just think that because I'm your sister. Boys aren't supposed to cook and look after their families, and yet you excel at that better than most women. Maybe she's your true mate."

He snorted. "Yeah, right. True mates aren't possible."

"You know what I mean." I recited it as if to a dunce. "Maybe she'd be your true mate if the curse hadn't suppressed all our animals, and we could actually function like real shifters."

He paused for a moment. "I don't think true mates ever existed. I've read the histories, same as you, and none of them confirm they're real."

"First of all, our library is small and limited, and before the curse, people weren't looking to learn about their shifter traits from books. They learned about that from their peers. So it makes sense that we wouldn't have many volumes on shifter functionality. I know that because I whined about it, and that's what I was told. Second, those that are carried are histories focused on the nobles and kings and queens and important people. They marry for money and power. They don't give a shit about love. Common people like us have a better chance at finding our true mate."

I didn't actually believe that, but I loved to play devil's advocate. I knew for a fact that my brother did wish to meet his true mate. That he would honor his animal's choice (should he ever meet his animal, locked inside of him), and mate her as nature intended.

I, myself, did not believe in destined anything. I wasn't the type to allow anyone to push me around, even if it was my own primal side doing the pushing.

Nor did I give a crap about love and mating. Not anymore. Not since I'd gotten my heart ripped out and stomped on two years ago. My ex had dumped me and then quickly gone on to mate a toothy girl dedicated to needlepoint and looking after him.

His reasoning for the breakup? He needed someone ready and able to run a house. He wanted a "proper" wife.

Apparently in his eyes, and in the eyes of most of the people in the village, a proper wife didn't hunt better than her husband, or at all. She didn't tan hides, play with knives, and wear trousers. Nor did she look after villagers ailing from the curse's sickness more than she would tend to her husband's less-than-dire needs. This was because she would've (apparently incorrectly) assumed her husband was an adult and didn't need a nursemaid to wipe his mouth and assure him he was the master of the universe. Silly her.

Clearly I would be single forever. It really wasn't a huge loss, though, given the dickfaces in this village. It was just too bad about the dry spell for the last two years. That wasn't so easily borne, especially with lust demons wandering around.

"I think true mates are incredibly rare," Hannon murmured.

"Well, yeah. There is one person in all of the magical world meant for us? And they have to be the same type of shifter, same overall power level, and same general age... Lots of 'ands.' But it *is* doable, or else we wouldn't have a name for it. Besides, Daphne is very pretty and *very* willing. I know how you like them curves, too."

I could see his cheek and ear turn bright crimson. He was very easy to embarrass. I made it my goal to do it at least once a day.

"I'm too young to marry," he grumbled.

"Yeah, right. That's not even remotely true, and you know it. Not since the curse. None of us have a long life expectancy anymore—we need to get life rolling. Hell, if that donkey hadn't dumped me, I might be mated with a bun in the oven right now."

"Still," he muttered.

I ignored the pang in my broken heart and tapped the counter. "Do you have a list, or should I guess what we need?"

"We don't have enough coin for you to guess."

"This is true. I'm pretty hungry. I go crazy when I shop hungry. Hurry up with that bread."

He glowered at me, the red in his cheeks just now starting to seep away.

"Oh hey..." He pulled the slip of oddly shaped, overly thick, beige-splotched handmade paper from the edge of the counter and held it out.

We didn't have normal paper anymore. We couldn't power the machines to make it. Instead, we either had to make it by hand from wood pulp, plants, and any paper left over from before the curse, or trade for it. Parchment could be made, as well, though that was more expensive and reserved for special situations.

In this house, we received it as a thanks for helping with the everlass or elixir. It wasn't pretty, but it worked.

"About Dash…" Hannon said.

I finished what was in the mug and set it beside the washbasin. I'd completely forgotten about Dash. I'd only managed a couple hours of sleep last night, and anything not relevant to everlass completely slipped my mind.

"Yes, what was that about?" I asked.

Seriousness stole over Hannon's expression. "One of his friends knows the location of the field. I guess you're not the only one who uses it occasionally. He took Dash and another friend. I guess the kid goes with his older brother to collect the leaves."

The blood left my face. "Are they insane? Why would they risk a ten-year-old boy?"

"They go at high noon, I guess. The least dangerous time. They sacrifice the potency of the leaves in the elixir for the safety of the kids."

I was having a hard time processing this. To risk the children at all. *Children!* They were all we had. They were the most important resource in this village. It was why Dash and Sable were pampered more than they probably should be. Overprotected. Watched more than was probably healthy. We needed the kids to keep up our numbers, or we were in danger of fading away.

"We have to do a better job of watching him," I said, mostly talking to myself. "He's going to get the spanking of his life. I don't care how old he is. I will put the fear of the Divine Goddess in him so that he never does that again."

"You were fourteen…"

"Four years older than him, and I was Nana's only hope. Not that it helped. Dash has no reason to be out there."

"I know," he said softly. "We do need to talk with him."

I let out a breath. "Well. Now we know. And we have plenty of leaves to keep us going until spring. We're good."

NOT LONG AFTERWARD, I walked down the sunny lane to

the little village market in the square. It mostly held produce and trinkets, some furniture, and one or two hides or pelts. We used to have much more, I remembered, back when I was a kid. Travelers would come to our market, bringing their special skills and wares, and the villagers created finer arts and crafts to sell to the outsiders. I used to love wandering by the various stalls, looking at the beautiful hand-blown glass, the fun designs on the needlework, and the art and sculptures. I would help my mother run our booth from time to time, offering some flowers I'd grown or pelts I'd helped Father cure. I'd say hello to the traveling people and watch their juggling on the grass in the square.

But our kingdom had disappeared from the hearts and minds of the magical world. No one could come here even if they wanted to. Worse, no one could leave. Many had tried over the years. Or so I'd heard. I had been too young to witness any of this firsthand.

Some had attempted escape through the communal forests to the east and south of the village. That land technically belonged to the royal family, but it had been allocated for the use of the village. As a result, it had not been directly cursed, like the Forbidden Wood, and no everlass grew there.

Regardless, a group of villagers had set out to leave that way. From what I understood, they made it a certain distance before they could go no farther. The air crystalized before them, scorching those who tried to push past it. Killing those who continued through the pain.

After that, the survivors—desperate, enraged, and frightened—set out for the castle. They carried pitchforks and bows, spears and torches, intent on demanding their freedom.

Not one of them returned.

That very evening, the demon king appeared in the village square. He announced that if anyone set foot in the Forbidden Wood, they would be punished. Steal, and they'd be hanged. Just like in the days of old.

He remained true to his word, or so people said. It was unclear if people were punished, hanged, or eaten by the beast or one of the other creatures, but in those early days, anyone who ventured in never came back.

We were trapped in this lost and forsaken place, shifters unable to shift. Unable to even feel the animals inside of us. Magic mostly kept beyond our fingertips.

It wasn't as bad for people like me, since I'd never known my animal and didn't remember much from the old days. I'd never known the primal power and strength and extra abilities that came with shifting. Someone older and more experienced was supposed to guide a young shifter through the change on the first full moon after their sixteenth birthday, but our powers had been suppressed long before my coming of age. I didn't know what I was missing.

For our elders, it was such a grievous loss that they wouldn't talk about it anymore. At all. I didn't know who used to turn into what animal. I didn't know details of a shifter's life, or what it felt like to change. I didn't know much of anything about what I was supposed to be.

I had learned one thing: a demon's offers always had strings attached. Their sugarcoated words had a sour aftertaste. Whatever deal our mad king had been *trying* to make, the one he'd eventually accepted damned us all. In suppressing our animals, the demons had also suppressed our ability to heal quickly. Our strength. Our fighting prowess. They'd cut us off at the knees. The nobility had tried to resist after the mad king's death, but they were cut down. Most of the army went next. Without their ability to shift, they were easy prey. Almost overnight, the kingdom was an island, all six villages and the castle at the center cut off from the outside world and at the mercy of the demons. What a wonderful life.

I remembered the onslaught of emotions I'd felt back then. The horror, anger, sadness, and desperation, but I was young. I learned how to adapt. I learned purpose. A purpose I still felt. A fight I would not give up until the day I died.

This would be my life until I went out screaming. And if people would just leave me alone, I could get on with it.

"Hello, Phyl," I said as the blacksmith walked toward me with a large hammer in his massive hand. He was the only man in the village who had never batted an eye about my love of sharp things.

He nodded with a smile, showing a large gap between his front teeth. "Well, hello, Finley. Lovely day, isn't it?"

"Very nice," I said, heading for the village center.

Devious Rita grinned at me from over the wooden counter in the tomato stall. "Well, hello, Miss Finley. Bed any demons lately? I hear the demon king likes virgins in particular."

"Oh yeah? Dang. I'm not a virgin. Unless assholes count?"

She laughed and packed up a few tomatoes and some lettuce. "Probably. Did I tell you? I saw Patsy Baker getting spit-roasted the other evening. That's when one is taking her from the rear, and one is taking her from the front."

Devious Rita liked to make the young people blush. She had a field day with Hannon. I was much harder to rile up, but I appreciated her efforts. It was another side effect of being trapped here—some people had just gotten…weird. I'd learned to just roll with it.

"That right? Was she having a nice time?"

"Until she was squirted in the eye. That's when—"

"I know what that means, yeah. No need to elaborate."

"I heard the demon king snuck into little Dalia Foster's room the other night and plucked her cherry. She's expecting his child."

"Gross. I hate that expression."

Her grin was wicked.

I didn't mention that "little" Dalia Foster was nearly my age and didn't have any fruit left to offer…from any of her orifices. She'd experienced physical intimacy early, I'd heard, and experimented heavily. Apparently, the birth-nulling tea had failed her. But at least she had a good excuse to tell her overbearing father.

Devious Rita tied the bag and handed it over.

"And when will it be your turn?" she asked, her gaze dipping to my flat stomach. "You're a pretty girl. Maybe the demon king will make an exception for you and sneak in your window. I hear he's an excellent lover."

"Oh yeah? Even with a knife in his gut? Because that's exactly what would happen if he tried to climb into my room."

She was talking rubbish, obviously. This village had seen the demon king exactly once, from what I had heard, and that was when he warned everyone to stick to the village or face death. He hadn't been interested in the women then, and he wouldn't be now. Not women from here, at any rate. We had always been the poorest village in the kingdom. He was also rumored to hate shifters. No, there would be no visits from the demon king in this place.

"If not him, then I guess you'll be happy to hear that a certain *someone* has decided to finally take a wife..."

Cold ran through my middle.

She had to mean Jedrek. *Ugh!*

He'd been after me since I was sixteen, wanting nothing more than to get in my pants. After the string of rejections, he'd decided he didn't just want a lay, he wanted to mate.

Delusion was strong with that one.

"You're joking," I said. This was all I needed. He was a tenacious fucker when he wanted something.

Her smile was cunning. "Not at all. I hear he was looking for you earlier. Very handsome, that Jedrek, isn't he? And quite the hunter. He owns his own home, and his wife will want for nothing."

"Except affection, her own free will, orgasms she didn't facilitate herself..."

"Oh look, he's coming now—"

I turned quickly and hurried down the way. Rita's cackles followed me past the line of stalls. I needed to cut this trip short before he saw me—

"Finley!"

Too late. Dammit!

Jedrek stalked up to me with the swagger of a champion, his thick arms swinging, his chin held high, and his shining black hair catching the sun. More than one woman turned to look, appreciating the view.

This dipshit had somehow beaten Hannon out for the questionable distinction of most eligible bachelor. Sure, he was handsome. And yes, he did have a house and viable income, but that was only because he hadn't done a damn thing to help his parents survive the sickness. Hannon could have those things too if he shoved his family out in the street and let Father suc-cumb to the sickness. He wasn't a weasel-faced fucker, though. That was the difference.

"Jedrek, hey," I said, looking at my list so he got the hint that I was busy.

"You're looking ravishing today." He gave me an appreciative pat-down with his eyeballs.

"Awesome. I was just grabbing a few things—"

"Did you hear?" He slid his hand through his hair, flexing his bicep as he did so.

"Your ego is so heavy you stoop when you walk?"

"It's time for me to take a wife. I have a nice little nest egg and plenty of room for a nursery." His gaze lowered to my hips.

Was he checking out my birthing hips?

"Well, good luck with that." I smiled with entirely too many teeth and tried to duck around him.

"Now, Finley, we both know we're the match of the village." He adjusted his britches, looking around at our audience. Apparently everyone had known this was coming but me. Super.

"And why would I know that, Jedrek?" I adjusted my sack so it covered more of my person.

He gave a flawless smile as he stepped a little closer. "Because we are the most desirable people in this village. It's only natural that we mate."

"Beauty fades, Jedrek. But faults remain, and I pride myself on having a lot of faults."

His booming laugh didn't fit my comment. "Nonsense, Finley. You will give me strong heirs with which to carry on my line."

"Oh good. For a second there, I thought it was going to be all about you."

He turned and slid his arm around my shoulders. "We will have the grandest wedding. A plate of meat for everyone. You wouldn't want to deny the village of a celebration, do you?"

Those within earshot, which was a number growing by the minute, perked up.

Fantastic, he was playing the guilt angle. How low was that? If I said no, I'd be the bad guy. That would make for a very pleasant rest of my life...

"I'll have to think on it," I said, wriggling away.

He grabbed my arm and whipped me around. I sucked in a startled breath as he leaned in closer, his eyes blazing. "You *will* marry me, Finley. I've made it clear in the village that you are my intended. No one else will touch you. I *will* have you."

His double meaning flashed in his eyes, his lust plain.

I kept the disgust from my face. He'd drawn an audience. I'd give them a show.

I increased the wattage of my voice.

"Who has two fingers, a thumb, and nightly orgasms? *This girl.* I wouldn't want to give that up for a boring ride on your tiny dick. Go peddle your shit somewhere else. This pail is full to the brim."

Gasps sounded around me. More than a couple of people chuckled.

I ripped my arm out of his grasp and continued on through the market. I didn't for a second think it was over.

# CHAPTER 3

THE COOL OF the library washed over me as I pushed through the door. Once inside and thankfully out of the public eye, I stood still for a moment and let the tension in my body unwind. Jedrek had really thrown me for a loop. He'd shoved me completely out of my game...in as much as I had one.

Books lined the shelf in the tiny room, not much more than a glorified closet. I didn't care. This was a place of refuge for me. A place of information. After a tough day, or a boring day, or really any day, I could come here and escape into another world and live a different life.

I swept my gaze across the rows, allowing the smell of well-loved books to permeate my senses.

I'd read every single one of the books in here, some multiple times over. We couldn't get new ones, so I had to relive adventures. Sometimes, though, that was just the ticket. Like today.

"Finley!" Kessa, the librarian, walked in from a side door. The next room over was nicely furnished, used as a sort of ladies' social club. It was a place of manners and tradition, with murmured conversations, tea, and little sandwiches. I'd never once been invited to attend.

It was for the best. I liked this side of the wall better, anyway.

"Hey, Kessa." I set my bag by the door and walked down the shelves on my right. I knew exactly what I was looking for, but I didn't want to advertise my quest for dirty, hardcore hate-sex right now. There was a time and place, and this was not it.

"Got any new books in?" I asked as a joke, running my finger across the spines of all these glorious books.

"As a matter of fact, I do." She stopped by a little desk in the corner and picked up a small stack of decently made paper. There were another three lying beside it. "Our favorite author wants to know what I think. Why he wastes his time and resources on this is anyone's guess. He needs a different hobby."

I laughed. At the next shelf I ran my finger down the spine of a history of our people. On impulse, I pulled it from the shelf and set it aside. I might delve into that one this week. I hadn't read it for a while.

"Think it's any better than the last one?"

"No. Nor the one before it. I give the notes, he takes the notes, and he doesn't incorporate the notes. It's basically the same story, over and over, with the same issues." She dropped the paper back onto the table. "It's unreadable. I'm not kidding. Why bother asking for my opinion if you aren't going to listen to it?"

"I think he'd rather you just compliment him and help him bind it."

"Bah." She swatted the air. "That's what happens when you mate a woman who is too supportive. You make a fool of yourself."

"At least he has a hobby." I looked upward to the top of the stacks to see if anything there caught my eye.

"I meant to tell you. Thanks for your help last month. Ernie is making a full recovery!"

I froze for a moment. I'd helped her make the nulling elixir for her mate, who was ten years her senior and had started the slide into sickness. He had some time, and with my help, he'd have more of it, but the elixir wasn't a cure.

I'd told her all this, but Ernie was her whole world. They'd never had kids, and she didn't have any family left. He was it. If she lost him, she was alone.

I didn't have the heart to set her straight.

"I'm glad it's helping," I said softly with a pang in

my heart. I needed to find a real cure. I had to.

After selecting two more books of renewed interest and grabbing my hate-fuck smut, I went home the long way. I didn't want to accidentally run into Jedrek or any of his groupie bros.

Letting my mind wander, I glanced at the brilliant sapphire sky above. Only two puffy white clouds puttered across the wide expanse.

Flashes of memory crowded my thoughts. Glittering golden scales against the blue. Buttery-yellow sunlight sparkling across golden wings. Fire belching out of a horned head.

Dragons.

We'd had a plethora of dragon shifters back in the day, all of noble blood. All tasked with protecting the kingdom. But only one of them had routinely stopped me in my tracks.

He had been magnificent, larger than the others even though he was much younger. His movements had been so graceful. So sleek and beautiful. His roar had sent a shock through my very core, soaking my blood in fire. Commanding me to heed his call. I still, to this day, had never felt anything quite like it.

Every single person would stop and gawk as he passed over the village. They would stand transfixed, just like I used to, their mouths open, their gazes pinned to that incredible sight.

The dragon prince. Heir to the throne.

He'd do us all proud, they'd said. He had amazing potential. We'd have the finest kingdom in the magical world.

And then everything had come crashing down.

Rumor was he'd forsaken our kingdom *before* the king's deal with the demons. The queen had died not long after, though I couldn't remember the cause, if I'd ever known.

Next came the end of all things—the curse.

In through the door to the house, I deposited my books on the table and took the food to Hannon. He came out of Father's room with a grim expression.

"How is he?" I asked.

He shrugged, taking the sack and heading to the kitchen. "Hanging in there."

"He just needs to make it until spring. Come spring, I will try everything under the sun. I am bound to find something that works."

He nodded, setting the groceries on the counter. "I know you will. It's just hard, all of this."

"Life is hard, but we'll make do." I patted his back. "Are the kids still at the schoolhouse?"

"They asked that we stop calling them kids, and yes, they are."

"Fat chance," I muttered with a smile. "Oh, guess what I heard today?"

"What's that?"

"Jedrek is ready to marry!"

He stalled, glancing at me with raised eyebrows. "And his intended?"

I pointed two thumbs at myself. "He thinks we're the most desirable of people and should therefore mate. I'll get the honor of carrying all his kids."

A smile tugged at his lips. "You two will be the handsomest couple in the village, with the surliest children."

I narrowed my eyes at him. "We *would* be, since there is no way I will agree to marry that assclown."

He smiled. "What would you do if he turned out to be your true mate?"

"Reject him in a heartbeat. If my animal insisted, I'd sever all ties."

He laughed softly. "Okay then, I guess we know where you stand."

"What do you need right now? Can I help in any way?"

His gaze darted into the living room and then out the window to the backyard. "No, I think you deserve the afternoon off. You'll be drying the leaves in the evening, right?"

"Yup. Magic hour."

"I think magic hour is at three in the morning."

"Oh really? Then what is twilight?"

"Twilight."

Made sense.

I scooped up the books in the living room and headed to my favorite sycamore tree at the edge of the village, facing the Forbidden Wood. With the daylight burning bright, keeping all the demon's creatures at bay, and that invisible barrier keeping the beast put, it was safe. I settled down on the ground against its trunk and spread out the books in front of me, deciding which I wanted to read right now.

The easy *no* was the book I'd grabbed about trees and their habitats. While I did want to study up on that damn birch, and the author had written these delightful asides about poisonous mushrooms and other poisons found in nature, I didn't have the brain capacity right now. I was tired from lack of sleep and anxious about getting those leaves dried just right later on. I pushed it aside.

The romance was high on my list for obvious reasons. I desperately needed that kind of escape. But my gaze kept drifting to the book I'd grabbed about the history of my people, the shifters. Although there were only three kingdoms of shifters now—well, two, since the curse had essentially wiped us off the map—there'd once been five. Two kingdoms led by dragon shifters, two by the wolves, and a lone bear queen and her people. Only the wolf kings and queens now remained, tenacious bastards.

There were other kingdoms, of course, near and far. A few faerie kingdoms with their court politics and intrigues. Hideous goblins with their heaps of stolen treasure. The land of night, ruled by the vampires. And, of course, the cunning demon king who was slowly cutting down all of his competition. Within each kingdom, various villages and towns housed the hardworking people, usually all the same magical type— shifters lived in a shifter kingdom, faeries in a faerie kingdom—but occasionally a star-crossed lover would move in for a little magical diversity, sacrificing same- ness for their love. That, or they'd escape beyond the veil to the human realm, disguising themselves within the mundane, often never to return.

The rumor was that the dragon prince had left our kingdom for that very reason. He'd fancied a noble faerie and moved away to her kingdom to be with her, shirking his duties as our prince and future king. Giving it all up for a chance at love.

I couldn't say I blamed him. Everyone deserved a chance at happiness, even princes. I doubted he had known the cost.

Maybe he still didn't know. Maybe the mad king had cut him off. We might have been erased from his mind.

It was impossible to know. Nobles weren't known for hobnobbing with poor commoners, and we were the poorest in the kingdom. We had the least fertile lands and worst commodities. We were one of the farthest out from the castle. Whatever had happened, I doubted anyone in this village had known more than mere rumor. It was probably why no one continued to speculate. Why I hadn't heard anything more about the curse once I was old enough to understand the larger picture.

The book from the library didn't talk about the prince's flight, of course. It was too old. Even still, it offered some sort of connection to our past, to the way things used to be, and I needed to believe they'd be that way again. So I pulled the book onto my lap and settled in.

After a while, a yawn took hold of me, and I bumped my head against the tree, feeling a wave of fatigue. Hopefully tonight I could catch up on some sleep. It was nearly time to go hunting again, and I'd need my stamina to face down those asshole boars. I was one of the only people in the village who routinely took on those beasts, but they had the best and most meat. It was worth the risk.

A moment later, I opened my eyes...and then blinked a few more times.

The light had dwindled around me. A cool breeze drifted across my face, signaling the coming evening. The book that had been in my lap had tipped halfway off, its edge propped against the ground.

I'd only intended to close my eyes for a moment, but I'd obviously fallen asleep.

I sat up, grimacing from the stiffness in my back and legs. If I'd wanted to nap, I should've done it in my bed. Not like I'd been planning it.

As I lifted my book and reached over to grab the others, prickles skittered up my back and crawled across my scalp. Eyes. Someone was watching me. A presence, likely dangerous. I didn't need a connection with my animal to ascertain any of that. Hunting gave a person a certain sixth sense.

I stacked my books nice and neat, a little away from me, and uncrossed my legs. If I needed to move fast, I could.

Nonchalantly, as though I didn't know anything was amiss, I stretched and did the ol' look-over-the-shoulder trick. No one waited in sight, though that didn't mean they weren't behind me.

I pushed forward to my hands and knees, like I was going to get up, and then peered around the tree trunk. Nothing. Deserted.

I'd half expected Jedrek to be lingering around. I'd rebuffed him publicly today. He wouldn't make the mistake of approaching me in front of an audience again, but a guy like him wouldn't relent, either. His ego wouldn't let him. I expected him to try to catch me alone and then scare me into acquiescing.

But he wasn't a small man. If he were the lurking presence, I would've seen him. Still…the prickles persisted. A strange feeling of heaviness filled my chest, just like I'd felt last night before…

I froze.

Nothing sexual came with it this time. Only a trickle of fire that seeped into my limbs.

I swept my gaze across the darkening trees, the failing light leeching the color from the area. Nothing moved within the lengthening shadows. The light breeze didn't stir the branches. All was still and quiet.

That did nothing to shake my certainty. Something lurked in the patches of darkness nestled between the branches in front of me. Something watched and waited.

Chills spread across my flesh.

Slowly I got up and grabbed my books. I didn't intend to hang around and see what the night would bring. Besides, I had things to do. I needed to attend to those leaves.

Turning, I thought I heard the shimmy of leaves.

I jerked my head back toward the Forbidden Wood and squinted as I peered into the gloom. Whatever it was, it was well hidden.

My nerve snapped. I clutched the books to my chest as though they would protect me—classic bookworm reaction—and hurried home.

I slammed the front door behind me and sucked in a deep breath.

"What's the matter?" Hannon asked, looking up from his own book in the front room.

"Nothing. Just…" I set my books on the little table by the door and plopped down on the couch next to him. "I got spooked, is all. The Forbidden Wood is messing with my mind."

"Good. That'll keep you out of there."

"I want nothing more than to be kept out of there."

"The day is dying," he said, going back to his book.

"In other words, get out of your hair and do something useful?"

"Yes. This is a good part."

"Where are the kids?"

"With their friends."

They'd be home soon. The setting sun was curfew for children, no exceptions. Even if a creature didn't wander out of the Forbidden Wood, there were still the demons that lurked in the village after dark. Since the curse, the night was too dangerous for children.

I peeled myself off the couch and headed outside to tend to the everlass.

Time passed in a series of familiar movements. At some point, Dash brought out a bowl of stew and then hung around, listening as I described what I was doing. Working with plants—this one especially—calmed me in a way I couldn't describe. I enjoyed the careful finesse it required. The way its properties changed with its environment.

In a few hours, I finally finished my tasks and shoved Dash inside so he could go to bed. This harvest would last for a while, thanks to the strong, healthy plants the leaves had come from. By the time I needed more, my plants would hopefully be thriving in the spring sun.

GLOWING GOLDEN EYES stared at me from the trees. Terror pounded a steady beat in my body. A roar sliced through my bones while also yanking on my middle.

I jerked awake, snapping my eyes open.

Damn that beast's glowing eyes. I was sure I dreamed of other things, but the only thing I ever remembered upon waking was those accursed glowing eyes, and now the roar, apparently.

A low, menacing growl curled through the air. Cold flowed through my veins.

*Please say I'm still dreaming. Please say I'm still dreaming.*

I was afraid to move, to turn my head to the side and look for the source of the noise.

The growl sounded again, deep and low, from the same place.

Right outside my bedroom window.

Dread pierced me, and I sat up slowly, fighting the fear freezing my joints.

This couldn't be what I thought it was. It couldn't be. The beast couldn't pass the boundary of the Forbidden Wood. Or at least that was what people said.

The deep growl sounded for the third time, rolling through the dense night air.

"Finley!" Sable lay on her side facing me. Through the hazy moonlight I could just see her wide eyes. She'd heard it too. It was no dream. This impossible situation was happening in real time.

The moonlight through the window flickered…and

then went dark, something enormous blocking the light.

"Goddess help us," Sable said with a quivering voice. "The beast has come for us."

"It's fine. It's going to be fine."

How was this possible?

I threw myself down and rolled onto the floor. It might be able to see in the dark, but it shouldn't be able to see much detail through our shades, even as worn and flimsy as they were.

"Don't move," I whispered.

On elbows and knees, I crawled to the rickety dresser in the corner. The light resumed streaming in through the window. The beast had moved on.

I pushed up to standing and grabbed my dagger off the top. A moment later, I hurried to the door and ripped it open.

A scream tore through my throat, cut off quickly by a hand clamped to my mouth. Hannon put a single finger to his lips.

I swiped his hand away and pushed past him. I wouldn't have needed the warning if he hadn't surprised the shit out of me.

Father coughed behind his closed door, his chest rattling.

*Let's not worry about that now, folks. Let's work on*

*keeping the whole family alive first.*

In the front room, I reached the front door and made sure the heavy wooden beam had been lowered. Its end rested in the metal cradle that secured it in place. Moonlight flickered against the white wood. Then the light dimmed…before it mostly went out.

I closed my eyes as my heart stuttered. Every nerve ending was pinging with electricity. Adrenaline had flooded my system.

Beside the window overlooking the porch, we had three windows in the front room. The two that faced the backyard were close together, and a third looked out onto the side yard between our house and another. Judging by the difference in lighting, both back windows had just been obstructed.

We didn't have shades on those windows.

Time slowed down as I turned. I knew what I would find.

My nightmares had come to life.

A large, glowing golden eye took up residence in one of the windows.

It was hard to breathe. That strange feeling in my chest rolled outward, fire leaking out from my center and into my limbs. But even as my body burned, my blood had turned to ice. I couldn't move from fear.

That eye wasn't more than fifteen feet away, much

closer than the last time I'd seen it. *Much* closer. Through my fear-induced paralysis, I couldn't help but take in every detail. A thin, vertical oval took up the center, the pupil similar to a cat's but rounder. A deep, brawny gold outlined the black before exploding outward in a sunburst of color, lined through with streaks of lighter gold, orange, red, and yellow. Along the edges, darker patches shone through, making the sunburst that much more dramatic.

It was beautiful.

It blinked, and I saw that there were two sets of eye-lids. The first looked like more of a sheen that slid over from the side. Then the human equivalent, top coming down and meeting the lower lid. The blink happened quickly, but the movement made me jerk.

"Finley?"

Dash's voice rang down the hall. The golden eye flicked in that direction, as if the beast had heard.

A different sort of fear ate through the first, and I was all action again, launching forward to intercept Dash running into the living room.

"Stay back," I barked, stopping in the center of the room to block his progress. I held out a hand. "Stay back! Stay out of sight."

That gorgeous but awful golden eye slid back to me, taking me in, pushing past my barriers and taking my measure. I could feel it, as if he'd ripped out my soul and placed it on a scale.

The eye disappeared, and the body followed, dark scales moving beyond the window. In a moment, the moonlight came back, flaring through the darkness.

The sound of shattering glass made me flinch and lift my arm in front of my face. Something thunked against the wooden floor and skittered to my feet. My pocketknife.

I stared at it as though from a different body. A different world.

It had retrieved my pocketknife. Then it had tracked me here. It knew who I was and what I'd done. It must.

And now it had come to collect.

*This might go very badly, everybody. Hang tight for the finale,* I thought desperately, my whole body shaking.

I needed action. I needed to break out of these fear-induced shackles and use the energy for something useful. But what? What the hell was I going to do against a creature this size? Hiding seemed to be the only thing available to me right now. Hiding…or a distraction.

Tears welled up in my eyes, but I didn't give in to them. To save my family, I'd do anything, including running blindly toward the Forbidden Wood so it would chase me. So that my family could get out.

"What do I do?" Hannon asked quietly from the hall.

"Keep them safe," I said in a hollow voice as I steeled my courage. I bent slowly and picked up the closed pocketknife with my free hand, avoiding the shards of glass on the floor. The light guttered out again, and there was that golden eye, taking my measure. Waiting, it seemed like. Offering me a choice. Give myself up or risk my family.

*Choose.*

With the window broken, I could now hear the beast. Its puffs of breath in the quiet night. The simmering growl deep in its chest.

It wasn't a choice. Not for me. It was an eventuality.

"Gather the kids near the large window in your room," I whispered to Hannon, a tear dripping from my eye. I slipped the pocketknife into the pocket of my pajama bottoms. "If it comes to it, you climb out with them and get them to safety. Otherwise, hunker down and stay put. I'll distract the beast."

"No, Finley." Hannon stepped forward as if to grab me and haul me away to safety.

I threw out my hand. "Stay put, damn it! You have the everlass. Chartreuse in the village square knows how to make the nulling elixir better than anyone else

besides me. Ask her for help. Keep Father alive. I'll…"
What would I do? What could I possibly do against a
beast? "I will get through this somehow, and I will come
back for you, okay? Keep them alive. All of them."

The tears leaked down my cheeks. My words
dripped with sorrow. We both knew I wouldn't be
coming back.

It was okay, though. He'd look after them better
than I could. He was the family rock in the ongoing
storm.

"I love you all," I said, turning and stalking quickly
for the door.

"What's she doing?" Dash whined.

"No, Finley," Sable said, all of them huddled at the
entrance to the dark hall.

I removed the wood blocking the door. I paused but
didn't look back. I wanted to go out a hero. I didn't
want the last image they had of me to be of a scared girl
headed out to meet her fate.

# CHAPTER 4

A FTER CLOSING THE door behind me, I took off at a sprint. I'd be damned if the beast would kill me in front of my family.

I didn't take the path through the neighbor's yard, either. It might barrel after me and take them and their house out in the crossfire. Instead, I took the lane down the center of the houses and around.

The beast's roar sliced through me, making me stumble, commanding me to stop. The force nearly locked up my legs and turned my body to wood. The effect tickled a memory, but my bleating panic wiped it from my mind.

Wood splintered, and heavy footsteps sounded on the path behind me. It must've crashed through our garden fence. Hannon could repair that, no problem. At least it was following me. That was the plan.

Putting on a burst of speed, I headed for the Forbidden Wood. I didn't dare look back. I didn't want to see the size of the thing. Besides, if it somehow snuck up on me, swooped down, and bit me in two, at least the end would be quick. It would be better than trying to fight a losing battle with a somewhat dull dagger.

Around the last house in the lane, I ran by the sycamore and randomly cursed myself for not telling Hannon to take those books back to the library. As though that were the most important thing in all of this.

Reaching the tree line of the Forbidden Wood, I wondered why I hadn't been caught. It should've reached me by now.

Maybe it hadn't followed…

I slowed to a stop and spun, expecting to see empty space. Instead, I very nearly wet myself.

Its progress had been utterly silent. Not one puff of breath or massive footstep had alerted me to its presence. But it had followed me all the same.

A massive creature stood just beyond the sycamore, looking down on me. Those eyes glowed in the semi-darkness, seemingly soaking up the moonlight showering its dull, murky black scales. A great head reached half as high as the peak of a tall tree, two horns curling away from the top. Its scaled face had a protruding jaw, and long teeth jutted from its lipless mouth. I'd seen its massive shoulders before, taller than me, with a deep, muscular chest. Two stout legs supported it in front, and the upper body sloped down to the hindquarters and slightly shorter back legs.

If I had my leather sheath, I would slip my dagger into it. It wouldn't help me against what I faced.

If I had more courage, I would stand my ground.

I spun and ran like hell.

I didn't even know where I was going. Nor did I look back to see if it was following me. I had zero control over myself right then. Panic was driving this wagon, and it was doing it with drunk horses.

I zigzagged around trees and stumbled over rocks. My shoulder rammed a tree trunk I hadn't noticed, and I careened into a tangle of briars. I gasped as a thorn ripped into my arm and tore my nightshirt. My breath came in fast pants, and the scene before me wiggled in my tear-soaked vision. Some hero. I'd slipped into full damsel, and honestly, I would not mind being saved. I would not mind it at all.

Beyond a set of reaching bushes, I suddenly realized where I was. The tall birch, seemingly out of place, stood before me a ways, marking the everlass field. Even in my blind panic, I'd had enough directional sense to get there. Given that I'd been caught thieving from this very field, it was probably the worst place for me to have led the beast. Then again, where the hell else was I going to go? I could hide in here all night and return home tomorrow…only to find the beast at my house again. I couldn't escape the village, and now I couldn't escape the beast.

*Time to face the future. How will our hero turned coward escape this time?*

Breathing heavily, I stopped in front of the birch and looked up. It took that as a cue to shake like a dancing girl, waving its branches and rattling it leaves.

"Would you shut up, you dickfaced cumsplat?" I yelled at it. "It can find me just fine on its own."

The low growl behind me was proof of that. I sucked in a deep breath and turned once again.

It stood nestled in the trees, mostly obscured by the branches surrounding it but for those eyes, like two embers surrounded by blackness. Its head lowered, and I clutched my dagger tightly, raising it just a bit. Might as well give the illusion of bravery.

The enormous beast reduced down in a blink, turning into a nude man.

My mouth dropped open. No. It couldn't be. This was impossible! The ability to shift had been suppressed by the curse. I hadn't heard of anyone in this kingdom who could still manage it. And while it was possible our village was the only one that had been so afflicted, I certainly hadn't heard that *the beast* turned into a man. That was something people would talk about. Warn others about.

He walked toward me, out of the trees. The moonlight fell over his messy brown hair and onto his wide shoulders and robust frame. Thick, well-defined muscle covered every inch of his tall body, not an ounce of fat to spare. He'd earned that muscle through hard-fought battles, I could tell. He looked like a man who knew exactly what he was capable of.

His movements were sleek and graceful, and his eyes—still that same animalistic gold hue—tracked me as he stalked forward. He was the hunter in this situation, and he knew it. The predator. He was sighting in on his prey. Me.

What caught me, though, wasn't his muscle or obvious power. It wasn't even the aura of danger that twisted my gut and made my legs tremble. It was his scarred appearance.

A mess of vicious scars cut across his physique. A ragged silver line on his pec ran beside his nipple, four parallel scars sliced through his side, and other lines crisscrossed his abdomen. He'd tried to cover them up with swirls of ink. It hadn't worked, though. If anything, it brought more attention to his past trauma, some causing puckered skin and others creating valleys from what must've been deep wounds.

He stopped a handful of feet from me, his brawn and power making my breath come out unevenly. Even as man, he was enormous. I was a tall woman, but his height topped mine by a foot. The point of my dagger wobbled back and forth, and there was nothing I could do to hide my shaking arm.

"You are trespassing," he said with a deep, scratchy voice. It sounded like he'd earned that, too. As though he'd screamed so hard and long that he'd damaged his vocal cords.

"You chased me in here. I hardly think that counts," I said, adept at biting back against all odds. I'd had a lot of practice.

"The price of trespassing is detention. The price of stealing is death."

"Good thing I didn't steal, then." I held out my arms to indicate my lack of stolen goods.

Clearly on impulse, he dipped his gaze down to follow the thread of the conversation. His eyes had started moving back upward, toward my face, when he did a double take and settled his attention on my chest. I belatedly realized that sweat had made my threadbare nightshirt cling to my freely hanging breasts, no time for binding before I ran from the house. The cold and fear had made my nipples stand at attention. He was getting an eyeful.

The pressure in the air increased. The weight inside of my middle flipped over, and more fire leaked out. My core tightened as his gaze slowly lifted to mine. Hunger flashed in those golden eyes. Lust. Dominance.

Something within me—something foreign but rooted way down deep—purred in delight. Desire warmed my body.

*What the fuck is happening, folks? This shit is no good.*

I recognized this feeling, though. It was the lust magic from last night. This still didn't feel the same as an incubus's power. Their power was lean and slinky and slick. Oily. This was...raw and intense and powerful. Dangerous. *Delicious.*

I pushed it away with everything I had, ignoring the sudden wetness between my legs and the unyielding desperation to be taken roughly. To have him pound that big cock into me over and over again.

"Finley, isn't it?"

Why did that rough voice suddenly feel like a sensuous lick across my heated flesh? I hated that I loved it. Hated that I suddenly craved his kisses between my thighs. His fingers banging into my slick sex.

"Fuck the goddess sideways, I am losing my ever-loving mind," I mumbled, trying to get a grip. I wiped the back of my hand across my forehead. It felt like his magic was unwinding me, one thread at a time. Why did it feel so fucking *good*?

"Do you want to be dominated, Finley? Your animal certainly does."

"Wh-what?" I pushed my palm to my chest, feeling that weight within rail against my ribcage, as though it were indeed a creature trying to break free. The fire kept seeping into my bloodstream, pulsing power into my limbs. I was drunk with it. Drunk on this feeling. Desperate to let this big-ass alpha push me down into the dirt right now and drive that big cock deep into my needy cunt.

"Enough!"

His bark of command was like a splash of cold water.

I blinked and realized I'd dropped my dagger and now stood right in front of him. His chest heaved like mine, his large cock fully erect between us. I hadn't touched him yet, but it was clear I'd been about to act on the things I'd been thinking. To demand he give me what I was craving.

The scary thing was that I had no idea when I'd moved or how I'd gotten there. Neither of those things had registered. It was like someone else had assumed control of my movements. Control of *me*. But at the same time, I remembered thinking those dirty words. Remembered wanting to act on them. Remembered feeling the ache in my core at the filthy, delicious thoughts.

Oh no, was it happening again?

Without thinking, I slapped him across the face. Then thought, *Oh shit, what did I just do?*

Before I could back-pedal or run or laugh manically, he snatched my wrist out of the air.

"I will give you that one," he said in a voice out of a nightmare. "I am partially responsible. I didn't control my beast as I ought to have. But you will get just the one. Try it again, and I'll break you."

"What disgusting type of creature are you?" I asked. "Are you the king of the incubi or something? You magically force girls to give themselves to you?"

"I am no demon, princess, I can assure you."

The pet name was condescending, as was his expression.

"You don't know what you have bottled up inside of you, do you?" he asked.

I squinted at him and, for the first time, didn't have a witty comeback. The bastard had completely knocked me off my game.

He flung my hand away and then shoved me backward, lightly enough to force some space but not enough to send me sprawling.

"That beast inside of you is going to get you into trouble," he said. "You need to learn to control it."

"What…what are you talking about?"

He huffed out a laugh, shook his head, and then looked up at the sky. "Fucking typical." It sounded like he was talking to himself. Or maybe he'd borrowed my invisible audience for the moment. He rolled his shoulders before squaring them. "You have stolen the everlass plant from these lands on multiple occasions. Why?"

"No, I didn't." Only an idiot would fess up without proof.

"Why?" he growled.

Fear wound through me, but I wouldn't give him the satisfaction of seeing it. That plant was clearly very important to him. This wasn't just about stealing—it was about stealing from him. His grudge was personal, and I did not want to incriminate my village. My secrets would die with me.

"Most people come to this wood in the hopes of escaping this rotting kingdom," he said. "They either hope to kill me or, lately, make a deal with the demon king. But you and some of your brethren steal the everlass plant. Your village is the only one to have shown an interest in it. Why?"

"I assume *others* do it because their gardens are too small and they don't have enough room to grow the plants they need."

He took a step forward, bristling with anger. "Do you need to make this so difficult?"

"Do I need to make my execution difficult? Yeah, kinda. It's not something I am looking forward to."

His stare beat into me, turning my belly to gravy. "You are trying to fight a battle that you cannot win."

"Life is a battle we cannot win. The question becomes, do we want to go down peacefully, or fight until our last breath? I choose to fight."

That weight in my chest—almost an actual presence—thunked within me. I felt its approval.

Could it really be my animal? Was that even possible?

The air between us crackled. "You leave me no choice."

A shock of power slammed into me. It throbbed, not sexual this time but commanding. Consuming. The compulsion to answer him washed over me. Pulled me down and battered me around. I opened my mouth to obey. I shut it.

I was not a puppet to play with. I was not a servant to boss around. I had no master, and I wouldn't take one now. If he wanted to kill me, fine, but I would not be compelled to give up my secrets.

I clenched my jaw to hold back the words. I dug the nails of my free hand into the heel of my palm, focusing on that bite of pain.

Anger and frustration sizzled from him. More power came, punching me. It set fire to my skin and scraped down my bones. Agony flash-boiled my blood. It hurt so badly that I thought I might black out. But still I resisted.

"Damn you, Finley," he growled. He reached forward and grabbed me by the throat, yanking me toward him. His golden eyes locked with mine. "*Why?*"

That presence within me poured out fire. Anger. *Rage.*

I had the pocketknife in my hand without thinking. Opened it without knowing how.

I stabbed him in the chest.

He hissed and tossed me away. A hand came up quickly to the knife now sticking out of his pec. I hadn't stabbed in nearly far enough. It was nothing but a flesh wound. Given the state of his body, he'd had plenty. Given his thick slab of muscle, it wouldn't slow him down much.

This was going to work out very badly for me.

I was up and running in a flash. I couldn't go home, though. That would just bring him back to my family.

Instead, I turned right and dodged around the birch tree, which surged to life. It shook and waved and did its jig. On the other side, I felt his pounding command to *halt*, but I ignored it. I ran out into the everlass, watching my footfalls until I got to the middle. There I stopped, breathing hard, and faced him again.

If the everlass was personal to him, he'd understand its fragility. He wouldn't want to tramp through the field and destroy it. Hopefully.

He appeared at the edge of the field with blood streaming down the new hole in his pec, dipping into the groove between his stomach muscles and lats.

He spread his arms. "Where are you going to go? If you run back to your village, I'll kill them all. Do you want that? Your life is forfeit, Finley. You stole from this land, and now you belong to me."

"And who are you? The demon king's puppet? His minion?"

Confusion crossed his face. He tilted his head and then started laughing without humor. He lowered his arms.

"This just keeps getting better and better," he said to himself. Then to me: "In the absence of the king, as the only noble left standing, I am the keeper of these lands. I am their protector. I am your jailer and your master."

"Their protector? Are you joking? People are dying. The sickness from that curse is killing them. If anything,

*I* am the protector. *I* am the one who keeps them alive when the curse's sickness tries to rot their bodies as it has rotted this wood. You should be thanking me, not threatening me. All you do is wander around these woods in beast form and kill trespassers. Who the fuck are you protecting it from? Its subjects? You're either misguided or an idiot. Exact your punishment and be done with it. You're wasting my time."

His fists opened and closed. He looked down at the everlass at his feet, then back up at me. It seemed like he was warring with himself over something. He walked forward, picking his way carefully. A sudden insight ripped through me. He'd said only my village was using this field, and none of them were great at pruning. *He* was the one who had been pruning and taking care of these plants. Showing them love.

I didn't have time for the confusion I felt.

I lifted a foot and braced it over the nearest plant.

He paused. "That's just one plant, Finley."

"By the time you get to me, it'll be a lot more than one plant. We both know they share a root system. If one of them is crushed, they'll all share the pain. They'll all dwindle if I take out enough of them. I know how many that has to be."

I wasn't sure that was true. I thought I had read it once.

He immediately froze, though, so perhaps it was

accurate. He slowly brought his palms up in a placating gesture.

"Your brother entered these grounds not long ago with two others."

My heart stopped beating. I lowered my foot in case I accidentally lost balance and crushed a plant anyway.

"His life—their lives—also belong to me. I will forgive their trespassing and theft if you cooperate."

"We can make a deal," I said quickly, licking my lips. "I'll tell you my secrets if you spare the village. They're having a hard enough time. They aren't trying to hurt anyone. They certainly don't have the resources to kill you."

He contemplated that for a moment.

"I will consent to spare those who treat the everlass well. Everyone else will die," he snarled.

It had to be good enough.

"Fine, yes, I've been here a few times out of necessity. Trust me, I didn't want to set foot in the wood. We use the everlass in an elixir I devised called the nulling elixir. Over the years, I've strengthened it so that it prolongs the lives of those who've fallen ill with the sickness from the curse." I swallowed. "I still haven't gotten it quite right. It isn't a cure. But while we used to lose a dozen villagers in a year, now we're down to a couple. Only one so far this year."

"You created this elixir?" I couldn't tell whether he was incredulous, but I could definitely tell he was sneering.

"Just because we weren't born with money doesn't mean we weren't born with intelligence. We all have our own gardens, but during the winter months, as you must know, the everlass hibernates. The leaves we pick don't grow back. Given we need a lot to keep a person stable, some of us with patients on the brink run out. When desperate, we either let them die, or we turn to this wood and risk confronting the beast that patrols it. Mr. Protector, as you call yourself. There, happy? We're just trying to save lives."

"I haven't heard of this elixir."

"Why would someone wander in here and tell you? We didn't even know you turned into a man. Or that anyone could still shift."

"None of the other villages have it."

"We are confined to the village, genius. I created the elixir. How would I share it with anyone beyond our borders? Mental telepathy?"

"I don't believe you."

"And I suppose you have a better theory. What did you think we came in here for, a dare? To stuff our pillows with extra fluff? Maybe a lovely little fragrance pot for the corner of our—"

He bristled again, and blistering heat crunched down on me. The consuming need to *shut up* washed over me.

"We struck a bargain," he said. "The past grievances of your village and your brother are erased. I will show them no wrath. Come now. You must pay for your sins."

The wind went out of me. I looked down at the everlass plants one last time as tears clouded my vision. I nodded, to myself mostly, and picked my way forward.

He waited beyond the birch, tall and stoic against the dark wood. I faced him with head held high.

"Do you want your weapons?" he asked.

I huffed. "Would they do any good?"

He didn't answer. Just stared.

I shrugged indifferently and collected them, wiping the blade of the pocketknife and putting it back in my pajama pocket, then hefting the dagger.

"You could've been incredible one day, Finley," he said.

The enormous beast emerged, and he lunged for me.

I swung my dagger on instinct, driven purely by fear. It clanged off his armored face. His glowing golden eyes blinked shut and then his teeth closed against my body.

# CHAPTER 5

I DIDN'T HAVE the breath to scream. The dull points of well-worn teeth pinched me between them as he ran, crashing through the trees. Branches *thwapped* my face, hard enough to sting but not to do lasting damage. If he let go, I'd have a long way to fall before I went splat. That was the only reason I didn't try to swing my dagger around and stick him in the eye or nostril.

We smashed through yet another wall of foliage, and his clawed feet crunched on the brittle grass beyond it, probably long since dead. Vines and thorns twisted through a gazebo off to the left, the paint peeling and the skillful woodwork splintered and broken. Arching, I could just see a grand entrance to what must be the royal castle.

He stopped before the grungy and cracked marble staircase and let me go.

I screamed as I plummeted toward the ground.

Before I hit, the large shape of the beast quickly re-duced down to the man, and his arms snatched me from the air. My dagger clanged against the ground, now out of reach, and he crowded me to his chest as he climbed the steps.

I had expected the smell of sweat and dirt and body odor but was instead surprised by a fresh, light, almost balmy smell of pine and lilac with a hint of honeysuckle. It was the same scent from the wood earlier, when all my senses had gone on high alert for a moment, and it was absolutely divine. It called up an image of a wind-swept mountain top overlooking a crystalline lake with a mirrored surface. It spoke of comfort and peace and familiarity, feelings so at odds with the moment and this horrible place that I froze as he barged through the doors into an empty foyer. Marble columns rose around us, and the ground had been cleaned to a glossy shine.

"Put me down," I ground out, trying to wriggle out of his arms.

He didn't budge, his hold too strong for me to break. Two staircases on either side of the cavernous space curved up to a landing above. He took a left, bypassing the stairs, and walked deeper into the castle, toward a set of closed double doors painted white. A dull thump vibrated through the air, pierced with occasional screams of mirth.

He kicked in the doors. Light was the first thing to hit me, glaring from what must've been hundreds of candles spread around the room and stuck in the crystal chandelier where light bulbs should go. I threw up my hand to cover my face as my captor walked forward. Next came the cacophony. Bawdy laughter and loud music filled the space. Frenzied movement accompanied a plethora of colors, none of them subdued. Feathers waved, and a string of what looked like beads flew across the air. Bodies gyrated to the music that must be powered by magic in some way.

Pulling my arm away, I took in more detail.

It was some kind of masquerade party. One woman wore nothing but a black feathered mask and robe. Her lips were scarlet, and her body was painted in elaborate designs, curling around her bare nipples and smeared on the inside of her thighs.

A man on the other side of the room wore a large headdress in bright fuchsia and yellow, jewels dotting the forehead and across the bridge of his nose. A large red robe draped down his front, the tie loosely knotted around his lower chest and the rest completely open. A metal ring surrounded his cock and balls, and red lines had been painted on each side of his erect penis.

Directly in front of us, two women writhed as they

danced, each completely naked except for their masks, one with her fingers in the other's mouth, and the other with her fingers in the first's pussy.

My gaze darted to an orgy of all men in the back. It was some sort of train, with four men attached with cocks in asses and in perfect sync, ramming forward and pulling back in opposites so they all had friction. Their timing was impeccable. One premature thrust and the whole party would disentangle.

I stared in complete and utter shock. I was no prude, but...

Fuck, maybe I *was* a prude. The pub in my village was *nothing* like this. This level of debauchery was beyond anything I'd ever imagined.

"What sort of outfit are you running here?" I asked.

A man trotted across the black checkered floor, wearing cloth hooves on his hands, which he kept tight to his chest, slippers fashioned to look like hooves on his feet, and a sort of horse mask with a bridle on his head. A leather-clad woman sat in the saddle on his back, custom-designed to be worn when he was upright, giving him slaps with a riding crop. He was enjoying it, if his hard-on was any judge.

One by one, the partygoers saw us, their large smiles slipping and their movements slowing and then stopping.

The lead guy in the dick train popped himself off his caboose and turned our way. I knew instantly that it was an incubus just by his posture and the sensuous way he moved. The crowd parted before him as he made his way toward us. He took the crop off the horse rider with a knowing little smirk on his face.

"Nyfain, how good of you to join us." His obsidian eyes sparkled with mischief and haughtiness. He stopped in front of us. "What have we here?"

He reached that crop toward my cheek. The goddess only knew where that thing had been. Whose sweaty ass it had spanked. No fucking thank you.

Before I could swat it away, the man who held me—Nyfain—kicked forward. His foot connected solidly with the middle of the incubus's chest. The incubus flew backward with an expression of surprise mingled with pain. He hit the ground and slid across the marble, his greasy backside not allowing him the traction to stop. He bowled over the previously dancing women and into a mixed group that had stopped to watch.

"Hadriel, step forward," Nyfain barked.

"Now, now, Nyfain." A woman strode toward us from the side, wearing a crimson lace bustier halter with garters and no underwear. Succubus. Of course they were behind this debauchery. They fed off lust and misdeeds. "The sun has set. You have no jurisdiction here."

"I don't need jurisdiction, I need Hadriel. Step forward!"

"Hadriel is otherwise occup—"

"Here!" A slim man in the center right inched out of a throng of people. It was a wonder that I hadn't noticed him earlier.

He wore a furry purple sort of…costume thing that made him look like a silly mock-up of the beast. His shaggy pants ended in black shoes that resembled hooves, kinda like the man posing as a horse. A black vee covered his pecker region, but then the costume opened up to bare the torso, exposing a couple of hairy nipples. His arms were covered with the same material as his legs, cinched up around the neck. Two stuffed horns curled up from his head.

"Oh goddess, that is a sight," I said with a small giggle. It was just the thing to slice through my terror.

"Here, sir." Hadriel inched a little farther forward and then wobbled. He clearly wasn't sober.

"Compose yourself and then report to the tower room," Nyfain barked.

"You don't have to go, Hadriel," the succubus said. "There is nothing he can do to you if you stay."

"There's plenty he can do to me," Hadriel murmured as he all but staggered in our direction.

I pulled away from Nyfain a little and tried to look down his body.

"What are you doing?" he growled, squeezing me to his chest so I'd stay put.

"Trying to see if you have an erection."

He huffed, heading back out to the stairs and up. At the third floor, he turned into a lovely, picturesque hall with arched windows along the left and stone on the right. Oil paintings lined the way, some with mustaches drawn on the subjects' faces and occasionally a few dongs. Clearly a few partygoers had gotten out of control.

At the end, he ascended a small staircase that wound up to a single heavy door. The tower, most likely. He planned to stick me there.

"I thought you were going to kill me," I said in a small voice as he put me down.

"Picking a weed is not really stealing, but your persistent trespassing warrants detention. Your sentence is for an eternity. Here is your cell."

He twisted the key before pushing open the door. Darkness waited within. He gestured me through.

"But…" I fidgeted with my collar as I stared into the inky depths. "You're going to keep me in a tower?" My voice kept rising. "In a room that locks from the outside?"

"Would you rather I throw you in the dungeon?"

"Is there a third option? Like a slap on the wrist and public humiliation?"

He grabbed me by the arm and shoved me into the room. I staggered, fear rising to choke me. He took residence in the doorway, his massive shoulders nearly filling the frame. His body was built for power, and he'd honed it with strength.

"Welcome to hell, princess."

The door slammed and the lock clicked. I dropped my dagger and pounded on the door, jiggling the handle and yanking. Nothing.

"That absolute asshole," I spat, turning and pushing my back against the door.

My eyes adjusted to the darkness. Thank the goddess for the nearly full moon. Weak light filtered in around heavy curtains. I started forward, waving my hands in front of me to feel what I couldn't see. My foot hit something solid and then the side of my arm did. Wood of some kind. A little farther, and I kicked and then practically fell onto a little table. Farther still, I finally reached the window.

I grabbed velvet and yanked. The metal curtain hooks scraped against the curtain rod. Light gushed in, and I got a first look at the view.

I was high off the ground. The stairs indicated I was

four levels up, but the castle was perched on a rise. The land on this side dropped away, and it felt like I could see forever. The tops of trees spread out in the distance with various gaps, some quite large. I wondered if those openings marked other villages or homesteads. It occurred to me how little I knew about the kingdom. I'd never been away from home. I had no idea what other places looked like and how they were set up. No idea what the castle was like beyond what I'd seen tonight.

As a young girl, I'd dreamed of such things. I'd make believe I was a queen walking out onto her dais, waving to the adoring crowds gathered below and adjusting my long red velvet cape. I'd travel to distant kingdoms and meet their leaders, smiling serenely and drinking tea with my pinky up, as befitted royalty. Other times I'd play the jester, doing handstands and juggling for the simpering royalty, then making jokes at their expense, which they were certainly too slow to grasp.

But then I grew up. My grandiose make-believe downsized into my habit of addressing an invisible audience whenever I got into trouble or took risks to put food on the table. My dreams had dried up. All of our dreams had, I guessed. I wasn't alone in any of this.

Well. I *was* alone in a tower in a castle, kept prisoner by the last surviving noble—

I sucked in a breath as I pulled back the rest of the curtains and looked out over the grounds. I did some quick math: the last surviving noble + in charge of protecting the land = dragon. Dragon!

I searched my memory for what dragons looked like. First came that glittering golden masterpiece in the sky from my youth. The dragon prince. But I'd never seen him—or any of them—close up, only from down below as they cut through the air with massive wings. There was no way I could compare the beast to what I'd seen.

There were pictures, though, drawn or painted by hand. In fact, I'd just seen some in the history book from the library. Nyfain did share some qualities with the dragons. The armored and horned head, the long tail ending in spikes, the clawed feet, the slope to his back.

But what had happened to his wings?

And why had only one noble been spared? A noble that apparently had jurisdiction here only in the daytime.

And why—

There was no point in tallying all of my questions. Throwing them out in the air would just crowd the space. I had no answers. Not yet, anyway.

A soft knock sounded at the door. My stomach

rolled over, but not that weird thing in my chest. My animal, Nyfain had called it.

A whole bunch more questions tried to shove their way to the surface.

"Hello?" called a muffled voice.

I turned. Was this the way it was going to be? I'd have to communicate through the door?

"Hello?" the voice called again.

Sighing, I crossed the room and leaned against the frame. "What?" I said, folding my arms.

"Oh. You're there. Fan-fuckin'-tastic. Can I come in?"

The slurring was evident. It must be the purple mock-up beast from the party. Hadriel.

I couldn't help a small laugh at the costume and his sheepishness in coming forward. He'd totally been making fun of Nyfain and not expected to get caught.

That didn't mean I would take it easy on him, though. For all intents and purposes, he was a guard. By rights, the prisoners were supposed to be at odds with their guards. For me, that meant lots of snarky put-downs. I hoped he was ready for it.

"You have the key, dipshit," I called.

"I do?" His voice trailed away. "Oh. I see. It's in the door. Wait...are you a prisoner? Why are you locked in?"

I raised my eyebrows and readied for a bandy of words, but…blank. His utter cluelessness made my mind go blank. He didn't seem any more enlightened about the situation than I was.

"Are you dangerous?" he called. "Should I be worried? The master didn't mention that I should be worried."

Again, I wasn't sure what to say.

"No?" I finally managed.

"You don't sound sure. Look, I'm not good at fighting. That's why I'm still alive. I'm a butler, for goddess's sake! I look after people—kinda. I'm not much good at it. That's also why I'm still alive, I think. There is safety in mediocrity. So if you're all ragey, I'm just going to have to ask you to simmer down for a while. I'm not the bad guy here."

A grin was pulling at my lips. Was this guy for real?

"I won't hurt you," I called.

"Are you sure? Now that I think of it, the master had a fresh wound. Did you give him that?"

"Yes, but he grabbed my throat. What was I supposed to do? And honestly, I don't even remember doing it."

"You don't remember doing it?" Now his voice was rising. "What kind of a nutcase stabs a person and doesn't remember doing it?"

"The kind who thinks they are going to die?"

A pause. Then, "Yes, okay. That makes sense, I guess. Fine, I'm coming in. I'd appreciate it if you wouldn't stab or hurt me in any way. I was having a very nice time a moment ago and don't want to ruin the buzz."

I shuffled away from the door and resumed my stance against the far window. There I waited. Nothing happened.

"Are you coming?" I yelled.

"I was waiting for a confirmation!"

Metal tinkled, the key working within the lock. The oval knob turned slowly. Just as slowly, the door opened a crack, and a fuzzy purple head topped with two stuffed horns peered in. His eyes darted around until his gaze came to rest on me. He looked me up and down for a moment, settling on my empty hands. The door continued to open until the fuzzy purple monster stepped in.

I tried to hide more giggles and failed. I'd gone from real life and nightmares to a nightmare life lacking any sort of reality.

"Hello…" He stepped in a little farther, his hands up. "I'm not sober. Just so we're clear."

"I wish I weren't sober. It's nearly the same thing."

He nodded and sidestepped to the little nightstand

by the bed. Light flared from a match that he put to a candle in a silver holder. Only then did I really take in the room.

A huge four-poster bed with a canopy pushed against the wall, the curtains collected to the posters with tasseled ropes. Intricately carved wooden nightstands bracketed the bed, and a large double-door wardrobe across the room bore the same design. The overstuffed chair in the corner, nestled between the floor-to-ceiling windows covering the east and south side walls, looked worn in and incredibly comfortable for reading. It was clear the little table at its side was for holding books.

A beige rug spanned most of the floor, but the design was lost to the dim light. The walls were mostly bare except for one oil painting depicting a misshapen goat and a sliver of a moon. It was either a modern take on art or done by an amateur.

Hadriel picked up the candleholder, the candle half burned from previous use with dried wax dripping down the sides.

"So. Here we are." He hiccuped and patted his chest then felt around a little. He dropped his head to look down. "Ah fuck."

"What?" I asked, unable to help myself.

"I forgot I wore this tonight. Do you think the master noticed?"

"How…" I contained a laugh. "How could you possibly forget you wore that?"

He staggered back a couple of paces and braced his fingers on the nightstand. "Once that demon magic kicks in, you stop caring what you look like. All you want is to…"

He narrowed his eyes at me.

I put up my hands. "I'm not judging. I know the effect it has."

He sagged. "Yeah. It's a good time. A real good time. But then you wake up, and you just feel dirty, know what I mean? I'm wearing a furry demon costume, hoping to bang any wet hole I come across. I don't even care who it belongs to or what body part it is, I just want to stick my dick in it. What am I, eighteen?"

I placed him in his mid-twenties, a bit older than me. He had tanned skin and a thin mustache above thin lips. He was somewhat toned but clearly didn't work out or fight for his dinner. He'd said as much.

"But it gets so fucking boring here," he went on, "that I keep venturing down to the party. Booze and sex were really fun for, like, five years. Then it was a pleasant distraction. Now…I'm just shame-fucking, you know? And if I'm not shame-fucking, I'm shame-eating. I used to do hobbies and shit. And, I don't know, make use of myself. Now I just do whatever that hot incubus tells me. He's got me banging ladies. I don't even like banging ladies! But I do it. Why not? It's not like I have any self-respect anymore."

I grimaced. "That's dark. How old are you exactly?"

"When the curse first started, I was twenty-six. And since we're frozen in time…I guess I'm still twenty-six? There are different schools of thought on that subject, but we're pretty sure we'll emerge from the curse how we went in, just with a lot of terrible sexual experiences under our belt. I'm going to be so vanilla after all this, I am not shitting you. Zero kinks after this. I'll be a new man."

"Wait…what do you mean, frozen in time?"

His brow pinched, and then cleared with a smile. "My apologies. I completely forgot your whole deal. Yeah, you guys age and get sick with the curse, right? We don't get sick, but we're stuck in time. Everything here just stopped. No idea why it's different between the castle and the villages, but there you go. I've been twenty-six for sixteen years."

I didn't know what to say.

"Anyway, yeah. Super dark." He pulled open the nightstand drawer before closing it again. "We need to get you some vibrators. You're not allowed to go to the parties—I wish I hadn't been allowed to go to the parties. Anyway, you'll probably want something to take the edge off. They're these little demon-magic-powered fuck sticks. They're awesome. I have one that, like, sucks my cock while spinning around, and—it's the stuff of legends. Or…it would be if I wasn't mired in a puddle of boredom turned self-loathing." He paused, pointing at me. "Are you into butt stuff?"

I made a sound like "Whuh" and envisioned myself clutching a strand of pearls in an iron fist. Now I knew what Hannon always felt like.

He nodded like that was an answer. "I'll make sure and get you one to try out. They're all clean, don't worry. We don't reuse or anything. The demons keep us in stock. What else?"

"Am I to be kept in this room…all the time?"

"She's going to need a fuck-ton of candles…" He headed over to the far wall and started poking around in a chest of drawers. "I don't know, are you?" He looked around. "I should hope not. Nah, I don't think so. He wouldn't confine you here. Not when…" His eyes widened, and he went back to poking in the chest.

"Not when what?" I edged forward.

He shook his head. "We have a magical gag. If we talk about…some things, the gag locks up and we suffocate to death. Do you know how many people have died from activating the magical gag? A lot, let me assure you. For a while, we would try to get others drunk and talk about…things they weren't supposed to talk about, just to see if they'd fuck up and die."

"So you tried to trick them into killing themselves?"

He lowered the lid of the trunk. "It sounds like a real shit thing to do when you say it like that. But at the time… Well, that was right about when I started shame-fucking. We'd all kinda lost touch with reality by that point."

"This place is…"

"It's a nightmare. Cheers!" He smiled and looked around. "Damn it. I don't have a drink."

It was clear that was a common theme around this place. In a way they were living a life of luxury, but the curse hadn't spared them. Whereas our people were physically suffering, these people were mentally suffering.

Sadness overcame me at the thought of my village, and tears welled up. Best not think about home right now. I'd end up in a darker hole than Hadriel, and it seemed that path led to shame-fucking.

"Goddess spread on a cracker, what *is* this…" Hadriel had the doors to the wardrobe open and was pulling out dresses like they were covered in chicken poop.

A frilly pink dress was thrown aside, puddled on the

ground like frosting. A blue number with ruffles and lace went on top of it.

"Whose dresses were these?" He threw a bright orange frock onto the pile. "Whoever made them should be stabbed."

"Was this...was this someone's room before mine?" A dangerous question for my mental wellbeing.

He shrugged. "Maybe before the curse? Not since the curse, though. Or at least not since Butler One was killed gruesomely and Butler Two was thrown from a window. Since I have been in this post, no, there has been no one new in this castle."

He scrunched up his face and slammed the wardrobe doors.

"Tower!" he shouted at me. "*No one new has been in this* tower*!*"

I put up my hands again, trying to digest this cascade of crazy. "Got it."

He gave me a dirty look before glancing at the overstuffed chair in the corner. Then the table beside it. "Are you a reader?"

I came to attention. "You have a library?"

He rolled his eyes. "Only the best library in the whole magical world. Well, until the curse. We haven't had anything new since then, obviously, since the rest of the world thinks we just faded away. Fucking demon magic." He held the candle out, better illuminating me. His eyes widened. "Holy fuck, you're pretty." His expression turned grave. "You're not allowed out after dark anyway, but don't go out after dark. No one here will force you—the punishment is death if anyone does that—but they'll be like flies on shit, mark my words. You're new and you're pretty and everyone will want to shame-fuck you. Boys who like boys, girls who like girls, boys who like girls, girls who like boys—they'll all want to shame-fuck the new hot girl. They will want to do things that you will need another decade *at least* to be comfortable even talking about. So just stick to your room. Read your books, fuck yourself with those vibrators, and pretend life is normal."

"I don't know how I can possibly pretend that."

"Man, I wish I were you." He shook his head sadly.

"You wish you were a prisoner in a castle, kept away from your family who needs you, all because you went in the Forbidden Wood to keep your father from dying?"

"But did you?"

"What?"

"Did you keep your father from dying?"

I blinked at him. "Short term…yes."

"Then at least your family is safe. Mine is dead. I came here at, like…" He put his hand out near his thigh, then raised it a little higher. "Little. My parents were nobles in the Red Lupine kingdom"—that was one of the wolf kingdoms still going, last I'd heard—"but they were exiled and then killed as they tried to leave. I was sent here. It was the only kingdom that would take me in. The former queen..." He put his hand to his heart. "She was a good, kind woman. She held this kingdom together. You know, I am a prisoner, too, just as much as you. I can go to the villages, but I'll get deathly sick if I stay too long. Or that's what I heard, anyway. I'm too much of a chickenshit to try it."

"That's why you're still alive."

He jabbed a finger through the air at me. "Exactly! Yes. That is why I am still alive. That and mediocrity. We're all prisoners in this kingdom, though, in one way or another. At least you get a change of scenery. And don't worry, the master is a royal cunt, but he won't let your family starve. He has these, like, principles. He stole you, and you clearly did stuff they needed, so he will make amends for that. He will. I know he will. It's his duty."

"As the last remaining noble?"

"As the last remaining anyone who gives a shit, yeah. And as the only guy who can stand up to that ol' demon king, may his dick rot off and fall into a grinder."

"Tell me about that—"

"No." He groaned and leaned to the side, like he was wilting on the vine. "*No!* I have to go get my nut off, then go to bed and sleep this off. I need there to be a point to dressing like this, otherwise it's straight to shame-eating and then necessary dieting and—It's a whole cycle. I just can't handle any more dark situations in my life."

He went to hand me the candle, thought better of it, and put it on the nightstand. He pointed at me. "Get a good night's sleep, what's left of it. We all get up a bit late here, for obvious reasons"—he spread out his hands to indicate his getup—"so you can have a lie-in. After that, we need to get your wardrobe sorted. The master will probably want to dine with you—"

"Fat chance. I'm his prisoner, not his escort."

Hadriel let his hands flop over. "O-kay. You have troubled seas ahead. Fine. More power to you. Please leave me out of your struggles. You'll still need clothes, though. I can see your tits through that top, and you're dirty as hell. We are a civilized fucking outfit here." He stared at me for a moment. "I realize that comment would've gone over a lot better had I not been wearing a purple beast costume with my cock hanging out."

"Your cock isn't hanging out."

"Well, that's a miracle. You have a washroom adjoining through that heavy drape thing there. We obviously don't have running water anymore—fucking curse—but there is a chamber pot, and tomorrow we can get you a bath and everything. It's a bit late tonight for all that. The lady's maid is a bit tied up. Literally. Anyway, fuck off. I'm going to go shame-come. Then either pass out or cry myself to sleep."

"Why choose? Do both."

He opened the door and nodded. "Yes, good point. Why not? Oh!" He placed his hand on the empty keyhole inside the door. Then looked on the other side. He plucked the key from the lock and held it up. "I'd keep this, if I were you. Demons are wily cunts. They sneak into all the crevices." He raised his voice to yelling. "*Ask me how I know!*"

He rolled his shoulders, like he was shaking it off.

"It's fine to leave your door open during the day; just make sure you or your lady's maid has the key. Keep your door locked at night, though, even when you're not here. You don't want to return to one of those fuckers lying in your bed. Their magic... Well. It's hard to resist, and they like to push limits. There is one skeleton key in this whole castle, and that is guarded by the master. As long as you keep your door locked, you're safe."

Safe from the demons, maybe, but it was already clear I wasn't at all safe from the beast.

# CHAPTER 6

A SOFT RAP sounded at my door. "Milady…"
I frowned. It was a woman's voice.

My eyes were swollen from the crying I'd done last night. I'd tried to go to bed, like Hadriel ordered, but thoughts of what I'd lost kept barging into my brain. For the first time, I was alone. Sable wasn't beside me. Hannon and Dash weren't just down the hall. Father wasn't in the next room.

Worse, they were mourning me right now. That or wondering if I'd somehow saved myself. I couldn't leave them in suspense. I couldn't kill their sunshine just because the beast wanted to play mind games with me. I needed to get to them and at least assure them that I was okay. It would be impossible to stay, of course—the last thing I wanted was the beast coming for me and taking his anger out on the village—but I could at least tell them not to worry…and make some of the incubus-be-gone draught. I did not want to get caught in some sort of fuzzy purple costume at the back of a train.

The problem was getting through the wood, of course. Hadriel had scared me off from venturing outside at night, so I might have to escape during the day.

Before I tried anything, though, I needed to get the lay of the land.

"Milady?"

Who in the world would be calling a commoner "milady"?

I sat up and stretched before slipping on what I was wearing yesterday and unlocking the door.

A woman in her late twenties stood on the other side of the door with large blue eyes, curly blond hair, and deep red marks across her throat.

"Are you okay?" I asked, pointing.

"Oh!" She waved her hand and blushed. "Yes, don't worry about me. That was asked for."

It looked like someone had tried to strangle her—Oh.

So she wasn't into fuzzy beast costumes; she was into the harder stuff. Noted.

"I'm Leala, your lady's maid. How are you this morning, milady?"

"Lady's maid? Um… I think there must be some misunderstanding. I'm not noble or anything."

She smiled pleasantly. "You're the master's guest in the castle, and therefore you need a lady's maid." She bustled into the room, heading first for the curtains. Bright sunlight streamed in, and I put up my hand to block it from my face.

"Right. I think that's the misunderstanding. I'm not actually a guest. More like…a prisoner."

"Well. We're all prisoners in some respects, aren't we?" She gave me a comforting smile. "If anyone asks, though, we're going to say that you're waiting to be executed for stealing. That's in case anyone gets chatty with the demons. The demons are…not kind to new people. They might go babble to their king, and we don't want *him* coming around. He is not pleasant."

"How often does the demon king come around here?"

She picked up the dresses Hadriel had dropped and opened the wardrobe. After stuffing his rejects away, she leafed through a few of the others. "Goodness me, these are…old." Her face colored a little. She shut the doors. "He comes around every so often—time is hard to keep track of here. Everything is the same. Day in and day out, it's all more of the same. He comes to harass the master, essentially, and make sure our lives are ruled by his demons. It's not a nice time when he visits."

Fire kindled deep inside of me. My animal moved within my chest, the first time it had happened without the beast—Nyfain—close at hand.

"I won't say a word. Chances are I'll still say something that'll piss Nyfain off—" I stopped at her flinch. "What?"

"It's just…" She curtsied, something I'd never actually seen done before. "We don't call him by his birth name. We call him master."

"You can call him whatever you like. I'll call him by his name, and if he doesn't like that, I'll call him a ballbag fuckbumper. I'll let it be his choice."

She made a face like "oh!"

"Anyway, the chances are that I'll piss off the ballbag fuckbumper very quickly, and he'll kill me in rage."

"Oh now, milady. I doubt he'll…" She pulled her lips to the side as she looked through a chest of drawers Hadriel had poked through last night. "He does have a temper, sure, but…"

"He grabbed me by my throat last night when I wouldn't answer his question."

"Hadriel mentioned the master had been stabbed. Did you stab him then, milady?"

"Yeah. It's why he let me go."

I didn't elaborate. Her look of triumph made me feel good about myself. I didn't want to ruin it by telling her that I hadn't been in control.

"You'll do just fine, then." She pulled out a set of leather pants and held them up in front of her. "The master said you might like a pair of trousers instead of a dress for day-to-day activities. Was he correct? I hope so, because there aren't any dresses suitable for your beauty. They are all designed to add flourishes for someone with a plain face. Also, they will nowhere near fit. Much too small."

I hadn't realized such considerations went into fashion. Then again, Mom had made our clothes, and she didn't care about such things. Hannon had taken over that duty after she had died, and he cared even less.

"Trousers, yes," I said as dangerous tingles worked up my spine.

Nyfain must've been paying pretty close attention to me the last time he chased me out of the Forbidden Wood. How else would he know what sort of attire I preferred?

"Well, then." She laid them out on the bed and looked through another drawer. "Thankfully you're a tall girl, or you'd have to stay in your room until we had something made up. Which reminds me. I've booked you appointments with both seamstresses for later today. They can start working on your clothing right away. They were *very* excited to have the opportunity to do something new. All they work on now is party costumes and servants' clothes."

"I won't be needing any party costumes," I said quickly. Too quickly. I needed to pry my fingers away from those pearls.

She gave me a comforting smile. "Of course not. The master has forbidden you to leave your room after dark."

That brought me up short, remembering what Hadriel had said last night as well. I wasn't *allowed* to go out after dark.

Nyfain thought he could rule me, did he? That I would obey him?

Clearly he didn't realize that Hadriel had given me the key and I could essentially do as I pleased. Maybe I wouldn't wear a costume, and I damn sure wouldn't partake in the festivities, but I would definitely leave my room after dark.

I just had to make that demon-be-gone draught first. These demons seemed more powerful than the ones in my village.

The pants were too loose at the waist and short in the leg, with extra room in the crotch and not enough room in the ass. The shirt was hanging off my shoulders and very loose around my neck, tight at my bust and then loose again. This was even after having the binding around my breasts.

"I'm wearing clothes for a male," I stated.

"Yes, milady. It's all we have, I'm afraid. Females around here don't exactly dress…"

She paused, and I knew she was searching for a word that wouldn't hurt my feelings.

Before I could help by assuring her that I had no feelings, she finished, "For comfort."

"I'm a bit of a social pariah for dressing how I dress," I admitted as she refolded the clothes she'd been looking at and shut the drawers.

"That just means you don't conform to the way you've been told to live your life. That takes courage, milady. In these times, we need people with courage. There aren't enough of them left."

Humbled, I sat on the edge of the bed and looked out the windows at the breathtaking view. A warm glow infused my heart.

She got me. She wasn't judging—she was supporting.

She suddenly straightened up and said, "Oh!"

Out of the corner of my eye, I saw her spin and curtsey. A blast of fresh fragrance assaulted my senses, pine and lilac with a hint of honeysuckle, so delicious I wanted to lick the air. It reminded me of balmy days in the sunshine as a child, memories full of happiness and laughter.

My mood soured.

"Master. Excuse me," she gushed, and I rolled my eyes. "I was just finishing up, and then I was going to get her ready and take her for lunch and show her the grounds, like you requested."

Nyfain filled the doorway. He wore a white T-shirt that stretched across the top of his torso and hung loose at his waist. A pair of faded gray jeans were plastered to his thick thighs. People in my village wore fabric trousers almost always, or leather if they could afford it or make it. I hadn't seen jeans in…a very long time. The fabric was hard to make, labor-intensive, and required expensive machinery—or whatever was used in its place now. Before the curse, I remembered trading for it in the village. Clearly the castle had the means to make it, but not the ability or inclination to trade it to the villages. Given how worn his jeans were, though, clearly they weren't making it too often.

"Prepare a picnic," he said curtly. His deep, dark sandpaper voice flowed over me. My animal pumped fire into my blood, awakening my senses. She moved within me, begging to be unleashed.

I hadn't realized she came with a leash. I wish I could find the fucking thing and tie it to a tree.

"Oh goddess," Leala said, clutching at her chest and falling against the chest of drawers.

I looked over at her in surprise. A serene smile crossed her face, like she was hugging a long-lost friend. She clearly felt her animal around Nyfain as well, but she seemed to like hers. I was still incredibly wary about mine. I was okay with randomly stabbing dangerous men who lurked in the woods, but not as on board with her other wishes—like randomly dragging said dangerous men on top of me and going to Pound Town.

"Deliver it to the west garden field," Nyfain said as though her reaction were normal. It probably was.

Garden *field*? Those were two words I hadn't expected to be smooshed together.

"Of course, sir." She attempted another curtsey, but it was awkward and one hand still clutched at her chest. "Excuse me, milady." She hurried from the room.

A few beats of silence passed. I let them, looking out at the fantastic view. Not one cloud marred the crisp blue sky. From here, the Forbidden Wood didn't look so dead and twisted. There still life within it, struggling to hold on. The gaps were indeed other villages. I could see roofs, even from this distance. Right below my window, way down on the ground below, was a forgotten garden, overgrown and tangled with weeds.

He walked into the room and stood in the empty space beside the bed, in line with me. He looked out at the same view I was studying.

"The Royal Wood used to stretch on forever, it seemed like," he said into the hush, and it occurred to me that he was talking about the Forbidden Wood. Obviously, that was the favored name on his side of the social divider. "It's dying, like the rest of this kingdom."

I nodded. That was certainly true.

After a moment, he gave me some side-eye. "Those garments don't fit you."

"Your observational skills are exceptional," I replied dryly.

"They were made for a man."

"Hence the extra space where a dick should go, I guess."

"You're too thin."

"Not by choice. I'd eat more if there were more to eat. Would you like me to start pointing out your faults now? How much time do you have?"

His stare beat into the side of my head. After a moment, he said, "Come with me."

His tone brooked no argument.

But I was out of fucks to give.

"Nah," I said.

He stepped away, out of view. "Will you make me force you?" he asked from somewhere near the door. I didn't turn to look.

"Didn't you try that already? In the wood? But look, if you want another stab wound, I'm in."

"Big words for a prisoner."

"Says the guy who *protects* the land by abducting evil villagers trying to save their families from the curse."

Silence greeted me. One moment turned into several. He waited so long that I wondered if he'd left.

Curiosity got the better of me. I glanced back.

Empty space.

He'd left! How did a guy that big move so quietly?

I sat there for a moment longer, wondering if I should take this as an opportunity to explore the area by myself. Except suddenly my body turned to fire. My skin felt like it was blistering, sizzling away from my bones. That presence inside thrashed and railed within me, trying to take over. The desperate urge to stand up and obey Nyfain was so strong that I could barely think. Suppressing it was taking all my will, and even that might not be enough.

"Breathe through it," I coached myself, pulling in a deep breath through my nose and exhaling slowly. "Breathe."

Pain twisted in my gut the longer I resisted. I ignored it. Shut it off. I'd been hurt plenty—if it wasn't life-threatening, I could shove it aside.

"Did you say something, doll?" Hadriel poked his head in the doorway, his eyes bloodshot and his face haggard.

"Nope, nothing," I said through a tight jaw, the unanswered command making me feel like my hair was being torn off and my eyes scraped out. The presence within clawed against my ribcage.

Still, I persisted, suppressing that animal. Handling the pain.

"How do you feel?" I asked. "Amazing?"

He wasn't a friend—for all I knew, he could be an enemy—but you couldn't get a greeting like he'd given me last night and feel like a stranger.

"I do not feel amazing, no," he answered, leaning against the doorframe and rubbing a hand down his face. "My mouth tastes like someone shat in it, and my head is *ab*-solutely pounding. I'm miserable. And while I am miserable, the master has decided he needs to make matters worse and have me take you to the west garden field. Dealing with him is adding a little more misery to my day. We need to hurry."

"I'm not going."

"Yeah, except if you don't go, I will be the one who's

punished gruesomely. So I will have to beg you to please, *please* have pity on your poor, humble butler Hadriel and accompany him to the west garden field."

"Do you always talk about yourself in the third person?"

"Only when it's a dire situation and I cannot think in a rational manner. This is an emergency, love. My goal of the day is not shitting myself. If he punishes me for not following orders, I will definitely shit myself, and then everyone will make fun of me for, like, five years or something. This is essential. Please. I will do anything."

He held his stomach as he said all of this with a straight face, and I couldn't stop chuckling.

"It's not funny," he said with a little quirk to his lips. "Do you have any idea how much I drank last night? That mead is not good for one's stomach, and then I had a greasy breakfast. I only did those things because I thought I would be inside all day today with nothing but a puzzle to do. Now I have to venture out into a high-stress situation away from the privy and a washbasin. I'm not able for this, my darling. These are my professional pants. I don't want to ruin them. I need you to do this for me."

I laughed harder; I couldn't help it. The situation was just so absurd.

"I'd really rather not," I managed.

"*Please.* I cannot handle his wrath normally, and I certainly cannot handle it today. I'll do anything."

My head had started to throb. If I gave in, I'd be owed a favor. It was a good excuse to end this excruciating torment.

"Fine," I said, sounding put out. I had to play the part, after all.

He sagged in relief. "I had you pegged as the stubborn, unrelenting type. Which, let's be honest, I absolutely *love.* There is nothing like a snarky jackass to color the day. I can't take the women who always get their feelings hurt and then act passive-aggressive about it. Who has the time? But just for today, I need you pliant, yes? Just work with me today. Be your badass bitch self after today."

Still laughing, I said, "You've convinced me."

"Oh, thank the goddess and her lubed-up men. Okay, here we go. Step lively. The master is already pissed off for some reason. It doesn't take much usually, but this is ridiculous. Who shat on his breakfast, you know?"

"The same person who shat in your mouth?"

"Don't joke about that. Worse things have happened in this place, and I'd rather they didn't happen to me."

I took in his outfit. Dark gray slacks and a gray jacket with a black velvet lapel.

"I'm missing the fuzzy purple beast—"

He held up a finger. "Don't say it."

"I loved the stuffed purple—"

"Don't you dare keep going. I woke up with my head in the toilet and my pants around my knees. I would say that was an all-time low, but sadly, it isn't even close."

"Dark."

"Tell me about it."

"And this is your…butler ensemble?"

He looked down his front, then farther until he could see his pressed velvet slippers, two shades lighter than the gray slacks. "Yes. I'm going for a modern look. I think I picked the wrong shoes, though. Otherwise, I am definitely selling the vibe, wouldn't you agree? I mean, when was the last time I had to properly butler? I don't even know how to do this fucking job. I was a stable hand before this. I only stepped up into this gig because everyone else was afraid of getting killed. If we ever get out of this, it'll be a great work history builder, you know what I'm saying?" He held up a finger as we walked down the stairs. "The important thing is mediocrity. Remember that. If you stay mediocre and mostly uninterested in helping the castle flourish, the demons won't treat you to an 'accident.'"

Anger burned through me. "They just randomly kill anyone who does a good job around here?"

"Yeah, pretty much. But there haven't been any deaths in a while. We've all pretty much got things under control. If someone is good at their job, like your lady's maid, they have some serious kinks that the demons like exploring. Since I am afraid of the more serious kinks, I've got being terrible at butlering down to an art." He ran his hand down his lapel.

"Yes, you do," I said to play along, grinning. He had a way of making a person feel better about their shitty situation. I really needed that right now.

"And you…" He did a once-over on my outfit. "You have already taken that note, it seems. Good work. You're still pretty, don't get me wrong, but this…clothing and the…dirt on your face really detract from your appearance. What is your hair even doing?"

I hadn't even thought about washing up. My life was upside down, and it hadn't occurred to me to do any of the basic things I did in a normal day. Since I wasn't in the habit of looking at mirrors anyway… Well, I guessed it could only help me in this castle. Bully for me.

"Did you literally punch yourself in the face, too?" he asked. "There are other ways to detract from your appearance than self-violence. Trust me. Do you think I *like* this hideous mustache? And this bow pulling back my too-long hair—you think I'm enjoying this look?" He lifted his eyebrows.

I erupted in giggles again. The mustache definitely detracted from his handsome face. The thing was comical, as were the outfit and the large bow holding his shoulder-length black hair at his nape.

"No, no self-violence. I thought it might be fun to cry myself to sleep last night."

"Ah. Well, it could be worse. You could've woken up with your head in a toilet, a purple costume gathered around your knees, and zero recollection of how you got there."

"Thank you for the cautionary tale."

When we reached the second floor, he pointed to the left, and we headed through a grand room out of a picture book. It was gorgeous, with large red curtains draping the massive windows, golden trimming, and cream walls playing host to oil paintings. Large chandeliers hung down from above, all the candles within burned nubs. I wondered if they burned those down every night or had just never replaced them. I wasn't sure how many demons loitered in this place at night. I was a little afraid to find out.

"Where do the demons sleep during the day?" I

asked. In the village, they all retreated to a house they'd taken over at the far end of town. They hunkered down in darkened rooms, waiting for the daylight to disappear. The sun didn't kill them like it did vampires, but it sapped their power. Only the very powerful walked around during the day.

"They are in the dungeons. Nasty fuckers. Why choose to lie low in such a vile place, you know? Then again, I guess they can shut themselves in. Maybe they're worried one of us will try to drag them into the sun and kill them all. Who knows. Not like the master would let us."

A man walking in the opposite direction slowed when he saw me. He beamed and waved before ripping his floppy hat off his head and holding it to this chest.

"Oh, go fuck a donkey, Liron," Hadriel called, waving the man away. "Don't draw attention to her."

"Eat my ass," Liron said with a snarl before smiling at me and bowing.

After we passed him, Hadriel murmured, "That guy fucks up every single threesome you try to get started. He literally does not know where to put his dick. He just walks around parties with his cock in his hand. He'd be creepy if he ever did more than look on with that dumb expression on his face."

"I can hear you," Liron yelled in a shrill voice, now

continuing down the hall.

"Like it matters," Hadriel called back. He rolled his eyes. "Clearly nothing wrong with his hearing. If you ever find yourself in an intimate situation with that guy, watch your arsehole. Because that guy will cornhole you. He will fucking cornhole you! All the ladies say so. One time I was giving head, and he just randomly walked up and tried to stick me in the ass. Only he missed and fell over me. Like—who does that, you know?"

My mouth had dropped open. I needed those pearls. I needed something to clutch. This was starting to get a little crazy.

He must've noticed, because he waved it away. "It's fine. You won't be out at night, anyway. If someone tried to fuck you, the master would probably rip his dick off and feed it to him."

"Is this how all of you talk?"

He laughed. "Oh, love, aren't you cute?" He looked skyward. "Remember when I thought talking like this was gross? Neither do I. Boy are you in for a world of crazy. This place is frozen in time with a bunch of single adults. Pregnancy doesn't exist—not in the castle. Only the master can impregnate a woman, and then only his true mate. That's it. The curse has shut everything else down. Add in the demons and their sex magic and endless quantities of alcohol, and that, my love, is a recipe for bad decisions and disaster. Dis-*aster*! The demons have steered this ship. Anyone who tries to turn the tide lands themselves in an accident that they don't walk away from. We're adrift. Only the master has been able to avoid all the sex stuff, and that's because he has a will of iron. Of absolute iron. I don't know how he does it. The rest of us… Well, this is our life. Welcome to it."

"You keep getting darker and darker."

"Yeah, right? I wasn't ever a ray of fucking sunshine, but I had my moments. Anyway, we have a shitload of hobbies here. After the master is done with you, I can walk you through them all and see what you might want to do. That assclown Liron teaches watercolors, if you want to give that a go. It's not as boring if you're drinking."

"I'm not a painter, I don't think."

"Neither am I. I painted pictures of penises. I couldn't even get that right. He kept commenting on my finished product, thinking I'd painted a bouquet of flowers or something. But really he was complimenting me on a bunch of dicks. I kept going back just for that. Eventually someone told on me and ruined all my fun."

I chuckled helplessly as he opened the door leading outside and waited for me to go through.

"One thing of note," he said, pointing at a wide set of stairs that had been freshly painted. We stepped down to a natural rise in the countryside, the base covered in colorful tiles that hosted a round wood table and matching chairs. Brown and brittle grass led away to a patch of trees much tamer than the Forbidden Wood. "I shouldn't be telling you this, but...well, I'm going to. If you plan to rebel against the master and leave your room at night, you should go to the salon. It takes place in the early evening before all the major stuff kicks off. It's the safest activity for you."

I put a hand up to my hair. It had only ever been cut by Mom or Hannon. I could probably use someone who knew what they were doing.

"No, not that kind of salon, love," he said. "It's not for the hair on your head. It's for the lady beard." He pointed at my crotch. "You can go in there and get shaved, and it's super delicious and erotic. Then, if you want, you can round it out with a little meow, meow." He winked at me.

"Is this the beginning of the road to shame-fucking?"

"No. This is just a way to treat yourself. Get that lady beard spruced up, get yourself a little meow, meow, and *relax*. You can lie with a cloth divider hanging around your middle, or at your neck or whatever, so they can't see who they are servicing. Then it's totally anonymous."

"Demons do this?"

"Yeah, but the really low-powered ones. They feed off your pleasure still, but they don't really muddle the head or anything. It's about as safe as you are going to get in that regard."

"I can make a draught that deadens the demon lust magic."

He put his hand to my arm as we walked. "Shut the fuck up. Are you serious? You can?"

"Yeah. I just have to find the right herbs. You can have some if you want."

"Um...*yes*! Are you some kind of stem witch or something? That's awesome."

"You've had your sex, and I've had my plants. I need to make a morning tea, too. I devised it to give the kick like coffee, and I could've really used it this morn- ing—"

He stopped and yanked me around to face him, ut- terly serious. "Do not lie to me about a coffee replacement or I will pull your hair. All these years and I am still desperate for a cup of coffee in the morning."

"It's tea, but it apparently gets the job done."

"Finley, you talented, smart, sparkling gift from the goddess, you. I could just *kiss* you." He started walking again. "We'll get you all the herbs you need, don't you worry. I will literally cut someone to get them. I'll cut them, I don't care."

I laughed as he pointed to the left on a diagonal, and we crested a little rise. On the other side, just within the trees of the nicer-looking wood, a field of everlass spread out before us. It wasn't as large as the one I'd used in the Forbidden Wood, but it was just as well maintained, with large, healthy plants and big, vibrant leaves. Nyfain bent in the middle of them, his shirt pulled up against his back to reveal four silver parallel lines not quite covered in new ink. He'd been both scored and tattooed somewhat recently.

Now that I saw him, the desire to get to him and the pain of resisting finally dissolved. He straightened up with a couple of wilting leaves, taking care of some pruning. That strange weight within—my animal— surged at the sight of him before settling down again until I couldn't feel her at all.

Only then did Nyfain turn and glance at me. Right at me, too, like he'd cataloged my approach and held off on acknowledging my presence until I was actively waiting for him. In other words, he was playing alpha dick slinger. That rat bastard.

"Finley," Dick Swinger said as he approached, and that goddess-damned voice slid over me like an intimate massage. I *hated* that.

"Nyfain," I responded casually.

That gorgeous golden gaze beat into me, and I soaked up the electric current crackling in the air between us. In the full sunlight, I could now clearly see his face. He looked to be in his mid-twenties. A straight nose cut through almost sharp cheekbones, hollowed at the cheek. Dark reddish stubble covered his defined jaw and dipped into the cleft at his chin. His unruly dark brown hair curled behind his ears and swept across his forehead. He could've been handsome, if a bit severe, if not for the scars slicing up his visage. One streaked through an eyebrow, and another pulled at his full lips.

His size was just shy of imposing. He was seven feet tall, at least, with huge, robust shoulders and thick slabs of muscle covering his large frame. I'd always felt big for my sex. Tall, thick. He made me feel absolutely puny. Dainty in a way I'd never thought possible. Jedrek had nothing on him. Hannon would be dwarfed, as well. Nyfain was a stack of lethal.

None of that mattered, though. What drew me in was his aura—the hard, raw intensity that slammed into me like a force all its own. It turned my stomach runny and bones fluid. Made my flesh tingle and pooled fire in my core. His obvious ruthlessness, his darkness, sent my heart racing, and I didn't know if I wanted to run from him or cling to him in mindless desire.

One thing was eminently clear: he was not a guy to turn one's back on.

His gaze flicked to Hadriel. "You may go."

Hadriel offered a deep bow. "Yes, sir."

When Hadriel had gone some distance, Nyfain turned and faced the field. "As I said last night, I had not heard that everlass could slow the sickness killing the people in the villages." His tone suggested he still thought I was lying.

I'd been called a lot of things in my time, but there were two things people always agreed on—I was brutally honest to the point of social awkwardness, and I knew my way around plants.

This guy was questioning the very foundations of my being. That rankled in so many ways. So much so that I stood there in silence, envisioning ways to ruin his day.

"What is this elixir?" he asked after a moment. "What is in it?"

It wasn't in me to hold back such useful knowledge, no matter how much I wanted to stick him in the ribs with something sharp. If I could help the other villages, I would. I described my process from beginning to end, explaining why I harvested when I did, how I'd come to that conclusion, and the effects it had.

When I was done, he looked at the field for a moment before he asked, "Where did you learn to work with the everlass?"

"Books. Trial and error."

He turned to me. "Impossible. One must be taught to work with everlass. It is passed down from generation to generation. Mother to daughter. Father to son."

"And then some smart fucker with daddy issues took his knowledge and put it in a book. Now I have it."

His eyes sparked fire. My spine felt like it was disintegrating within that menacing stare.

When he spoke next, his voice was low and dangerous. "Are you afraid of me, princess?"

"No." *Lies.*

"No? You should be."

"Well, aren't you knowledgeable in shit I don't care about."

"Keep at it with that smart mouth, and I'll be forced to fuck it."

His words shocked into me. My body lit up like it had been dead all this time, and *he* had brought it to life. Liquid fire pooled hot and spicy in my core, suddenly throbbing and desperate for hard, brutal contact. My nipples tightened and shivers coated my sensitive flesh. Within it all, the presence inside me—my animal— roared and twisted, struggling to get free so she could sink to her knees and grip his thighs. I could actually feel her desperation to suck in his big cock and choke on it. That bitch did not need a strand of pearls to clutch. She was here for it.

I struggled for breath, struggled to stay standing as my knees weakened and my body trembled. My whimper of desire was incredibly embarrassing, but I kept fighting the beast inside, my hands balled into fists and my arms shaking.

"Say shit like that to me again, I'll burn your bed...with you in it," I ground out.

It came out like a purr. Damn it all. Hard to be tough when you sounded husky and wanton.

A smile slowly pulled at his lips. "You'll need that fire before the end. Mark my words, princess, before this is all over, I will ruin you."

I narrowed my eyes. "Is that a threat...or a challenge?"

At hearing *challenge*, he sucked in a startled breath. His golden eyes burned into me as they settled on my lips. Another surge of his power shocked through me, trying to bring my beast to the surface.

My panties flooded with wetness, and my core tightened until I nearly had to clench my thighs together. I barely stopped from moaning at the flurry of heat playing within me. Barely stopped myself from plastering my front to his. I knew he'd let me, even if he didn't want to. I somehow felt his desire almost like a palpable thing. I knew he'd be pissed at the lapse of control, just like last night.

Would he push me away before or after he filled me with cum?

I struggled against his alpha's call—because that's exactly what this was. He was using his power to try to dominate me, like alphas used to do before the curse. I'd heard it talked about. I'd read about it in books. People back then hadn't seemed put out by it.

I was not fucking having it.

I struggled to suppress it, but the ferociousness of the alpha serenaded my newly awakening animal. He was hitting me on multiple levels, and it unfortunately didn't matter that he'd plucked me from my life and was holding me captive. I wanted to pull him down between my spread thighs and accept him deep, *deep* into my body.

# CHAPTER 7

T HIS DESIRE WAS something I would have to ignore, because I was not going to reduce myself to fucking this dickhead.

Maybe I did need to check into the salon for a little meow, meow.

"You done?" I asked him with a bravado I didn't feel.

He closed the scant distance between us, his big body dwarfing mine, his sweet breath dusting my face. Fire and rage and lust charged the air between us. His breathing was shallow, matching mine. Unsaid words— dirty, filthy, sexy words—hung around us.

A vein pulsed in his jaw. His eyes bored into mine for a tense moment. It took everything I had to force my animal down.

"You'll want to stay away from me," he said in that

voice out of a nightmare. "I was not lying—I will ruin you. I will destroy your virtue. I'll taint your goodness."

Why did part of me want that so badly? What were these crazy desires this man was bringing out in me?

I clenched my jaw so tightly my teeth hurt. I believed his threat, and I didn't want to set him off. I didn't want him to flood me with another burst of power. I didn't know if I could stop myself from giving in.

His eyes roamed my face before he finally nodded. With a stiffness belying the state he was in, he turned and walked farther into the everlass field. He ran his fingers through his hair, rendering it more unruly.

I let out a breath and turned the other way. I needed to get my bearings.

Hadriel stood back with Leala, a picnic set up and waiting. Even from a distance, I could see the worry on both of their faces. A memory of the night before floated up—Nyfain grabbing my neck and yanking me to him, demanding information I was not willing to provide. He clearly had an incredible temper.

If only that was what I was worried about.

Once again under control, I turned back around. He was working through the field again, checking the plants and pruning as he went. His graceful movements looked like a well-practiced dance. He didn't just pull away dying or flagging leaves, either. He fluffed up the plants, touching them almost tenderly before moving on, giving an extra bit of love and attention.

"Does that work?" I asked, working closer. "The random touches as you go?"

He glanced back before continuing on. "I don't know, honestly. This knowledge was passed down. I didn't question it."

"I can test it, if you like."

He straightened up, straddling one of the rows. The sun beat down on his wide shoulders as he glanced out over the field. "Do as you will. I want you to make that…nulling elixir, you called it. I want you to drink it first, to make sure it isn't poison. Then I want to distribute it to a few people to see if it really works."

"Please," I said.

He glanced my way. "It's an order, not a request."

"And if it weren't going to save people, I would tell you to shove your order up your dickhole."

Surprisingly, he smiled. "We aren't going to get along, Finley."

My name in his voice flowed over my body. I shivered, now incredibly annoyed again.

"I think that was a given as soon as you took me prisoner," I replied.

"It was a given long before that." He worked his way

back toward me. "You say you need to harvest at night?"

"Yes. Midnight seems to work best."

"Have you tried three o'clock? That's when the demons are strongest. If you say the elixir works better when harvested at night because of their magic, then three o'clock would be the optimal time."

I pulled my lips down in thought. "Good tip. I don't really know much about demons."

"Then you didn't...tangle with them in your village?" he growled, as though the very thought of me intimately touching a demon enraged him.

I frowned, no clue why he'd care. Maybe just an all-around hatred of them, which I completely understood.

"No," I said, wandering the field and looking at the various plants. I wanted to choose the ones I'd harvest from. "Speaking of, does this place have an herb garden? I want to make the draught that nulls the incubi's magic."

"What did you say?" That got his attention.

I huffed out a laugh. "Hadriel was excited to hear that as well. That and the coffee replacement. All this time on your hands, and none of you thought to experiment? I developed that demon draught almost immediately after turning sixteen. Those bastards came on strong. I didn't want to accidentally get caught out too late and run into one. What a thing to lose your virginity to."

I made a sound like *yuck*.

"Not all of us have the gift of healing."

His tone was somber with traces of sorrow and a hint of pride. I glanced up to gauge his expression, but he had turned away, wandering the field.

"Right, well, if you have an herb garden, I can make enough of that for everyone, if you want. Whoever wants it. If there's enough supplies, obviously."

"You are very giving in your antidotes." Again that somberness. That sorrow.

"Maybe I'm just trying to poison everyone." After a few moments of quiet, I let curiosity get the better of me. "Do you tend this field on your own? And the one in the Forbidden Wood?"

"Mostly. There is one gardener left on the grounds. He helps where he can."

"Who taught you to work the plants? Not books, I imagine."

"My mother," he said softly.

He'd done a nearly perfect job with these plants. They were all happy and healthy. They'd make a very strong nulling elixir, except that we didn't have any rainwater collected. I'd have to figure out a different way.

First things first—harvesting.

"I haven't noticed any correlation between the demons' strength and the various moon cycles, have you?" I asked as I stopped near a struggling plant. I crouched down, studying it, resting my forearms on my knees.

"No. The moon doesn't affect them."

I pulled my lips to the side, thinking, before looking up at the sun and then all around, marking this spot in my mind so I could avoid it.

"It affects shifters, though." He stepped down in my line of sight, having clearly followed me through the field.

"I know that."

"Does it affect you?"

"How could it? My animal is—or was, I guess—suppressed like everyone else's. It's only now, since you, that I can feel it. Her, I think. It feels like a female presence."

"You didn't feel your animal at all before me? Not even a whisper?"

"No."

"And yet you can resist my commands."

I didn't mention that it was not a fun time resisting him.

"No one could ever resist me," he said.

I pushed up to standing. "Maybe you're not as

147

strong as you once were. Maybe that's why you can't break the curse, whatever it is."

"It isn't up to me to break the curse. I am powerless within it."

"We're never powerless," I muttered, a sentiment I'd always repeated to myself when I did, indeed, feel utterly powerless. Usually hopeless, too. I pointed downward. "This plant is being crowded. I assume you know what that means?"

His eyebrows stitched together. It took him a moment to look where I was pointing. He didn't comment, and judging from our previous interactions, I took that to mean he didn't know what to say.

I really wanted to punch him, just in general, but instead I took a deep breath and readied the lecture. This was something he needed to know if he was going to work the everlass. Something his mother should have told him. The plant's location suggested it had been planted this way on purpose.

"This plant is basically getting bullied, to put it simply. That creates a sort of…acidic quality that's bad for healing. It can be poisonous, actually. Someone in my village used leaves from a crowded plant for the elixir we spoke of, and it killed her husband within a few hours. She claimed to have chosen the leaves—multiple—by accident, which means it was definitely on purpose. Given she refused to marry again and spent a lot of time after that with demons in the pub...well. She's suspect.

"Anyway, the book I read said it was often thought that crowded plants were cultivated that way on purpose, nestled among the others in the field, hidden in plain sight. Only a person who knew what they were looking for would know the crowded plant's true nature."

I used my finger to outline the rows. Little dips happened all over, like the horse hadn't walked in a straight line when the fields were plowed. Only sometimes the rows dipped enough to create a crowded plant. I counted thirteen of them, a superstitious number.

"The layout of this field is masterful." I raised my eyebrows at him. "You?"

"The former queen."

That was surprising. I hadn't thought royalty actually worked. Not in any physical way.

"Well, she knew what she was doing," I said. "Too bad she wasn't the one who taught you. To un-crowd the plant, you simply prune those around it and give it more breathing room. It'll spread its leaves and flourish. It won't hold a grudge. Overall, your garden won't suffer in production, either, since all the plants are firing on all cylinders. If you then wish to crowd the plant again so you can off your husband, prune it back a little and let the other plants creep in. Easy."

"You learned all this from a book?" He sounded incredulous.

"From a few, actually. A book on everlass, one about myths and legends, a history of the kingdom, a book on faeries, and finally just trial and error. I definitely filled in a lot of blanks."

He stared at me for a long moment, balanced on the balls of his feet. Braced for something, or against it, I couldn't tell which. Whatever it was, the struggle seemed internal.

He gritted his teeth against a strong emotion. For once, he didn't shove his drama at me, for which I was grateful.

"Our gardens aren't up to par for a witch," he said with disdain, but I could tell his heart wasn't really in it.

"I hear sometimes it's more work to be a dick than to be a nice guy," I said softly.

"Do you know from experience?"

"No. For me it's always been easier to be a dick. Nice people make me nervous."

A genuine smile stretched across his face, softening his severe appearance. He'd definitely been a looker at one time, before all those scars crisscrossed his skin.

"If you can shift, why don't you also heal?" I asked, curiosity getting the better of me as I helped him work through the field, pruning and now lightly petting the plants. Very high-maintenance, this everlass. Worth the effort.

His expression fell, quickly turning broody again. His muscles tensed. "I can only shift because of sheer determination and a tight connection with my animal. I refused to lose my grip on him, and he was able to force the shift. Our bond is strong, and together we are more powerful than the demon king. We paid the price, though. The magic sheared off our wings with that first change, leaving us ground bound and disfigured. My healing ability is mostly suppressed, too. When I sustain wounds, they last. What woman would want to be stuck with a ground-bound dragon and a scarred man..." He turned and bent, his back to me. "If you had stabbed through my heart with that pocketknife, I would've died. You would've done what no one else has been able to do these last sixteen years. You would've ended this eternal nightmare."

Pain lanced my heart. Not just for him, but for all of us. I wished someone could explain the curse to me so I could figure out a way to end it. So I could do more than fuss around with finicky plants.

"What would happen if I'd killed you?" I asked,

walking closer to him.

"The curse would end and the demon king would finally rule. After that, he'd likely turn everyone into servants or just kill them outright. I don't know."

The breath left me. "Well…" I stood and looked down at the plants for a moment, hopelessness welling up. As always in my past, I only let myself dwell for a moment. I let the feeling sink in, and then I rallied. "Where there is life, there is hope. You're not dead yet, and neither am I. We can find a way. What happens if we kill the demon king?"

He straightened and turned, his beautiful eyes devoid of anger for once. "The power he wields over us will be transferred to the next in line for the demon throne."

"And if we kill them all?"

A grin worked at his lips. "We don't have the resources for that."

I braced my hands on my hips. "I'll figure it out. There must be something that can be done."

"Would you sacrifice your life to save this kingdom?"

His voice was thick, and it sounded like a trick question. Regardless, I didn't need to think about the answer.

"Of course," I said. "I thought I was sacrificing my

life for my family. To do it for the kingdom would be an honor."

"As easy as that, huh?"

"Yes. I mean, don't get me wrong, I'd be scared out of my mind, and I'd try to run and escape like I did last night, but in the end, I'd do it. Of course I would. Anyone would."

He sneered. "Not anyone. Some people aren't as honorable or selfless as you claim to be." He squared up to me, rage once again burning brightly in his eyes. Something else glimmered there as well. Pain. "You should be more careful when you make such claims, princess. You don't know of which you speak. There are worse fates than death."

"Like being disfigured?" I met his stare. "Like losing your wings? At least you can change into your animal. Most people long to do that and can't. What woman would love a wingless, scarred dragon? A woman who doesn't give a shit about appearances, that's who. Why don't you ask what you're really afraid of—what woman would like you for you? You're not a noble anymore. You're not a dragon anymore. You're just as fucked as the rest of us. Sure, you prance around this castle and patrol the *royal* grounds, but the demons run this place. You're in make-believe land if you think otherwise. The demons run your life as surely as they control the rest of us. The lines between commoners and royals have been blurred. Now it's just you and me and everyone else. So, no, you're not worried about being disfigured—you're worried about the ugliness of your personality being the only thing people have to judge you by."

"You dare to speak to me that way?"

"Tell me I'm wrong."

His fists opened and closed, and his temper broke. Suddenly he was storming toward me, rage and power let loose. He stopped in front of me, still careful of the everlass plants but not careful of me. A fast movement, and his fingers curled around my throat. I didn't have my knife. I did have my foot.

I hopped up so that he would take my weight, all of my body held up by one of his hands. My air completely cut off, but I didn't waste the opportunity. I swung my foot as hard as I could.

My boot smacked between his legs. His breath swooshed across my face with the impact. He squinted in pain and nearly crumpled, groaning as he lowered.

My feet hit the ground, and then I threw his hand off me. Normal people would've run away, but normal people didn't have a kingdom resting on the strength of these everlass plants.

"Keep standing," I commanded, and my animal swirled within me, lending power to my words.

His wobbling knees locked straight, jerking him upright. His upper body still bowed, though, as he cupped his balls.

"Do not crush these plants." I hooked my arms around his middle, and he draped over me, his weight a bit more than I could comfortably handle. "Get a hold of yourself. It's just your dick. Deal with the pain."

He issued a shaky laugh before coughing. "That was a damn good kick."

One of his big, scarred hands rested on my shoulder, and he straightened up painfully. He looked down at our feet before pulling one of his back a little, giving the everlass plant more room. His gaze then tracked up my body, searing heat following in its wake. His smell delighted my senses. His other hand traveled up my arm and over my collarbone to the base of my neck.

"So fierce," he whispered, tracing his thumb across my heated flesh. "So strong." He breathed out, our breath mingling now. His fingertips brushed my jaw line before applying pressure, making me look up at him as he bent. "So powerful."

I braced my hands against his chest to push him away even as my eyelids grew heavy and desire curled through me.

His lips neared my ear. "Do you want me to touch you, Finley?"

His tongue traced the edge of my earlobe, and I shivered.

"Tell me," he commanded softly, and my stupid animal surged power through me. Tried to take over.

"Hmm," he groaned, tightening his grip on my jaw, keeping my head tilted up to him. "That's right. Let your animal feed your arousal. I can feel her in you. I can feel how much you want me."

The hand on my shoulder slipped down my collarbone and over the swell of my breast. His thumb pressed against the bud of my nipple. A shock of pleasure speared me.

I clenched the fabric of his shirt and willed myself to push him away.

His thumb moved in lazy circles, stroking my inner fire. My lips opened wider as I panted.

"Where do you want me to touch you?" he coaxed, pulling away from my breast so he could push the fabric off and down my shoulder. The neck was so big that it slid down easily. His tricky fingers edged down again, gliding across my bare flesh. At the top of my binding, he ran his finger just under the fabric.

I jerked my fisted hands a little, yanking him a bit toward me. I gritted my teeth and stopped myself. My animal tried to surge up, but I was ready this time. I pushed her down, suppressing the power that rolled through me, trying to keep my head.

His chuckle was dark and sinister as he worked my binding lower. His other hand held my face, and he bent until his lips grazed mine. A shock of electricity lit me up as our lips touched.

"I want to taste you," he murmured.

I clutched his shirt tighter and braced myself, in a battle for control. Logic said to push him away. My animal had me locked up tight, though. She wanted this, and she was about to take over and get it.

His tongue darted out, skimming the seam of my lips. I opened my mouth before I could stop myself. His lips curled, and he finished pulling my breast free, now reaching in my shirt. He pulled back, our gazes locking, as he pinched my taut nipple.

I whimpered at his touch as he manipulated the hard bud with the rough pad of his finger. His pupils dilated, showing his delight in the effect he was having on me.

"Um...sir?"

The voice was insistent. Anger kindled within me that anyone would interrupt. My animal beat power through my blood.

Nyfain pulled my shirt farther down. Fabric ripped, giving him more access. He bent and raked a hot tongue across my nipple.

I groaned, lost in the sensations now.

I moved my hand to the side of his face and arched, pushing my breast toward his mouth. He enveloped it, sucking greedily.

With me holding on to his neck, he freed one of his hands and reached between my thighs. His firm touch rubbed right where I needed it, building me up higher. I gyrated against it, utterly out of control.

"Sir? Sir!" The voice was incessant, and I vaguely recognized it.

I also wanted to kill the owner so he'd fuck off.

Nyfain licked and flicked my nipple as he rubbed the seam of my pants, working me. Building.

"Master, sir. Sir!"

Nyfain pulled back with a growl, my nipple popping out of his mouth. He clutched me possessively, as though there was danger from this third party and he didn't intend to let it reach me.

"Sir." Hadriel was waving from the edge of the field. "Sorry to interrupt, but sir, it's time to go."

It took a moment for Nyfain's eyes to clear. His eyebrows dipped, and he blinked rapidly. When his gaze swung back to me, it was accusatory. He pushed me away as he pulled back. He glanced down at my feet, checking to make sure I wasn't trampling the everlass.

"I told you to keep a tight hold on your animal," he

snarled, his face flushed.

Cold washed over my previously fevered skin. I shivered with the change, pulling up my binding. My nipple throbbed against the fabric, still shooting pleasure through my body. Tingling from his hard, delicious suction.

"Are you fucking kidding me?" I pulled my shirt so it looped around my neck again, now stretched out. "Which of us has ever even met their animal? You're the one with experience. This is your fault, not mine."

"Stay away from me, Finley. I'm not a nice man. I will destroy you." He walked toward Hadriel.

"Stay away from—I wasn't the one with my nipple in his mouth," I yelled, the sting of rejection tight in my chest.

This was a good thing. Him pulling back and walking away was *good* news. I should've been the one to do that. I should've pushed him away almost immediately.

So why did it feel like I wasn't good enough? Like I was dirty?

I walked farther into the everlass to quiet the mad thoughts. My animal was messing with my head. That's what was happening. For some reason, she had taken a liking to that dickhead, and she was taking me along for the ride. His animal was pushing him, too, I guessed. But that man and I just did not get along. For one, the fucker had imprisoned me. Granted, yes, he could've killed me and didn't. And sure, it was technically within his jurisdiction to pass judgment and execute a punishment. But people were dying left and right, and I'd only trespassed in that field to save my family. What sort of asshole would imprison someone for that? It was nothing but a power trip.

Second, he simply was not likable. He was brooding and angry and tough to get along with. If he wasn't pissing me off, he was trying to force me to do something. Um…no thanks.

So any feeling of rejection was just ridiculous. I needed to pull on my big-girl panties and let logic rule. My animal was cut off, and as soon as I could figure out a way to further suppress her, I'd do it.

The pang of remorse and guilt that followed that thought was unexpected. Fuck it all, I just couldn't win.

"So, how'd it go?" Hadriel asked in a singsong voice with a grimace. "Get those plants sorted?"

My face burned with embarrassment. In the moment, I hadn't thought about people watching. I wouldn't have cared.

"You didn't turn away, did you?" I asked as I sat down to the lovely spread of food on the bright pink and orange blanket.

"Turn away? Love, please, you must be kidding me."

He sat down with me. "I couldn't look away! I didn't know if he was going to bang you or break you. It was wonderfully tense."

"Hey." Leala batted his shoulder. "What are you doing? That's for her. You're not supposed to sit with them."

"She's not a *them*, first, and I will let her eat it. But you heard the master; I'm supposed to keep her safe...somehow. If she gets into trouble, he'll kill me." He smoothed his hair back. "So I've got that going for me now. It's like...I think my life can't get any worse, and then *bam*. Here's a shit sandwich, Hadriel. Enjoy your lunch!"

I stared at him incredulously. "When did he tell you to keep me safe?"

"Just right now when he went away. I'm to let you find a garden that you can grow your herbs in. And I'm to watch over you. If you get into trouble, he expects me to call him immediately."

"That's not keeping her safe," Leala said. "That's just tattling on her."

"Keeping her safe, tattling on her—either way, he has his eye on me and wants me to report to him. And do you know what will happen if the demons find out?" He gestured between him and me. "We'll both be killed."

I held up my hands. "I do not understand that guy. He essentially just told me to fuck off and leave him alone, and yet he's setting someone to guard me? To tattle on me?"

"Oh, no way can Hadriel guard you, milady," Leala said, laughing. "If anything were to go down, he'd probably soil himself as he ran away."

Hadriel turned to her. "Leala, honey, eat glass."

"Walk off a cliff," she responded pleasantly.

I chuckled. "What sort of trouble can I get into?"

Hadriel pointed at the everlass field. "You just made out with the most dangerous, unhinged guy in this kingdom—"

"Except for the demon king," Leala said. "He's more dangerous."

"He is *not* more dangerous than the master," Hadriel shot back.

"Of course he is. He can control the master."

While I listened to them bicker, I selected a sandwich and took a bite. Cured ham and cheese. Delicious.

Hadriel half turned toward her. "The demon king can only control the master by using the curse as a leash. The master isn't even supposed to have jurisdiction, remember? In the beginning, he was just supposed to stick to the castle like the rest of us did. But he killed any demon that tried to keep him from the Royal

Wood. Tell me that the demon king is more powerful than that!"

"But the demon king does have the curse as a leash, so *technically* he is."

"*Technically* you're a waste of resources."

"Suck an asshole."

"Whoa, okay…" I put my hands out.

"My point was"—he gave Leala a poignant stare; she rolled her eyes—"you clearly don't make the best decisions."

"What about the girls he bangs?" I asked. "Do they have a guard detail, too?"

An awkward silence greeted my question. I lifted my eyebrows.

"He doesn't bang girls," Hadriel responded as Leala said, "He hasn't been with anyone since the curse, I don't think."

"Wait…" I lowered my half-eaten sandwich. "What?"

"Yes, you might have to take a second with that one." Hadriel patted my knee. "I cannot even fathom what his blue balls must be like. I mean, shame-fucking warps the brain, yes, but being backed up for years and years? That would drive a man mental."

"He has some…issues," Leala said carefully. "He won't have sex with a demon because they moved in and ruined our lives. He has a lot more self-control than the rest of us do, obviously. I didn't want to touch those demons either, I really didn't. But the incubi are really handsome, and eventually I got tired of everyone else, and then…"

"Shame-fucking," Hadriel finished. Leala shrugged and nodded. "That leaves the household staff. We assumed he was secretly fucking some of us, but all the secrets and then some have come out by now, and no. He's not fucking anyone in the castle. So then we assumed he might be fucking some of the villagers. Stands to reason. They feed him information, and then he probably gets a little whisper and a poke down that way. But he seems to only meet with men."

"He's not into men," Leala said.

"Right. He's not into men."

"Wait a minute." I pushed my last bite to the side of my cheek. "He's meeting with villagers?"

"That's how he gets his information," Leala said. She put her finger to her mouth. "But don't tell anyone. If the demon king found out, he'd kill the villagers. It's happened in the past."

"He doesn't meet with anyone from my village," I said, strangely offended.

Hadriel pulled his lips to the side of his face. "He clearly should've been, huh? Because you have that elixir thing. I'm supposed to bring you down to harvest the everlass tonight. Good thing, too, or I might've gone for the hair of the dog, and then the demons would've made a fool of me."

"You make a fool of yourself just fine without the demons' help," Leala said.

"I know what you're doing." Hadriel held up a finger. "You're trying to rile me up so that I'll get behind the paddle next time you want to be spanked. I'll say it again, Leala, I am not into that kinda kink. I do not find spanking a tied-up girl a good time. It stresses me out. So stop coming at me about it."

"But you really put your all into it. I can feel your passion."

"That's anger, Leala. It is anger, and I'm being very violent when I do it."

"Hmm," she said with a little smile, and ran her fingers down the side of her neck.

He shook his head and looked away. "I don't understand hate-fucking. If I hated you, I wouldn't want to fuck you."

I felt my face flush as I thought of my complicated feelings for Nyfain. Our anger, our rage, our mutual dislike for each other, and how damn good his tongue had felt stroking my nipple. The pounding of desire as his fingers rubbed between my thighs. I was pretty sure hate-fucking him would be a real good time. A *real* good time.

I was also sure something was wrong with me, and Hadriel was right—I was not making good decisions! I needed to stay away from that guy. At all costs, I needed distance between him and me.

"I'm not clear on the rules here," I said, rubbing my temples as though that would get Nyfain out of my head and the simmering heat out of my core. "I thought the beast couldn't pass through the edge of the Forbidden Wood."

"Well, that's where the power thing comes into effect," Hadriel said. "Back in the day, the magic fortifying that line was potent. It hurt the master a great deal to cross it. But the magic has dissipated a bit over the last sixteen years. The demon king has not re-fortified it, and the master can make the crossing without too much pain now. He just has to do it sparingly because he doesn't want any of the demons to find out. Luckily for him and unluckily for us, we keep the demons pretty well occupied. As do the villages, I hear."

"And so when he goes to meet these villagers…" I squinted an eye.

Hadriel flung out his hand to silence Leala, but he was too late.

"They usually meet him in the wood. The villagers can come and go without the magic affecting them. Which is also supposed to be a secret from the demon king. I mean, he probably knows, but he doesn't think villagers pose any threat anymore…"

She trailed off. Hadriel looked at me with a blank face. As well he should have.

"And just how many other prisoners has he taken?" I asked in a measured voice. This time I let my animal rise to the surface, fueling me with power. My senses strengthened, smell and eyesight and hearing more acute. That might come in handy. "How many?"

"Um…" Leala cleared her throat. "We're really not at liberty to—"

"Tell me," I barked.

"None," they both said quickly, clutching their chests. Hadriel's eyes widened, and Leala smiled and bent a little, looking inward again.

After a moment, Hadriel took a deep breath.

"Never, and I mean never…" He stuck up a finger. "*Never* do that in the presence of the demon king. Ever. Or he'll take you away without a word."

"Do what?" I asked, allowing my animal a little more freedom now that Nyfain wasn't kicking around.

Hadriel gave Leala a *look* before pushing to standing. "Nothing. The master will figure it out. Right. Let's get cracking, doll. I'll show you around to all the hobby stations so you don't go crazy and give in to the demons, then we need to find you that garden for your herbs—I hope you can work miracles—and get you measured so you don't look like a fourteen-year-old boy running around the place. We have standards around here."

"So he took me prisoner—"

"Don't." He held up his finger again.

"But seriously, he's—"

"Nope." He shook the finger.

"Why am I—"

"Zzzzzip it." He grabbed my arm and pulled me up, leading me away from Leala, who would presumably pick up the largely uneaten picnic, and to the side of the back door.

"Listen to me," he said seriously. "There are three people you can trust in this place, okay?" He ticked off a finger. "There is me because I had no choice in the matter." He ticked off a second finger. "There is Leala because she is a damn fine lady's maid and will keep every one of your secrets. Don't tell her I said nice things, she'll just taunt me." Third finger. "Finally, there's the master." He spread his hands. "That's it. We're the only ones you can trust. Just us three. And that isn't because the rest of the house staff mean you harm. The problem is that the survivors are mediocre at best. Remember me telling you that? We tend to make things worse instead of better. So if you tell someone something, they'll spread it around. If they don't tell a demon during a pleasure session, they'll tell someone else on the house staff, and *they'll* pass it on. When it comes to you, we do not want any details getting around. As far as they are concerned, Nyfain found someone stealing, and he's going to use her as a plaything before he kills her. That is something the demons will understand. They'll think they're finally getting to him. They'll give him a little leeway with it. At least"—he grimaced—"he seems to think so. I guess we'll just have to wait and find out, huh?"

"But…I still don't understand. If he never takes anyone else prisoner, why me?"

"Sometimes to protect something, we need to hide it in plain sight."

"Protect me from what?"

"You'll have to ask the master. I'm not at liberty to say, and if you go too far in making me answer your questions, you might accidentally ask the wrong one. I'll try to spill things covered by the magical gag, and it'll kill me. Your grievances need to be taken up with the master and no one else. Preferably where you can't be overheard."

I brushed my hair out of my face, nervousness swirling in my gut.

"Fine." I lifted my chin in defiance. "I will take it up with him directly."

So much for staying away from Nyfain. I just hoped the next meeting didn't end up with my tit in his mouth.

# CHAPTER 8

"OKAY, WHAT ARE we thinking, my darling?" Hadriel walked me down a wide hallway with towering vaulted ceilings. Mostly closed doors lined our pathway, with windows at the very top of the wall beneath the ceiling line, showering down light.

"What are we doing again?"

"We're choosing hobbies. You need something to do during the day besides piss off the master."

"Oh... But..."

"This is needlepoint." He pointed at a door somewhat ajar. "Fancy making a lovely picture by poking fabric with needles? Or, in my case, a horrid rendition of a pond? It turned out like a swamp. By then word had gotten around about the watercolors and everyone accused me of failing at making a penis." He put a hand to his chest. "I said ex*cuse* me, if I wanted to make a dick, I *could* make a dick, even in needlepoint. But I left in a huff and never returned because, honestly, I wasn't totally sure that was true, and I didn't want them to call me on it."

I barked out a laugh before poking my head into the room. A middle-aged woman sat in a rocking chair. Glasses perched on the end of her nose as she pulled a string through a white strip of fabric. Two other women sat near her, one of them sitting in front of a white rectangle of fabric on some sort of stand, creating an intricate flowery design.

Before I could back out, the woman in the rocking chair glanced up. Her eyebrows sank low, and she startled.

"Maxine!" she shouted, stopping her rocking. "Max-ine, am I dead?"

"What?" A woman up in years glanced over with a scowl. "What are you talking about?"

"I see an angel. Am I dead?"

"I see it, too," the third woman said, her hair piled up into a bun at the top of her fuzzy head. "Is it a battle angel? Why is it dirty?"

I pulled my head back out and backed away. Hadriel filled my spot.

"Hey! Did you ladies see that ghost?" he said. I heard a collective gasp. "That was a ghost, wasn't it? I'm pretty sure it was! It looked like that woman…" He snapped a few times and glanced at the ceiling. "That cook's assistant from back in the day. Remember her, the one that dove off her horse and got trampled?"

"Oh!" one of the women said. "Yes! I believe I remember."

"That never happened," another said. "I would've remembered if that happened."

"It *did* happen!" the first insisted. "Remember—"

Hadriel shut the door and turned back, chuckling. "That'll give them something to discuss for at least a year. Andrelle has been obsessed with death since the start of all of this. She constantly thinks she'll be the next to go. She hunts the grounds for ghosts, assured they are real. What she doesn't believe in? Demons."

"How does she not believe in demons? They're in the castle. They have their own kingdom."

He laughed as he stopped in front of another door. "Isn't that a kicker? She doesn't actually go out at night! She doesn't partake in any of the sex stuff, yet she still turned out nuts. There was no hope for any of us, I'm telling you. She goes into her room at sundown and reemerges at dawn. Or thereabouts. Sometimes she sees demons, but she ignores them as if they weren't there. It is the absolute strangest thing. I mean, in the beginning, we all thought it was just her way of getting through it all. After sixteen years, though?" He tilted his head. "It's anyone's guess. Also, you should get used to the taunting. We're all dejected and miserable. Taunting each other is all we have anymore."

"It's a nightmare…"

"Cheers!" He scowled at me. "Damn it, don't do that when I don't have a drink. It just makes me want to go find a party. Right, okay, what about candle making? You can do scented ones, colored ones, and… I think that might be all."

"No, thanks. I'm not really good at any of that kind of stuff."

"Right. But you can get good. That's the point."

"Yeah, but…I have no interest."

"Me either. Okay, what else? There is a puzzle room. I've been working on one for three years now."

"Are you…not so good at puzzles?"

"No, I'm great at them, actually! I really love puzzles. It's just the rest of these bastards aren't any good, and they've mixed up all the pieces. So I'm essentially doing all the puzzles in the castle to try to sort everything out." He pushed open a door into a jungle of small and large tables covered in partially finished puzzles. Pieces were strewn all over the place. Little pathways led in between them. Two people were currently sitting on the floor, bent over a section.

"Those are the misfit pieces! Don't mix up the misfit pieces!" He pushed into the room quickly, walking as carefully through the puzzles as I had the everlass.

While he was busy, I continued a little farther down the hallway, wondering if I had the courage to try one of the other doors. Ahead, at the end of the hall, one of the double doors stood slightly ajar. I could just make out a shelf of books on the wall. My heart filled with joy, and I started that way.

"No, wait!" Hadriel jumped in front of me with his arms out. "Sorry, I can't show you that yet. Master's orders."

I narrowed my eyes. "Why doesn't he want me to see the library?"

"He takes great pride in that library. There's a system for checking out books. He wants to go over it with you."

I rolled my eyes for show, mostly. I couldn't honestly fault Nyfain for that. With all of the shenanigans that went on here, he'd need to have a very good system for keeping track of books.

Still, I itched to check it out, to run my fingers across the spines. There was probably so much new knowledge in there it would make my head explode. If the only viable hobby for me was to read through that library, no one would ever hear a peep of complaint from me.

However, it was yet another thing I needed to see Nyfain about. Staying away from him wasn't looking so feasible.

After a deep breath, I clued in to Hadriel rattling off other potential hobbies.

"Knitting?" he asked. I shook my head. "What about making pots out of clay?"

"How about archery? Or sword work. Fighting in general?"

"Anyone good at that stuff was killed. Obviously. Love, have you heard nothing I've said? They were the first to go."

"Hunting? Surely you all need to eat?"

"The master takes care of hunting. But…maybe? I'll mention it. What about…" He walked us a little farther along.

"What if we just look in the library? I won't take anything."

He made a pouty face. "Not this time, I'm afraid. He's not a fun one to piss off. Soon, though, I promise. I will mention your desire. He loves those books. He'll make the time for a fellow enthusiast, I guarantee it." He looped his arm through mine and pointed right. "How about dancing or singing? Do you fancy learning a musical instrument?"

"It just feels like I should be doing something more useful than taking a class."

He pulled back from me, his brow furrowed. "Maybe don't say stuff like that. Oh, goddess save us, how are we going to keep the demons from making you have an accident we don't walk away from? Notice I said *we*? Yeah, because I'll end up perishing with you."

Fire shot through my blood and my fingers tingled, my animal making it very clear about where she stood on demons trying to kill us. I agreed wholeheartedly.

"And that, yeah." He touched his chest while shaking his head.

"Do you not usually feel your animal?"

He slapped his hand to my mouth. "No," he whispered, standing closer. "Damn it, I knew you didn't know much, but I wasn't told you knew nothing at all. We're all still suppressed. Everyone but the master. He can occasionally pull our animals to the surface with his power, but it's rare, and in no time at all they go back to being suppressed. I'm not sure why. How you're doing it so much is beyond me. Whatever you have lurking in there is powerful, and she never got to make her debut like other animals. She's probably frustrated and restless and eager to work her way out, right? She's driving you mental?"

I swallowed and nodded.

He glanced behind him. Seeing that no one was there, he continued to whisper. "When you flex your power, I can feel her lurking. The combined—"

His eyes widened, and fear leaked into them. He reached up to his throat, fingernails scoring his skin.

Alarm rang through me. I reached for him, grabbing his shoulders as he backed against the wall. My animal scrabbled to get out. Hadriel's face turned red, and he opened and closed his mouth like a fish. No breath could force its way out. He must've activated the magical gag!

"Breathe," I said in terror. I had about five minutes until his brain would suffer. I had to act fast. "*Breathe!*"

I felt his throat, wondering if I could slice a hole and get him air that way. Would the magical gag cover from chin to chest?

Probably.

Everlass?

My mind shot through all the possibilities as my animal bled fire into me. She shoved her way forward, up and up through my middle until she was throbbing against my limbs. As worry and panic consumed me, I slipped in my hold of her.

She filled my body like a person pulling on a latex suit. Power roared through me, and my senses heightened, the scents and sounds I was processing so complex I couldn't make sense of them. But *she* could.

It was like I was a passenger in my own body, but instead of blanking out the way I had before stabbing Nyfain, I could see all that transpired.

She picked up Hadriel like he weighed nothing, draped him over our shoulder, and went running through the hall and then down a couple sets of steps. She stopped instead of continuing on to the door we'd used to enter. Inhaling, processing those complex smells, she turned left and put on a burst of speed.

A woman who'd been walking toward us stopped in confusion.

"Mind your business, Florence!" my animal roared as we passed by.

The woman, who probably wasn't called Florence because I'd never seen her before, jerked as though she had been slapped. She stumbled and fell onto her butt as we ran by.

*Florence?* I thought.

*Hadriel said these people were simple.*

I tried to widen my eyes, but they weren't solely mine just now, and she had more control than I did.

*You can speak to me?* I thought. *He didn't say they were simple; he said they did a mediocre job.*

*Whether or not she is simple, now she's confused. She'll hopefully forget all about this. I get the sense that we are a rarity in this place, and we need to keep a low profile. You're doing a piss-poor job of that so far. Great work.*

She sounded like me, only surlier. I doubted my personality needed more salt, but here we were.

We entered a small hall off the side of a little den, the ceiling low and the walls tight. Servants' hall, probably. At the other end, she kicked through a wooden door to the outside.

*How did you know—*

*Smell,* she interrupted me. *You need to allow me more room so you can access my power. That delicious alpha is letting me out of my cage. Use it until we can abuse it.*

*Yeah, except you clearly want to get in his pants. That's a nope. He's not a nice guy.*

*Fuck nice. I have a dark and damning need for that alpha. I want to take a running leap, wrap my legs around his head, and force-feed him my pussy. This bitch needs some cock. Wham, bam, call me ma'am.*

Great goddess. What the hell kind of creature did I have inside of me?

We ran out into the deadened grass and around the castle. Hadriel kicked and writhed over our shoulder, trying to get air. She inhaled and then changed direction, running faster than I'd ever moved in my life. In a flash, she darted into the Forbidden Wood, choosing our footsteps carefully. Twigs crackled and branches whipped out behind us. The side of one foot caught a rock, and I surged up and adjusted our weight so we could drop into a roll. Otherwise it would've resulted in a sprain. I was an old pro at accounting for missteps.

*You've kept us in great shape,* she thought. *Our body has great tone and dexterity. Nice job.*

*Kinda had to. Wild boar would have been the death of me otherwise. Bastards.*

She hit an animal trail and turned right, putting on another burst of speed. I caught Nyfain's delicious smell, the effect vibrating through my person.

*Yummm,* she purred.

*He took me prisoner. He's the enemy.*

*That just makes it hotter.*

I was really annoyed that I couldn't roll my eyes.

We burst through a wall of thorny bushes, scraping our skin. She growled in challenge.

*It's a fucking bush. Don't challenge a bush.*

*You can hold a machete, can't you? It won't be a bush for long.*

Again, it would really be helpful to my overall well-being if I could roll my eyes.

Nyfain bent within yet another small field of ever-lass, nude from having shifted, brushing one plant gently before moving on to the next. He plucked a couple of dead leaves and checked the soil before brushing this plant as well. I'd always been labeled weird for how much I babied the plants. Compared to him, I was nothing. I wanted to stop and watch, to soak the sight in, but Hadriel wilted on our shoulder, giving in to the darkness.

*Hurry,* I thought, covering the distance between the bush and the everlass field in a few quick strides. Nyfain hadn't looked our way. *Why doesn't he hear us? Or smell us?*

*He is clearly lost to his thoughts and has nothing to fear out here. He is the predator.*

I wondered what those thoughts might be, causing him to act with such gentleness and ease when he was usually rough and surly. I quickly shifted my attention, though, as we laid Hadriel carefully onto the ground, his lips turning blue.

In a moment I was totally myself again, my animal slinking back so I could take control.

"Nyfain!" I yelled.

His head snapped up. He stood in a rush, withered leaves sprinkling from his hands. In a moment, he quickly picked his way to us.

"I think it's the magical gag," I said as he crouched beside us. "My animal took over. She brought us to you."

He studied me for a second, and it was hard to breathe within that intelligent golden gaze.

He nodded. "Ease her out. Just enough that you can maintain control."

I took a deep breath and did as he said, ready for the onslaught of lust when she emerged. It didn't come. The fire I'd grown to realize was her power coursed through my blood, but her focus was solely on Hadriel.

We glanced at Nyfain, needing direction, and for the first time I could feel his beast. Raw need, desperate desire, and something so strong I couldn't quite define…

The world tilted. Everything inside of me tightened up. I felt my presence shoved down, but it only took a moment for me to push my way back into myself.

"Work with me," Nyfain said urgently, holding out his hand.

I watched as we took it, mine so dainty in comparison. He put his other hand on Hadriel, who'd gone still.

Fear and sorrow ricocheted through me.

"Please," I said to no one in particular. "This is my fault. Please, he needs to live."

I spun, looking at the everlass.

Nyfain used our joined hands to yank me back around. He leaned closer, his eyes claiming my focus.

"You have been using some of your power all your life without knowing it. You can heal. *You* are life. You don't need the plant right now. You just need me for strength. Pull him away from the demons' magic. Think of what your soul wants and will it. Take from me, Finley. Use me. I am yours."

*Pull him away from the demons' magic.*

The thought echoed through my mind. My animal pushed power into me.

Together we focused on Hadriel, and our power continued to build, pulling up from my roots, bubbling and turbulent.

"Now," Nyfain commanded.

For the first time, I didn't push back.

I sank myself into the thought: *Breathe. Please, Hadriel, breathe!*

A shock of power reverberated within me before blasting out. I could feel Nyfain's power swirling and merging with mine, becoming a tidal wave of force that stole my breath. Then, to my shock, it swung back around and slammed into my middle. I nearly fell back from the force. My vision wavered and my animal roared, bucking and jumping within me. My skin prickled and fire rolled over it. It felt itchy, somehow, my skin. Like it was stretched too tightly. I needed to shed it.

"Easy now," Nyfain commanded, his rough voice washing over me comfortingly. "Take it easy. Use the power, but not to shift. You cannot shift with the curse in effect. I will not let it disfigure you as it has done me. Just settle into the power. Push anything you can't handle back into me. Use me, Finley."

The raging storm within me thrashed. My vision was peppered with black, and I did as he said, leaning against him as I tried to shove some of the power away. The haze cleared a little, but it didn't calm the raging inferno.

"That's my girl," he murmured, his voice seeming to hum within me. "That's it. Hold on to it."

I whimpered under the strain as his arm came around my shoulders and pulled me in tightly. His heat caressed my skin and then settled deep and low. Throbbing. Electricity fizzed within our touch.

His head dropped a little, and I swore I heard the softest of moans, like a decadent sigh.

"Will it again," he whispered against the shell of my ear. "Use your will to pry him away from the demon magic."

I closed my eyes, feeling my animal basking in the glow of our combined power. Shivers raced up my skin and across my scalp. Again, I did as he said, clutching at him and taking in a bit more power, the swell stretching my skin unpleasantly. Raging to the point of destruction.

*Breathe, Hadriel,* I thought, my eyelids fluttering.

My power scrabbled against something slick and oily, like a sheen over garbage. I clawed through it, wild and raw. Ripped it away.

Hadriel sucked in air, convulsing upward. He gripped the ground, his fingers digging into the dirt like claws. He coughed and bent, flopping sideways.

"Hadriel?" I reached for him, but Nyfain's grasp kept me immobile. Those strong, scarred fingers clutched my chin and he pulled my face his way.

He searched my features for a moment before landing on my eyes. It seemed as though he was looking for something. An answer to some question. His brow dipped, and he suddenly released me and stood.

The unexpectedness made me lurch forward, falling to my hands.

"Get him cleaned up, and then let's go," Nyfain barked, striding away right and behind the trees.

By now his mood swings and shitty behavior weren't new or shocking. The guy took brooding to a whole new level.

Shaky from the power, which was now dissipating quickly, I bent to Hadriel.

"Are you okay?" I grabbed his arm.

He coughed again, curled up in the fetal position.

His chest rose and fell. "You guys saved my life," he rasped out, clutching his throat. "That was a close one."

"Too close." I waited until he was ready and then helped him up.

He sucked in a deep breath. "Fuck, I thought I was going to die. When you started running me into the wood, I thought it was to hide my dead body."

"My animal was in control."

"Thank the goddess and her secret kinks that you have access to her and chose to listen, because yeah." He stood with his hand pressed to the base of his throat for a long moment, looking out at nothing. "I don't really want to comment because I don't want to go through that again, but..."

He gave me a pointed look and nodded.

Butterflies fluttered up through my stomach, although I had no idea why.

"You can tell me about the curse now," I said, gesturing to the castle. "Maybe I can help—"

"No way." He waved his hands. "I wasn't even talking about it directly, and it did that. It might have been worse if I'd said more. Stronger magic, maybe." He shook his head adamantly. "I'd seize up before I could give you anything of note, and even if I did..." He paused, clearly going over what he would say.

"Even if you did, there's no need." Nyfain walked back into the area, still completely nude.

I tried not to let my gaze wander down his sculpted body and end on his large—

I jerked my head away so my animal didn't try to fight to the surface and jump him.

"She can't help." He stopped a few paces away, scowling.

Hadriel studied his feet and didn't comment.

"Can't I?" I asked with a sudden rush of anger. "Clearly I have some worth. Maybe I don't know how to fight as well as you do, but I'm told you have a big library. If you'd fill me in on the checking-out system, I could find something to help me. I know I could. I learned about the everlass from books, about making elixirs and draughts. I can be ready when the time comes."

Hadriel looked up again with a furrowed brow, tilting his head slightly. I didn't know him well enough to interpret the expression.

Nyfain closed the distance and snatched my upper arm. He jerked me to face him. "You can be ready when the time comes, can you? To what? Sacrifice your life and your happiness to protect your village?"

I gritted my teeth, making a note to start carrying a knife around him.

"Obviously," I said through a tight jaw.

"Sacrifice your future? Reduce yourself to nothing more than a cause?"

"Your staff isn't simple, *you* are," I said, balling my fists. "Sacrifice my future? What future? All we have to look forward to is sickness and death. Seeing our loved ones die horribly around us. You call that a future? Of *course* I will sacrifice myself, you great ape. Why do you think I left my house when you showed up in your beast form? I'd endure any fate to see my loved ones survive this. I'd pay any price to give Sable and Dash a chance at a real life—a *real* life where they can travel and see other kingdoms and marry for love."

He stared at me for a long time, doubt plain in his eyes. But also…pain. Sorrow. Regret. These were old hauntings, I could see that. His torment wasn't just because of the curse.

"What happened to you?" I asked softly, unable to help myself.

His eyebrows lowered. "It makes no difference. I'll be damned if I let it happen to you."

"Why do you care? I thought my life was forfeit…"

Emotions warred on his face. Then he stepped back, and suddenly the beast grew before me. His sheer size and power shocked terror into my bones. I pushed back as Hadriel did, driven by a primal warning to *get away*.

The beast opened his mouth into a great maw filled with large teeth. I quaked, turning. I didn't get far.

The teeth closed around me for the second time in my life, and then he was running me back to the castle.

# CHAPTER 9

H E FLUNG ME into the tower room. I fell against the bed. He stood panting in the doorway, having run me to the castle in his beast form and then carried me up the stairs in an unbreakable hold.

Now, back in my room, he stuck out his hand. "Give me the key."

I straightened myself up, looking around for my knife. Leala must've cleaned up and put it somewhere.

"Your weapons won't help you now." Menace flowed from him in heady waves. He stepped right in front of me, his size and power pounding down on me. "Give me the key, or I will search you and take it."

I ignored the desire to cower and instead squared off. I would not allow him to see the effect he had on me. "Don't you dare put your hands on me."

His chest rose and fell, his breath quickening. "I

don't have time for this. Give me the key, princess."

"Ah. We're back to *princess* again, are we? Just before you lock me in the castle tower."

He closed what little space was between us. His voice rumbled from his wide chest, caressing me.

"This is your last chance," he murmured, his gaze roaming my face and settling on my lips.

Heat flash-boiled my blood. My core tightened, fear and lust and yearning creating a confusing mix.

"I will not be locked in this place against my will," I managed, defiant.

"You will do as you're told."

He moved so fast that I couldn't even flinch. He grabbed my wrists and tucked them behind my back, transferring both to the hold of one of his large hands. I squirmed, trying to get out, but he leaned me against the bed with his body, his erection pressing against my lower stomach. His free hand flowed up over my upper thigh, feeling for my pants pocket.

I slammed my head forward, catching him in the mouth with my forehead.

His head jerked away, and his free hand flew to his face. He took one step back, pulling me sideways. I yanked my right hand out of his hold and punched. My fist connected with his nose, but I didn't have the balance to put any weight behind it. He barely moved from the blow.

His eyes flashed, and my insides went wobbly. I'd just excited him. Oh shit.

"You want to do this the hard way, then?" he asked in that deep, terribly scary, strangely erotic voice.

Surprisingly, he dropped my hand. A small smile worked at his lips. He wanted us to start on equal footing. As if there were such a thing.

Panic blared, and suddenly I was in survival mode, wanting to get away, my animal wanting him to catch me.

I feinted right, then broke left to run around him. He took one lazy step and reached out. His hand landed between my breasts, and he shoved me back, launching me onto the bed. I fell on my side with my legs sprawled out, a very bad position under the circumstances.

Acting quickly, I flipped and scrabbled to get off the other side of the bed. I needed my knife!

"My clothes look good on you, princess. But wearing nothing would look so much better."

I was wearing his fucking clothes? Why hadn't Leala said something? I would've rather worn a potato sack than parade around him in what must be his childhood clothes.

An iron grip latched around my right ankle. I flipped back to kick, but he pulled me toward him.

His tantalizing power slithered across my tingling flesh. My animal purred within his dominant manhandling. My pussy was so wet it dribbled into my panties. Damn my body! I would not give in to this insanity of lust. I needed logic here!

I struggled against him as he dragged my legs off the bed and dropped them. They swung down until my knees bumped the mattress. He leaned forward, his hard length resting right where I needed it. Where I hated that I wanted it.

My animal thrashed against my hold and my hips bucked back, in her control. Shivers coated me as I rubbed along his cock, momentarily dropping my head and closing my eyes, focused solely on that delicious sensation. He growled, his free hand gripping my hip and keeping me still while he rocked, the glorious friction dripping liquid fire into my desperate pussy.

"Hmm, Nyfain, fuck me," I moaned.

My eyes snapped open at the realization of what I'd just said. Not what my animal had made me say—what *I* had said.

Had I no self-preservation? My mind had gone completely haywire.

"That's not what I meant! I meant, take what you want and go," I said, fighting my animal again. Fighting myself. Fighting the glorious sensation of his weight against me, pushing me into the mattress. The hard peaks of my nipples rubbed against my binding as I wriggled, my eyes fluttering as we rubbed against each other.

"Take what I want?" He reached around and down, sliding his hand against my stomach and then pelvis. He dipped farther, and his first two fingers slipped over my swollen clit.

I bit back a moan. The feeling of his beast rolled through me, dominant and possessive. It was almost like the dragon was in control. A moment later, power followed, lending me strength. Was the man giving me the ability to fight back against the dragon? That was what it felt like. Like Nyfain was fighting his beast, too, and trying to help me stand on my own.

*Just a bit longer,* my animal purred as his firm fingers made circles against my—*his!*—pants. His cock slid against me, the two working in tandem. My body was tightening up, rocking with him.

I did want to wait a bit longer. Goddess help me, I wanted him to flip me over, tear off these pants, and sink deep into my greedy cunt. My body was so keyed up. My pussy swollen. Eager.

"No," I said to myself, using that power and twisting.

I threw off his hand and managed to pull up a knee.

Before he could grab it and spread my legs, I kicked as hard as I could, the sole of my foot hitting him in the sternum. I expected his eyes to widen as I knocked him back, but instead a flare of pride soaked into that golden gaze.

I didn't have time to wonder about it. I jumped from the bed and shoved him, careful not to let his reaching hands take hold of me. He staggered back toward the doorway. I fished the key from my pocket and held it out.

"You want to take me prisoner? Fine. Here's your key."

He stood panting for a moment, his huge cock erect, the tip glistening. I tore my eyes away from it, then away from that perfect chest, cut up from his many battles. This man was impossible, but he was affecting me in gut-clenching ways. It wasn't fair. I'd always thought I'd land a nice guy who would smooth out my crazy. This bastard hands down made it worse.

"But tell me this—why me?" I asked. "Why take me prisoner and no one else? What did I do that was so wrong?"

He stalked forward, slinky like a predator. My body trembled under his gaze. He plucked the key from my fingers.

"Maybe someday I'll tell you. I'll have Leala come

up and bathe you and bring you food. Get some rest. I'll be your escort when it is time to harvest."

He closed the door behind him. The key turned over, locking me in. Metal clinked, and I knew he was taking the key with him this time.

Annoyed, frustrated, and pissed off, I paced across the room and spread my hands on the windowsill. That overgrown and half-dead garden waited below, rose-bushes reaching out in every which way without one bloom to cheer me up.

He'd said I could choose a garden and bring it back to life for my herbs. I'd choose that one so that when I was locked in here, I'd at least have something to gaze down at. For now, I shed the clothes that were not mine and put on a slip of fabric that had been left at the edge of my bed. It was likely for sleeping, but it would do until I had something else. No way was I going to try those cake-frosting dresses. They were probably from a past girlfriend of his. Or maybe he liked dresses as well; it was impossible to say. I just knew that they weren't mine, and I wasn't going to look a fool anymore.

LATER THAT NIGHT, after a relaxing bath, meal, and bed, the swell of desire washed over me. Nyfain's fingers wrapped around my ankles, the memory morphing into a dream. I groaned as his large hands spread out and took the inside track of my legs, reaching my knees and pushing them wide.

I lay flat on my back in bed as the moonlight soaked up the darkness. The slip of fabric draped over me, light and soft against my fevered skin. The covers had been pulled back, and Nyfain sat between my spread thighs, nude and gorgeous despite his scars. It looked picture perfect, like this was actually happening. Like I'd come softly awake without realizing it.

He worked his hands farther up, bunching my nightgown as he went. His touch seared the insides of my legs. I arched back, spreading wide for him, desire drenching me.

"Do you want me to fuck you, pretty girl?"

His voice was different, not the scratchy sandpaper laced with power and confidence and pain that I was used to. Now it was silky and sensual, winding my desire higher.

"Do you want me to thrust my hard cock into your wet depths?"

"Hmm, yes," I whispered.

His touch slid along the tops of my thighs, and he bent forward. His tongue slid through my wet folds before getting to the top and teasing. He sucked in my clit, and the pleasure made me roll my eyes back into my head. I ran my fingers through his unruly hair, grabbing on and yanking a little. He sucked and licked, dipping two fingers into me and curving upward.

I groaned, writhing beneath him.

He worked harder, lapping at me eagerly, setting a fast pace. I gyrated my hips against his mouth, running my hands up through my nightgown and over my hard nipples.

He kept going, faster now, pushing me to the edge. Finger-fucking me.

Two hands on his head now, my fingers tangled in his hair, I moved against him, fucking his face, needing a little more so I could fall over that edge.

He stopped, moving to kiss farther up my body. Sucking on my flesh. It still felt like he was sucking on my clit, though, ramming his fingers into my cunt with reckless abandon.

"Fuck me, Nyfain," I begged, dragging him up my body, writhing against that ghostly touch. "Please, Nyfain. I need you."

"Take what you need," he whispered, and this time his scratchy voice echoed in my mind like a memory. "Use me."

He reached my mouth and kissed me dominantly. He took my breath away with his bruising kiss. And then he thrust into me, filling me to the point of bursting. I cried out, pain and pleasure and desire and no looking back. I clutched his shoulders and wrapped my legs around his middle, wanting to be taken hard. Wanting him to stamp his brand into me and claim me like an alpha should.

"Do you want my forked tongue between those sodden pussy lips, pretty lady?"

The words struck me wrong. The tone.

Nyfain pulled back, looking down on me. His eyes weren't right, though. The beautiful sunsets were gone, replaced by bright yellow eyes with small black slits. Horns curled from his head, but they weren't the same as his beast's.

I gasped and jerked awake, sitting up in my bed. Moonlight streamed through the windows, but Nyfain was nowhere in sight. My nightgown, which Leala had given to me after a bath, was undisturbed, and the blanket still covered me to my chest.

A dream. It had all been a dream. But I still felt the pleasure curling around me. The thrusting inside my body.

It felt wrong. It felt like a violation. An incubus, it must be, but one more powerful than I'd ever felt. Usually they just made you want to bang, but this one acted like it was doing the banging with invisible hands.

My guts twisted in disgust. I pushed my knees shut to block it out. It didn't turn me on. It made me feel sick.

*Help,* I called to my animal, clearing the way.

She filled me in a rush of fire and rage. *What kind of filthy fuckery do we have going on here?* she thought as she assumed control.

I let her take over without complaint. I wasn't equipped to handle something like this. My brain recoiled from the thought of what was going on. I could rise to the occasion for a fight, but this was a whole different thing entirely.

She sniffed the air as she pushed back the covers, and we slowly climbed out of bed.

"I have your scent now, you filthy fuck," she said in a voice I hadn't known I could make. A throaty sort of voice brimming with confidence and menace. A voice promising death. I really liked it.

We stopped next to the door and felt for the key, just in case it had magically appeared.

*No such luck,* she thought. I thought the opposite. I'd raged about Nyfain taking that key earlier, and commanding Leala to bring it back to him when she was done helping with my bath, but right now I was grateful. If that thing had gotten in, it would have tried to take what it wanted, and I had no idea what sort of fighting prowess it had.

"Come out to me, pretty lady, and let me lick that delicious cu—"

The creature cut off right before a loud *thunk* rattled the door.

We caught the familiar smell of pine and lilac with a hint of honeysuckle on a balmy summer's day. Nyfain.

The *thunk* came again, rattling the wood in the frame. A third time, something being slammed against the wall. A loud wail suddenly cut off before intense quiet filled the space outside the door.

Metal tinkled in the keyhole, and the lock clicked over. I took a step back as the door swung open, revealing Nyfain in a blue T-shirt and tight, ripped jeans.

Every instinct in my person said to run at him and tuck myself into his safe embrace. I held back with everything I had.

"What was that—" I caught a glimpse of it lying behind him. A human-looking guy, nude, about my age and incredibly handsome. His head had been bashed in and was cocked at an unnatural angle. A shoulder looked out of socket and three fingers were clearly broken. Nyfain had done some damage. Which obviously included death.

"It was one of the most powerful types of incubi in the demon kingdom," Nyfain said in a rough voice.

"They feed on lust and shame. There are three in this castle—two now—designed to slowly drive the staff into self-destruction."

He captured my chin and analyzed my face. His nostrils flared.

"It aroused you." It sounded like an accusation.

"I was sleeping when its magic reached me. It turned my dream erotic, but it felt wrong, and I woke up. Some idiot locked me in the tower before I could make the draught to block that sort of thing out. Though I think I might have to make it a lot stronger to handle stronger incubi. That one was...gross." I shivered.

"Some idiot is right," he murmured, so quietly I stared at him for a moment to see if I'd imagined it. "Get some clothes on. It's time to go."

I looked down at my nightgown. "I don't have clothes. That was also on the list of things to do before the idiot locked me in the tower."

"Same idiot, I reckon?" He quirked his eyebrow before brushing by me. Since when did he have a sense of humor?

He glanced at the bed as he walked around it, his movements stiff. Without a word, he opened the chest of drawers.

"No. I'm not wearing any more of your clothes."

"I doubt you want to walk around this castle at night without clothes. At this point, that's seen as an invitation. Has for…at least a decade, I believe. People will touch without asking permission, and I'll be forced to kill them."

My animal shivered in pleasure, responding to what was obviously the alpha in him. I scowled in annoyance at them both.

"I'll wear the nightgown."

"That nightgown is basically see-through, and while I love the view, so would everyone else. We'd be back to the me-killing-everyone scenario. I don't want to lose more staff, and killing a host of demons will result in a visit from the demon king. No one wants that, least of all you." He continued sifting through the drawers. It seemed like he was looking for something particular. "Don't worry, it's been a very long time since I've worn any of these. My cooties are long gone."

My scowl this time competed with a budding grin. His personality shift, however small, was making him more likable. That was bad news. I was having a hard enough time sticking to anger instead of desire.

"Here." He pulled out some leather bottoms and a black shirt to go with them. "Where is your binding? I'll protect you from everyone else, but you'll need to protect yourself from our animals. The binding makes it take longer for him to get our mouth on your perfect breasts."

My animal's shiver coincided with mine this time.

"Why am I always the one told to control my animal?" I opened the wardrobe and yanked out the binding. "Where's your accountability in all of this?"

"That's a damn good question." He saw me pause, not wanting to slip off my nightgown in front of him. He turned his back and looked out the window. "Usually there is a pretty even divide with our animals. My animal controls the beast for the most part, with me looking on, and I control this body. Our connection is open enough that I have access to his primal capabilities, and he has access to my logic and deductive reasoning. But with you..."

I struggled to get the binding clasped at the back. This was different than the type I had always worn, better quality and more secure, but also designed for someone else to help apply it. Leala had handled that earlier.

"I can't... I need help." I held the fabric tight as he glanced back.

He took a deep breath before coming over. "Turn around."

I showed him my back. He kept talking as he worked the clasps. His fingers brushed my skin lightly, gently, as though he were working with the everlass. Goosebumps spread across my flesh.

"He desires to claim you."

I shivered again, damn it, remembering my dream this time. Remembering him moving within me.

"That's a nope," I said quickly, pushing the memories away. The sudden wetness between my thighs couldn't be helped. "You've already abducted me without proper explanation, pushed me around, talked a bunch of shit—I'd rather not wear an alpha's shackles on top of it."

"I know that. Believe me. While he has access to logic, in this case he clearly isn't using it. He doesn't care that you're lowborn, for example. That your family doesn't have a pot to piss in and your village is poor and mostly useless. He doesn't care that a noble of my standing would never lower himself with a woman like you. He just wants me to fuck you good and proper so that you'll never, ever be used by another man. He wants our claim on you. He hates that you're resisting it. That *I* am. He feels your animal trying to get to him, so he's been taking matters into his own hands. It's a battle every time, and when your beast wins, *he* wins. Our animals are feeding off each other, and it is too powerful for me to stop unless you work with me on it. Which you aren't doing. It's throwing everything off."

Broody McFucker was back. A growl laced every word. He clearly blamed me for his lack of control. Wasn't that how it always went for a woman?

He jerked my binding, roughly, before pushing me away. He went back to looking out the window, his good humor dried up.

I put up a finger and then laughed. His return to being a cuntcycle was honestly a little relieving. I knew this guy. That other guy, with the playful words, light humor, gentle fingers... That guy was intriguing and, because of that, dangerous. That guy had the potential to thaw my attitude toward him. Given he was my jailer for unspecified reasons, that was a troubling thought.

"There is so much wrong with that speech of yours, it's a little tough to unpack." I pulled the black shirt over my head. It stretched across my bust and then hung down to my waist. "My village is mostly useless? Aren't you asking me to recreate an elixir that came out of that village? A *life-saving* elixir? I think you are."

I stepped into the pants and worked them up over my thighs and to my hips. That was where they stopped.

"These aren't going to work. Younger you didn't have any shape."

He glanced back, his gaze catching the slip of lacy fabric posing as underwear. There wasn't much to them, and apparently that was what Leala liked about them.

They could be torn off easily. For such a polite girl, she did like roughness. She'd given me this pair because she hadn't worn them yet.

Hunger burned brightly in his gaze. He tensed, every muscle going taut. With stiff movements, he bent to the chest of drawers.

"Your beast doesn't want any other men *using* me? Is that all women are good for, our vaginas?"

"Women are good for nothing," he snarled, but he didn't even remotely sell it. He was trying to deflect his arousal—*his* arousal, not his animal's. I could tell because my animal hadn't risen to the occasion. This was all him, and that knowledge took the sting out of his words. I had power over him. He wasn't untouchable.

"And yet you keep coming around," I said.

"After tonight, that's a situation I hope to rectify."

"Hmm."

He tossed me another pair of leathers. Did he have any other types of pants in there? "How often does this happen with you? Your animal wanting something you don't?"

He turned, gave me a hard scowl, and crossed the room. "Hurry up. The night is wasting." Then he gave me his back and stepped into the hall.

I'd struck a nerve. Interesting. Was there a lost love

at one time that had rejected him? *Something* had certainly happened to make him this way.

These pants ended at my shins but mostly fit everywhere else, except for the extra room in the dick department. After putting on shoes and remembering to slip my pocketknife into one of the large pockets, I tied up my hair and met him in the hall. The demon had changed from a very handsome man to a hideous humanoid form covered in slick green scales. It had a serpentine face, twisted horns, and hands ending in claws.

"The glamor washes away when they die," Nyfain said, his lip curling in disgust.

"The glamor... You mean he doesn't actually change into a man? He's always like that, we just can't see it?"

"Yes." He took me by the upper arm and steered me away from it. "If a person is in their right mind, they'll feel the difference." He walked us down the stairs. "The demons that feed off lust *and* pain have barbed penises or barbs in their vaginas. They coerce their victims and feed off the result."

I touched my hand to my chest, revolted. I hadn't heard of demons like that. I was glad I hadn't. It would've given me nightmares.

I guess it already had.

"There are a lot of different types of demons," he went on when we hit the next set of stairs, "but the demon king has taken most of the warring kinds away to defend his kingdom. They've done their job of thinning us out, making us vulnerable to attack. If we ever managed to escape this curse, he could take us over without a problem. We wouldn't be able to fight him off. We're done for; we're just waiting for the funeral march."

I ripped out of his grip when we hit the second-floor landing. He reached for me again but stopped when he realized I didn't plan on running. I looked up and met his turbulent eyes, anger, frustration, regret, and most of all sadness swimming in their depths.

I kept my voice a whisper, for his ears alone. "Don't you dare give up hope on this place. I will not watch as my family and everyone I know dies because you gave up. You're the only hope we have left. I don't care if you fly or run—you're *powerful*. You need to keep faith and be patient. There is a way through this. I think you're a dickface, and I'd rather punch you instead of talk to you, but I will fight by your side to the bitter end to pry this place out of the demons' hands. Do your job and lead your people. You're their rock. You *cannot* lose hope, do you understand?"

His body tensed as he stared at me, emotions flickering in his eyes so fast that I couldn't get a clear picture of what he was thinking. Energy crackled between us, and his power slithered across my skin, desperately sexy. I held my ground, though. I would not be deterred from delivering this message.

He leaned forward just a bit but then braced himself, and I didn't know if he wanted to kiss me or hit me. I prepared to dodge either.

Instead, I heard a silky voice say, "Well, hello, Nyfain."

Nyfain exploded into action, sweeping me behind him as he turned, pushing me to his back. I very nearly stepped out from behind him—I didn't need a shield—but thought better of it. I was supposed to be weak, or at least mediocre. A dead shifter walking. It wouldn't do to assert my independence and get killed for my courage.

"What do you want?" Nyfain snarled.

The faintest whisper of movement was the only sound as the demon circled us. Nyfain turned as it moved, keeping himself in front of me. Still, I caught a glimpse. Sleek and handsome, much like the man upstairs. Dark, long, flowing hair cascaded over his shoulders. His pointed nose ended close to large lips, like pillows affixed to a face, no real shape to them. His long fingers ended in manicured nails, and a silk robe adorned his lean body.

His magic tickled me, a dirty sort of sexy, slipping under my clothing and across my bare skin. I sucked in a breath and clutched Nyfain's shirt. His body went fluid, like a fighter preparing for battle.

"What have we here?" The demon moved until he could see over Nyfain's arm, taking me in. He looked down, not able to see my top half but clearly taking in the leather pants and boots. "Ah yes, I heard about her. You brought her in last night, correct?"

"She was stealing from these lands. I am the one who caught her, so by rights, she belongs to me."

The demon's oily smile showed stained teeth, as though he'd drunk too much wine or habitually fed on blood. "Yes, that is part of the deal. And instead of killing her outright, as you have always done, you brought her here. I wonder why. You prefer plain, willing women, do you not?"

Nyfain didn't comment.

The demon laughed. "I could have sworn you did. But if that were the case, you wouldn't have stolen a great beauty from her village and confined her to the castle. You were carrying her in, I believe, correct? And earlier, when she tried to escape, you locked her in the tower?" He clucked his tongue, his gaze still on me. "When you can, come see me, girl. I can pry you away."

Chills spread over me, and I very nearly shot back a

response. Instead, I pulled farther back behind Nyfain and buried my face in the groove of muscle in the middle of his back. I wasn't sure that was the right play—was I supposed to be a wilting flower, scared of demons, or should I act terrified of Nyfain?

"If you touch her, I will kill you," Nyfain stated, his voice even and confident. It wasn't a threat—it was a statement of facts. My small hairs stood on end.

I peered around Nyfain again as the demon spread his hands with a sly smile. "You are losing, Mr. Alpha. You've lost all your prized people. Your ability to protect anyone has diminished. Soon that girl will realize she exchanged her body for empty promises."

Nyfain flinched but didn't comment.

"When that happens, she will turn to us," the demon went on. "And when *that* happens, we can grant her safety from your...wrath. Or whatever it is you do to her."

"Are you done?" Nyfain asked, turning slightly and pulling me out from behind him, still keeping his body protectively between the demon and me.

"Mr. Alpha is so proud," the demon said with that oily smile. "So delusional. One day I will enjoy watching the light dull from your eyes. You are on borrowed time. You will die, and your kingdom with you."

# CHAPTER 10

NYFAIN WRAPPED AN arm around me and gripped my hip possessively, keeping me close. I glanced back as we continued down the hall. The demon stood in the middle of the space with his robe now open, showing his hairless and shiny nude body. Tendrils of his magic fluttered across me, making my skin crawl.

"Well, that guy was a charmer, huh?" I said with a grimace.

Nyfain glanced down at me. "You don't find him attractive?"

I studied his flat expression. "I can't tell if you're kidding."

He looked straight ahead, not noticing the two people ahead of us—one dressed like a tiger, the other like a rabbit—getting busy between two dragon statues.

"I also can't tell if they are joking."

The tiger with the large, fuzzy head stood behind the bent-over gray rabbit with floppy ears. The tiger growled as he thrust, making the rabbit mew happily.

"Wrong sound for a rabbit," I said, aghast, as we passed. "Won't that get the costumes all gross? There'll be jizz and juice all over the place."

He chuckled softly. "It's been a long time since someone…rational was in this castle after dark. I can't imagine what this must look like to you."

"I've seen a lot in one day. That's for sure."

"I doubt you've seen much of anything. I once walked in on an entire room filled with people in costumes like that. There was so much fur and movement that I just backed out. A woman trying to give a blowjob through a hole in her squirrel mask… My brain wouldn't make sense of it. I didn't push the issue."

"Does their sexy magic affect you? The demons?"

"If I let it."

"But you never give in?"

"No," he growled. "Never."

"You have a strong will, then?"

"A strong will and a large stubborn streak." We reached the door leading outside, and he stepped forward to open it for me. He guided me through, his hand still on my hip.

The chilled night air greeted me as I stepped out.

"To answer your question, no, I did not find that demon attractive. Wait…"

He paused, his hand snaking around to my belly to keep me at his side.

"No, I meant wait, as in halt the conversation." I tried to pry his hand off me, but he slid it back to my hip. Apparently, he wanted to keep up the possessive pretenses when in public. It couldn't hurt with the strength of the demons wandering around. I huffed and gestured him on. "Keep walking. I was telling my brain to wait. You're too literal."

He resumed his unhurried walk toward the everlass field.

The supplies I'd need rolled through my head. I'd need to grab something for transporting the leaves, as well as check out the setup to work with them.

"Wait," I said.

He kept walking.

"No, this time… Would you just…" I twisted and spun to get away from his hold, then put up my hands. "Where will I be drying the everlass? It needs to be done in the evening tomorrow, and the leaves should be kept flat and wet—"

"We have a large station for working with the plants," he said, hooking his thumbs in his belt loops. "You'll have at least two of everything you need, with enough room for multiple people to work with you. If you want."

I looked around. "And who would that be?"

Was it just me, or did his body language scream *uncomfortable*?

"I was hoping you'd let me shadow you. I realize we…have our differences, but I could be of use. Also, it's been a long time since I worked with someone knowledgeable. It would be a special favor to me." He paused for a moment. "That I would be willing to trade for."

I nearly waved that away, rather enjoying the idea of having some help, but stopped myself. "Okay, fine, but you better hold firm on that trade, the terms to be decided later." I immediately thought of talking to my family. "What about something to hold the leaves as we pick and then transport them back?"

"It's all set up."

I narrowed my eyes. "We'll see."

He grinned but didn't say anything, snaking his arm back around me. I tried to wiggle out of his hold, which didn't budge, and then decided to let it go. We were still within sight of the castle. There might be one or more demons looking out, watching their newest prey. Me.

Getting back to his other question, I said, "That demon gave the impression of someone who is attractive. His face wasn't too attractive, though, so it must've been his glamor affecting me, right?"

"You're a quick study."

"When it comes to my survival…or chastity, yes."

"You're not chaste. At least, you're not a virgin," he said matter-of-factly as we walked down the stairs to the deadened grass beyond. His flat expression gave nothing away.

"How do you know?" I asked.

"A virgin would be a lot more nervous about what we've done. About things in the castle. You might not be experienced, but you're not a virgin." He blew out a breath and ran his fingers through his hair. "Change of subject."

I grinned maliciously but didn't taunt him. I knew where that would get me. It seemed our beasts were happy to stick to the background at the moment, and we needed to keep it that way.

"His magic left me feeling disgusted, though, not turned on. Same with the other one, once I realized what was going on."

"That's the…" He looked away. "Your animal. It'll fight off the effects. It won't totally null them, though. You need to make up that draught."

"I've chosen the garden. I just need time outside of my tower to start working."

"You'll have it. Tomorrow. During the daylight."

I wasn't going to argue with him about that, not after tonight. I'd be a target for that oily demon, especially after it learned that Nyfain had killed the other one, and I didn't trust myself to stick to the wilting flower routine.

"I hated not being able to talk back to that demon," I said, looping my hand around his forearm. I just needed a little solidarity. That had been gross. I'd tolerated the demons in the village because they weren't worse than the sickness, but this... I wasn't going to be good at tolerating this. "There were so many things I could've said that would've knocked him off his high horse."

"I could feel your frustration as you burrowed into my back." A grin lit his face, transforming it. "There's no point in it, though. They want to taunt. To get a rise out of people. Once they know what affects you, they'll keep pushing. I say very little to them if possible. I would advise you to do the same."

"Easier said than done."

He chuckled softly. There he was again, the guy who allowed himself a little levity. The man who was pretty damn hard to resist.

"What has you in such a good mood?"

He took a deep breath and slowly rubbed his thumb

along my hip. "Some of my fondest memories are of working the everlass fields with my mother. She loved to garden and work with plants, and I enjoyed sharing her passion for it. She didn't have an easy life in a lot of respects, but when she was in the fields, she would smile and laugh. Being out here together lifted our spirits. It was the thing we did together. The thing no one could take from us. I miss those times."

"I should warn you that I'm a hack. I doubt my methods are going to be anything like your mother's."

"You have passion for the plants. I can hear it in your voice when you speak about working with them. The method might be different, but the joy of it is the same. I can't wait to see how you do."

"Why haven't you kept it up?"

He looked down at me, his face cast in shadow. I couldn't see his eyes well enough to read the expression in them. We approached the field, but he still didn't let me go, slowing.

"Not everyone has the gifts that my mother did. That *you* seem to. I know how to take care of healing plants—that's a duty within a dragon line—and I know a few rudimentary draughts to help heal wounds. I'd be dead without those. After that, I'm a novice at best. I need guidance. Most people do. The faeries use everlass to give their potions and elixirs unparalleled strength, but what you claim to be doing with the nulling elixir sounds like the work of a master."

"I'm hardly a master. Still, you'll learn that I don't make unfounded claims. Come on, let's get cracking."

"I can't wait."

It sounded like he actually meant it.

Sawhorses holding large wooden trays with lips about the length of my pinky had been spread out along the edge of the field. The moon shone down, at its full strength and providing plenty of light. The night breeze ruffled the leaves, and a night bird screeched in the distance.

I smiled and closed my eyes for a moment, taking it all in.

"A copper for your thoughts?" Nyfain said quietly.

I spread my hands and took a deep breath. "I have all this everlass to work with, at the right time of night, and I don't have to worry about a great beast or some other creature killing me. I don't have to be jumpy or always looking over my shoulder. It's like a dream come true."

"Or would be if you weren't doing this to negate the nightmare in which you live."

"Way to steal the moment." I ran my fingers along the inside of one of the trays and then felt the lip. "Cedar works better for trays. This tray is pine, if I'm not mistaken. That's second best."

"I've heard the opposite."

"The book said the opposite, as well. There are limits to secondhand information. Your mother said pine was king, and so you went with that. Your mother's mother probably said the same thing. The guy who penned that book clearly heard it too. They had no reason to question it. Had I not been using oak before I read that, which was worse, I wouldn't have thought to experiment either, but the differences were stark enough to make me wonder about the impact of other types of wood. Through trial and error, I discovered cedar worked the best, hands down. It's the most forgiving, and it produces the most potent leaf."

He didn't comment, as I'd thought he might. I'd probably want to argue if someone told me that my mother's knowledge was mistaken. Then again, it wasn't like I was telling him to change out the trays. He had clearly grown accustomed to letting the demons rattle on. That was probably what he was doing with me, too.

I paused when I ran my fingers along the top of the last tray.

I lifted it and tossed it to the ground. "Someone polished that one. That'll wilt the leaves at twice the speed."

He crossed his arms, still watching me.

I paused. "That was a test, wasn't it?"

"Yes. Was that in your book?"

"No. I learned that one the hard way. I tried to increase production once because a neighbor was on her deathbed and her husband, who usually made the elixir, was injured hunting. My mother was gravely ill then, too. I tried to double the batch. I used the neighbor's tray and damn near lost all the leaves."

"Did you save the neighbor?"

"I didn't save either of them. I haven't saved anyone. Just given them more time."

"And yet you still think you'll be able to save them all."

His tone had turned rough. Mr. Broody Fucker was never far away.

"I'm at least trying. Are you going to help me or not?"

"What's your process?"

"Given the size of those trays, you're going to have to follow along behind me, holding one until it's full."

He picked the first one up without another word, and I started harvesting leaves—one per plant, the biggest and healthiest ones I saw. As I went, I took care of any pruning he'd missed, adding the plant fluffing into the routine. Taking care of these plants was relaxing in a way. Meditative. Probably because giving them love and care meant I'd be able to give family and friends love and care.

Halfway down the row, I heard a soft tune in a deep, rumbling voice. The notes rose and fell delicately, beautiful and intoxicating. A glance back said he was in the same headspace, peaceful and meditative. It was like he'd started singing without realizing he was doing it.

"Louder, please," I said as I deposited three leaves on his tray. I met his deep, soulful eyes.

"My mother used to sing that song when she worked the everlass. I didn't mean to sing it out loud."

"It's beautiful. Did your mother die before the curse?"

"Yes."

"Then she was spared the nightmare."

"This is the only nightmare she was spared."

I layered my hand over his on the tray, running my thumb across his knuckles. I didn't really know what to say, so I repeated, "Sing louder, please."

He sang with words this time, in a language I didn't know. An ancient language, it sounded like, with rolled vowels and soft consonants. His pitch-perfect voice was still deep and scratchy but pleasing in an unexpected way. It lifted my spirits and soothed my anxiety. His tone was full of sweet sorrow and soft lament, his voice now billowing larger, lazily sifting through the air.

Before I knew it, all three trays were as filled as they

safely could be. He pulled over two carts with space for two trays each, and we loaded the trays up, each of us wielding a cart. Only when we reached a large shed with two tables spanning the length with various stations for working with plants and herbs did he finally let the song die on his lips. The absence left a pang in my heart.

"Was her version sad, as well?" I asked as he helped me deposit the trays near the end of the nearest table.

He studied me for a moment, something he'd been doing a lot lately. "I always thought so, but she said it was supposed to be a joyous song."

"Do you know what the words mean?"

He shook his head as we grabbed buckets to collect water from the pump. "She was from the mountain region in the Flamma Kingdom, ruled by the wolf king, Cincious, and his queen, Elmerdonna. They had a regional mountain language. It was allowed in that kingdom, but the king here outlawed it. He said it would be too easy for her to pass secrets."

"Wow. That sounds crazy."

"It wasn't just at the end that he was mad. He'd never been quite right in the head—it was just kept quiet."

"And look how well that royal secret worked out for everyone."

I held the bucket in front of the pump, but he took it from me. "This is a man's labor."

"Pumping water is a man's labor?"

His smile softened all the harsh planes and vicious scars on his face. He flexed his bicep. "Me strong. Hold water for smart lady."

I laughed and stepped back as he worked. "Earning your keep, then?"

"I always had the grunt jobs as a kid. I was big for my age and lacked the natural dexterity to work the plants and healing remedies. My strength is in…well, strength. Brawn. Power. My role as a dragon male is to protect. And while I formed a brotherhood with the other dragon shifters through training and after, we were always at odds with each other. We were taught to compete—Can you handle that?"

I picked up the water bucket with two hands. "Yes, thanks."

He nodded, easily holding one bucket in each hand like they weighed nothing. Meanwhile, I'd probably have to come back for more after I spilled half the contents of mine.

"We were taught to compete with each other for placement. To dominate each other. There was always an underlying hostility with us. The women working the plants…it was different. They always worked in harmony. They helped each other instead of trying to show they were better than each other. It was probably because I spent so much time with my mom, but I gravitated toward that mentality. My dad hated it. He called me weak because of it." His smile dwindled. He set his buckets on the table and reached down to grab mine.

"And are you?" I asked.

He poured the water into the first tray, and I went about reorganizing the leaves.

"Wait, whoa—" I held up my hand when the water was at the right depth. "Not too much. They don't like being too deep, like in a flood. Just enough to keep them damp."

He nodded and worked on the other trays. I wasn't sure if he didn't plan to answer my question or just needed time, so I didn't press.

"You leave these inside?" he asked.

"At home? Yes, because I didn't have sawhorses, and I didn't want any wild animals getting to them or desperate neighbors stealing them or demons pissing on them. A backyard isn't as secluded as one might hope. As you know, since you invaded mine before kidnapping me."

"But they would do better left in the moonlight?"

I pulled my mouth down at the corners. "I don't know, actually. Let's put one out and try it. It'll need to be brought in at dawn, though. Do you trust me enough to leave me a key?"

"At the moment, yes. In an hour, likely not. But I'll bring it in. You might spill everything."

He had a point. They were large and heavy trays.

He insisted I stand back while he set up a little table and placed the tray on it. That done, he put his hands on his hips and looked out at the fields then glanced at the sky.

"What?" I asked.

He was back to studying me again. "I should probably take you back."

Part of me didn't want to go. I wanted to stay out here and find some new things to try with the everlass. Or maybe go check out that rose garden with him following behind. Or maybe just…stay with him a little longer. Listen to him sing in the moonlight or tell more stories of his past. Maybe tell him a few of mine in return. When he was calm like this, it was so easy to keep company with him. Easy to talk to him. It felt like we could maybe get to a place of joking and banter. Of being friends instead of enemies.

*Watch, folks, as the abductor dupes the abductee into thinking he's an okay guy. Don't worry, she'll get the hint when he locks her back in the tower and refuses to let her see her family…*

"Yeah, probably," I murmured.

We turned toward the castle, and he slid his arm around me, resting his hand on my hip again. Even though it probably wasn't necessary for him to do so, I didn't resist. Tomorrow we could go back to being enemies. Right now, I wanted to create a memory to savor.

"No," he said when we were halfway to the castle. "I am not weak. Cultivating life and health with women does not make a man weak. If anything, it made me stronger, because it made me pliant. It allowed me to see a different perspective. It made me tolerant in the way battle training never could have. But there was no explaining that to my father. He didn't have a great relationship with women. In truth, he didn't think much of them as a whole."

"Sounds like a real treat, this guy. And your mother married him why?"

"Arranged marriage. You must know that nobles don't have much choice in such things. We consolidate money and power, both socially and magically. Our parents make careful choices in our alliances."

"Did your parents choose someone for you before all this?"

"Yes. It wasn't a choice I would've made for myself."

"What happened?"

"In the end? The curse happened."

He didn't elaborate as we reached the steps to the patio. Then again, he didn't really have to. He was the only noble left. Clearly his intended hadn't made it.

He slowed, looking at the door. Several glass panels were embedded in the wood, and a bare ass was pressed against one of them. As we watched, the back of what looked like a woman pushed against the glass pane above. Just beyond, two legs faced it, the knees bending before the flesh against the window shifted. Two palms flattened against the glass. They were fucking against the back door.

"Let's go around," I said quickly, knowing he'd probably want to force that door open and ruin their time. He clearly wasn't ignoring these shenanigans like he had the furry situation earlier.

His fingers dug into my hip angrily. A nerve jumped in the side of his clenched jaw. He did turn, though, heading around the side of the castle toward another entrance. Nearly there, he halted. His arm constricted around me, smashing me to his side before he swore softly and abruptly turned.

"What's hap—"

"Say nothing," he whispered furiously, moving his hand to my shoulder and pushing me toward the trees.

I hit a rock with my toe and tried to correct, but he caught me first, dragging me upright.

Once in the trees, he whispered, "They're looking for us. It either means they are suspicious or they want to taunt me. We need to ensure it's the latter."

"What do they want to taunt you about?"

He ducked behind a tree and dragged me with him, pushing me against the bark. He stood close, caging me in with his body. Showering me with his heat.

"I take my honor very seriously, and I've been celibate since the curse came into effect. There are a few reasons why, but one of them is that I will not allow them to twist me sexually like they have twisted everyone else in that castle. Now you're here, and they will think I am starting to break. That I have seen my true fate—failure and death—and decided to forgo my duty and let go of my honor. They think I have captured you for stealing and intend to use you sexually until I've had my fill. I want to propagate that illusion. They will taunt me to play on my supposed guilt. They want to twist the knife and, in so doing, twist my mind. Once they see that they are having an effect, they will go after you to incite my animal."

"Why would that incite your animal?"

"Because I do not share, Finley. If I lay a claim on my chosen, there will be no other. Not for me, and not for her. My animal will not stand for it, even if I could. Through me, they will aim to ruin you. But I will not let them hurt you, do you understand? I will not let them touch you. You are here under my protection, and I will do whatever it takes to keep you safe and whole. Whatever it takes."

"But you need them to think you're defiling me, and I need to play along. Otherwise the cover is blown and you'll get me killed or worse."

He lifted his hand slowly and ran his thumb along the edge of my jaw. My heart fluttered at that delicate touch.

"The plan was to keep you to your room at night. But your nulling elixir could save lives, and so the plan has changed. I told you I was not a nice man, princess," he murmured with a bite of gravel in his voice.

He tensed and turned his head to the right just a little.

"They've caught our scent," he whispered. "They're winding closer."

My animal prowled in my chest. I chanced tugging on her a little, needing her access to scents. She stepped forward in a hurry, the familiar fire washing through me and a musty sort of funk immediately accosting my senses. I crinkled my nose.

"Yes. That's the scent of a powerful demon," he said. "The higher they are on the power scale, the mustier they are to our senses. This might be hard for you to understand, but I need you to act like this isn't your choice. That I'm forcing the issue."

"To make them think you're losing your morals and degrading yourself, thus convincing them they are finally having an effect on you?"

"Okay, maybe it won't be hard for you to understand."

"It wouldn't be hard for anyone to understand. You literally just spelled it out a second ago."

"You haven't been in this castle long enough, clearly."

He grabbed my hands and pushed them above my head, trapping both wrists in one of his large hands. He pushed closer until every inch of that hard body was pressed firmly against mine. He settled his free hand on my hip and dipped his head, running his lips along the side of my throat.

"Make a show of resisting," he murmured, bending a little and rocking his hips forward. His hard bulge rubbed against my pelvis, not where I needed it. I ran a leg up the outside of his thigh and over his hip. He caught my knee and rocked his hips forward again.

"No, please," I said in a husky voice and moaned as he sucked in the fevered flesh on my neck. His lips skimmed up to my jaw and ended at the outside of my mouth. He gyrated again, rubbing against my leather-clad pussy.

He chuckled darkly. "You're not a good actress."

He moved slightly, adjusting so his lips were right in front of mine but not touching. Our breath mingled. He thrust forward again, his bulge rubbing just right.

My eyelids fluttered shut. I was so turned on I couldn't help myself. Damn me, but I wanted more of the sensations he elicited in me. Of his delicious body rubbing against mine. More friction. More heat. More, *more...*

I rocked my hips. My body tightened up.

He ran his free hand up my side and in, over the hard peak of my breast. He rubbed through my clothing with his thumb, sending shocks of pleasure straight down to my sodden core. I groaned, delirious with desire.

"It's too bad things are as they are," he murmured, trailing his lips along the outside of mine, holding my wrists firmly, grinding his cock into me. "I'd love to fuck you so hard you beg for mercy."

"Yes." I pulled my other leg up, wrapping it around him. My hips jerked frantically into him.

He pushed his hand up under my shirt and ripped at my binding. Fabric tore. It yanked down under my breast. He stroked my flesh with his rough hand.

I didn't know if it was my animal coming out in me

or the desperation to end this terrible ache throbbing in my core, but I went full-tilt filthy.

"Fuck me, Nyfain," I begged. "Destroy my needy cunt with that hard cock."

He growled and crushed his lips to mine.

The world spun then dropped away entirely. In this moment I didn't give a shit about our problems and my current prison. That was a chore for tomorrow. Right now, I just needed that big cock pounding the stress and worry out of me. I needed an escape from my life, and his big-dick energy would provide it.

He twisted my nipple between his fingers. The bite of pain made me suck in a breath, but in a moment it turned to sweet, sweet pleasure, and I struggled to get my hands loose so I could feel his perfect body.

"I need you to fuck my wet pussy, Nyfain," I said huskily. "I need you inside of me."

"*Fuck me*," he said, pain lancing his words. "You're so fucking sexy."

He gave me a dominant, bruising kiss. I opened my mouth in a moan, and he filled it in a rush, his tongue sweeping through. Oh, holy goddess, he tasted so good. Like liquid smoke and fresh spring mornings. Like the thrill of the hunt.

Lost to sensation, to the feeling of his hands on me and his body trapping mine to the tree, I pumped my hips wildly. He hooked his hand around the back of my knee and pushed his body closer. His cock rubbed hard against me, our clothes in the way. This consuming ache made me desperate.

"You're supposed to be resisting," he said against my lips, his breath coming fast now.

"No!" I called as I gyrated, struggling to get closer. "Stop!"

He kissed me again, ragged and desperate, then shoved against me harder and growled into my mouth. His tongue thrust in time with his hips.

"What were you dreaming about earlier?" he asked, pushing my legs away and going for my pants. "The demon made you have an erotic dream. What were you dreaming about?" He yanked the button away and pushed down the zipper. I spread my legs in desperation.

"Let me have my hands," I begged. "I want to get at your cock."

"What were you dreaming about?" he insisted.

He shoved one side of my pants down before the other, managing it with one hand.

I struggled to get my hands free. "Let me get at your cock. I want you to force that big dick all the way down my throat, then flip me over and ram it deep into my pussy."

"I will not fuck you, Finley, no matter how much I want to. I will not be the ruin of you."

It almost sounded like he was begging me to understand.

"The best I can do is pleasure you," he said. He dug his hand into my pants and between my thighs.

My mouth dropped open as his fingers traced along my panty line, right next to my sopping cunt. The world paused as he dipped a finger in. Hungry chills spread across my flesh.

"Yes," I whispered, widening my legs for him. "I mean…" I raised my voice. "No, please, no. Not yet. *Or ever.*"

My eyes fluttered as one finger slowly ran along my slick folds.

"Fuck, you're so wet," he growled. He dipped his finger in before rubbing my wetness against my clit. "I'm going to make you come for me, princess."

My movements were reduced to little jerks of pleasure as he returned to my pussy and threaded in two fingers.

"I'm going to make you come so hard you can't think of any other name but mine."

He kissed me, pushing his tongue inside. His thumb massaged my clit as he started finger-fucking me, hard and fast.

I groaned, gyrating with him, my senses on overload.

"Tell me what you were dreaming about," he commanded, his power blistering through me. My hard, bared nipple rubbed against his chest. His fingers pumped in and out of my pussy, his thumb circling my clit.

"You," I admitted with a cry of pleasure, my body impossibly wound up. His fingers slammed through my wetness. "I was dreaming about you fucking me. I want you to fuck me. So bad. So hard."

He growled, and his whole arm was moving now with delicious roughness. I spread my legs and arched, giving him as much access as my pants would allow. His thumb massaged. I was right on the edge, just…about…

"Well, my goodness, what is this?" a voice said.

Nyfain's animal surged aggressively, the feeling like a string yanking on my middle. Fire soaked my already heated body as my animal tried to push up as well. I forced her down lest she get me into trouble, and Nyfain ripped his hand from my pants. He yanked me away from the tree and crushed me to his side possessively.

I let out an anguished cry, and I was not acting.

# CHAPTER II

"TSK, TSK, NYFAIN," cooed the demon, the same guy that we'd seen at the bottom of the stairs. He had followed us out. "When you need to restrain your love interests, it means they aren't having a very good time. Or maybe you think you can sex your way into her good graces? That is very demonic of you."

Once again, I bit back a snarky response. But honestly, did he really think the sounds coming out of me as I barreled toward orgasm suggested I wasn't having a good time? Did he never get women off?

Instead, I clutched Nyfain like the damsel I was trying to be, attempting an expression of uncertainty and fear. I probably looked like I'd smelled something sour. And with the stench of this demon hanging around, it wasn't far off.

"What do you want?" Nyfain asked.

"Oh, nothing," the demon replied with a grin. "I was just coming out to see if your lady wanted to sample another flavor. Like me, for instance. I can show her a good time without any need for restraints."

Nyfain's body tensed, and his fingers pressed into my flesh aggressively. He turned and yanked my pants up before fastening them gently and ensuring my shirt covered my exposed breast. His gaze roamed my face for a moment, and he smoothed my hair away from my cheek before wrapping his arm around my body.

"She touches no one but me," he snarled, directing me from around the tree and starting toward the castle.

"For now," the demon said silkily.

With my binding still askew and my swollen pussy throbbing from his deliciously rough treatment, I was staggering and walking askew. My core pounded, built up to impossible heights and then left wanting. I licked my tingling lips, remembering his kiss. Spank the goddess, he was a good time when he got going.

"What am I doing with you?" he growled softly—to himself, it sounded like—going to the back entrance where the couple was still pressed against the glass.

"Playing a dangerous game with my life, it seems like," I retorted, my current situation making me a little saltier than usual.

He slammed the door forward. The couple flew into

a heap of limbs on the floor. The man's eyes were hooded and on fire, and the woman's were soaked with arousal. Another flood of desire poured into me, sending my brain back to moments ago, when I'd been trapped against that tree with those tricky fingers deep in my pussy.

Goddess give me strength, I wanted more. Lots more. My body was not on the same page as my brain. Logic was completely absent where Nyfain was concerned. I needed to go sleep it off, preferably after a good self-love session.

Couples littered the hallway and my gaze skittered between them. A man with his face between a woman's thighs. Two women writhing together in a corner. Another woman in the middle of five men, using every hole the goddess had given her and two hands to make up the difference. She was clearly excellent at multitasking dongs. Three men on the bench, one guy bent over sucking while a third took him from behind.

"Holy shit," I groaned, staggering into Nyfain.

He glanced down at me, looked around, and then swept me up into his arms. He'd apparently been ignoring all of this. All the sex around us hadn't made him flinch. I couldn't even fathom that, because suddenly I was a wanton mess. Again.

"Let's go finish what we started," I purred, tracing

my tongue along the shell of his ear.

"You'll hate yourself for it in the morning."

"Probably." I ran my lips down his neck, delighting in his deliciously balmy smell, in the heat of his skin and the feeling of his strength wrapped around me. "I've hated myself for less."

"I doubt that is true. We aren't attracted to each other, princess. It's our animals. We need to heed logic where they will not."

"Are you sure? I didn't feel your animal until the demon showed up." I skimmed my lips against his jaw and lightly kissed the corner of his mouth.

He flinched away before hoisting me up and throwing me over his shoulder. "I always stay connected with my animal. I have to, or I might lose him. His desperation to hump you seeps through. Don't let it go to your head."

His words sounded hollow, as though he were willing himself to believe them.

He put me down roughly in front of the tower door and fit the key into the lock. The demon from earlier had been removed. I wondered if that was why the other demons had decided to go looking for us.

"I won't always act like the damsel, you know," I said defiantly, shoving away the residual desire.

"Good. It's beneath you. But it's important right

now. It will stall the inevitable."

"What's the inevitable?"

"The demon king coming and the enemy closing in. You will need your grit by the end."

Shivers arrested me. I breathed through the sudden uncertainty clutching at my chest.

"I need to learn to hand fight better," I said. "I'm great with a dagger, and despite what the men will tell you, I'm the best hunter in my village. I'm good with a bow and a spear. I'm not so good with my fists, though. Also, I could use more strength."

"You were just fine with that knife when you stabbed me."

"That was my animal, I think. I don't really remember doing it."

"You have plenty of strength. You could use more conditioning with your animal." He turned the key.

"And if you are going to lock me in this cursed tower every night, I need access to the library."

He pushed the door open and shoved me inside.

"And if you don't stop manhandling me," I said as I stood in the room, "you're going to be sorry."

A grin pulled at his lips. "Is that a challenge, princess?"

His rough voice and the excitement I could see glittering in his eyes fired me up in ways I couldn't really explain. Fear and arousal created a heady mix.

I didn't have a reply, so I turned my back to him, waiting for him to leave.

"Strip out of your shirt, and I'll help you out of your binding. Your lady's maid will be…busy at present."

I groaned in annoyance and pulled off my shirt. My face heated, and I made sure to stay still so he wouldn't see the evidence of my embarrassment, my vulnerability. His presence moved up behind me, and a soft tug pulled at my middle as his heated breath washed over my exposed flesh.

"You didn't get to come earlier," he rumbled, his fingertips tracing lightly over my shoulders.

"Just another one of your torture devices, I assume."

His touch traced down to the clasps of my binding. It tightened and then opened, falling down my chest. The breast that had still been tied up bounced down with the other. He didn't move away. The electricity between us flowed over my skin.

I closed my eyes and felt his hands touch down on my shoulders again, kneading softly.

"You're tense," he whispered.

I couldn't stop my hands from floating backward, bumping against his legs. I grabbed his thighs, craving that anchor. Something about him made me feel grounded. Despite all the shit he'd dragged me into, his presence, his smell, his possessiveness made me feel safe in a kingdom that was anything but.

"I've had a lot of stress lately," I murmured.

"I checked on your family earlier tonight. They are sad for your loss, but they are well. Your village is safe, at present."

Something hard and uncomfortable thawed within me. I let out a sigh of relief. "You spoke to them?"

"No. I watched them like a creep. I will hunt for them as soon as I can. I know that was the task you used to do."

I ran my hands upward a bit, stopped myself, and let them drift back down.

"Thank you," I said softly.

He skimmed his touch down the outsides of my arms. He pulled his hands away and then reached under my arms to my waist. His rough palms traced my skin, drifting across my stomach and upward. They bumped into the bottoms of my breasts as I moved my hands farther up his thighs again. He traced up my soft skin with his thumbs, inch by inch, maybe wondering if I would stop him.

I should've, goddess how I should've, but my body was blisteringly hot, and the electric sensation of his touch flowed over and through me, like lightning striking down and engulfing me in its energy.

His thumb flowed over the center of my breast. A jolt of pleasure coursed through me.

"What was I doing to you in your dream?" he asked, taking each of my nipples in his fingers and lightly pinching.

"I awoke to you between my legs." I groaned, bending my elbows so I could work my hands higher. I stroked his upper thighs, reveling in their strength.

"Then what?" He cupped my right breast and worked the other hand back down my stomach.

I reached in, massaging his upper thighs now. Working inward. "Then you bent to lick my pussy."

He reached down and opened the button on my pants. "It turns me on to see you in my clothes," he said huskily. "It turns me on more when I strip you out of them."

He pushed them down my thighs until they dropped at my feet.

"I like these lacy little panties." With one quick yank, he tore them off me. "I think I'll keep them."

I stood bare in front of him. I slid one of my palms over his hard bulge.

I didn't get it—he wanted me; he didn't. He rejected me, then he came on to me. He touched me with such passion, and then he went cold. It was mind fuckery, and for some messed-up reason, I was excited by it. I liked the unexpectedness of it. I liked the constant need to react and adapt. I knew I could walk away at any time, and he wouldn't push the issue. I knew he would respect my distance if I asked for it (and kept my animal under control). But right now? I was here for the challenge of it.

Or maybe I just wanted to finally get fucked. The man was a cunt-tease of the highest order.

"Spread your legs a little," he commanded, his power blistering through me.

I moaned and did so, rubbing at his hard cock trapped in his pants.

He slid one hand back to my breast and the other lower, dipping it between my thighs. His middle finger traced through my slick wetness.

"That's right, princess, get nice and wet for me." He sucked in a spot on my neck, hard. A bite of pain quickly mixed with pleasure as his finger made lazy circles across my clit. "What else did I do in your dream?"

"You finger-fucked me, like you did against the tree."

"Did you like it?"

"Yes," I breathed.

I whimpered as he worked a finger into me, pulling more wetness to work against my clit. The pace of his strokes increased, and he bit into my neck. The pain and the pleasure, the heat and the sparks, lit me on fire from the inside out.

He pushed me forward so fast I staggered, grabbing the edge of the bed to keep myself upright. He braced one of his hands against the center of my back and with the other reached down and pushed two fingers into my wet depths. He started thrusting. My body roared to life, nearly picking up right where it had left off after the tree situation.

"I need to taste you." He dropped to his knees behind me, slapping against my ass and taking a healthy grip. He pushed me forward and spread me wide as he licked up my center. I shivered, moaning his name. It felt so much better than that dream. So much better than anything I'd ever experienced.

I pushed my butt back at him, and he sucked down my folds. His tongue played with my clit until he sucked that in too, pulsing the suction. I groaned in bursts, gyrating. He slid his hand over my butt cheek and snaked his thumb in between. He moved the pad gently over my puckered hole, and a strange thrill arrested me. He didn't go farther, though. He stood and flipped me, then pushed me farther onto the bed.

His hair was tousled and his eyes hooded as he raked his gaze down my naked flesh. I let my knees fall and dropped my fingers between them, stroking within my wetness.

I thought he would unfasten his pants and free that big cock, but he just adjusted himself before he flung my hand away and bent eagerly. He worked his fingers into me and sucked on my clit. With his free hand, he reached up and rubbed my breast, playing with my nipple in a way no one else ever had. Circles and loops and little pinches. It enhanced the pleasure of his mouth. Drove me out of my skin.

I arched into his hand, jerked my hips against his mouth. I grabbed his hair in a hard grip to keep him put until I was finished.

He growled and worked harder, faster. My body melted and then started to fray. The pleasure crowded me, blocking out the room and everything else. Everything clenched and then I fractured, coming in a thick, heady burst of raw sensation.

He slid his hands down my sides but didn't push up. His kisses against my pussy softened. His tongue stroked in the aftermath, giving me pleasant shivers. He ducked a little, pushing my knees up, and licked down farther still, over that forbidden hole. The tickle made me squirm, and I wondered if it would hurt for him to take me there, or if it would be pleasurable. I wondered just what sort of kinks I might have. It was impossible not to in a place like this.

I wondered if he'd always had the same sort of thoughts but never let himself explore them.

He shoved my legs over and stood, wiping his mouth with the back of his arm. Even that was sexy for reasons I couldn't explain.

"Get some sleep," he barked, before turning. "And don't bitch at me when you regret this in the morning."

With that, he pushed through the door and yanked it closed behind him. The key turned.

I laughed softly at his quick personality shift. The guy was clearly battling his arousal. He might not like me, but he clearly wanted to fuck me. It wasn't just our animals, or why had he taken my panties? We were in the same boat. And given I didn't want to ruin my incredible high from that orgasm, I'd deal with it tomorrow.

I pulled my animal to the forefront, sharing space. She gave the feeling of stretching lethargically, and I crawled to the head of the bed.

*Fuck, that male is so alpha,* my animal purred. *I love when he asserts his dominance. He has a lot of power. He'll be good protection for our young.*

*Yikes. That's not going to happen.* I tucked myself into the covers, looking out at the brightly lit night. Soon the moon would wane and I'd have to be better about lighting candles. *We need to stop letting him touch us, actually. It's fun, I'll admit, but it'll likely end badly for us.*

*Probably. I get the impression from his beast that the man carries a lot of guilt for his actions before the curse. That he has resigned himself to this half-life as a penance. He is duty-bound but doesn't want to drag anyone else into his misery. His beast needs you to save the man. I implied that the man has to save himself. That didn't go over well.*

*When did you talk about all that?* How *did you talk about all that?*

*We didn't talk. There are many ways to communicate—speaking is just one of them. You need to learn.*

I rolled my eyes. I hadn't even shifted. I'd only felt and known my animal for a day. How the hell was I supposed to know anything about being a shifter?

I let it go, though. I was too sleepy.

*Save the man.*

That wasn't really my specialty. And even if I did, it wouldn't help those dying from the sickness.

No, first I needed to figure out a way to save the people. I agreed with my animal—Nyfain needed to save himself.

I closed my eyes, supremely relaxed. Goddess help me, I felt really good.

My mind drifted back to the tree situation. Usually I did not allow people to strip me of my control. With the ex, I'd never wanted my hands bound. I hadn't trusted him with my vulnerability.

But with Nyfain earlier... I'd trusted him completely. I had been completely at his mercy. Yet instead of being scared, I'd been incredibly turned on. I'd trusted him without a thought.

I'd still push back when he was being Broody McFucker, but I believed in his ability to protect me. I believed that he wanted to. Hell, I even liked when he got all possessive over me with the demons.

He was getting to me. Damn it. I shouldn't have let him help with the everlass. He'd wormed under my skin, and now he was starting to fester. That couldn't be good.

Save the man. Save the kingdom.

*Why are men so breakable?* I thought as my eyes drifted shut.

*Because it gives us room to swoop in and save the motherfucking day,* my animal chimed in.

She had a point.

# CHAPTER 12

"STEP LIVELY, MY darling. Lots to do."

Hadriel greeted me earlier than normal the next morning, dressed in the same weird butler's outfit but with a little grease plastered across his scant mustache. That was new. I pointed at it.

"Why?"

"Oh yeah." He lightly touched it. "Ridiculous, right? After the close call yesterday, I thought maybe I'd better up my efforts at standing out in a bad way. I plan to wear this to the party tonight and let the demons make an *ab*-solute fool of me. They love doing that. It's the price we pay for not suffering at their hands."

"But you *are* suffering at their hands."

"Well, right, but not eternally, know what I'm saying? Oh…" He paused as he noticed the marks on my neck. "Did he…bite you?"

My face heated. I'd seen the effects of last night in the mirror this morning after my bath. "Yeah. Apparently the hickey wasn't enough."

"Did he just bite you on the neck, or…maybe the shoulder, too?"

"Why?" I covered my shoulder with my opposite hand. "He didn't do it hard enough to—it wasn't like grabbing my throat. This was…a different thing."

"Sexual, yes, obviously. But did he also bite—Here, just let me see." He pulled the neck of my shirt a little, peering at the juncture between my shoulder and neck.

I swatted his hands away.

"Just the neck," Leala said as Hadriel persisted.

"Ah. Well. That's strange." He gave me a smile. "Lame kink, right? Anyway. You've eaten?"

"I brought her up a tray before her bath," Leala said, turning and clasping her hands. Her wrists had angry red welts. She had certainly been busy last night.

"I wondered about the…you know…" I circled my finger around my crotch. "The salon. For the lady beard. But maybe not the demon part. Maybe I can just…trim things up a bit? Just for…cleanliness and…ease of…getting to…things." I grimaced and my face flamed.

Leala ducked her face to hide a smile.

Hadriel tilted his head and clucked his tongue. "Ah,

aren't you cute? When is the last time we've had someone bashful around, Leala?"

"A long time," she replied demurely.

I rolled my eyes to distract from my face continuing to heat.

"Well." Hadriel squeezed my shoulder. "We'll definitely look into that. But for now we need to do a bunch of other things. First, we need to meet the seamstresses." He led me out. "Now, I warn you. One of them is very sweet. Very professional. And the other is a real shitbox. It's hard to stand the awful bollocks. But he is amazing at what he does, and so we'll have to suffer him. Try not to hurt him."

TWO HOURS LATER, I stood in a middle-aged seamster's messy workroom. A chaos of fabric swirled around me, draped from poles, slipping down from desks, flowing in the wind next to two open windows letting in the cooling air. A pincushion lay on the ground at the base of the pedestal on which I perched. Bright red against the beige floor, it kept attracting my gaze for reasons I couldn't explain. Pins stuck out at odd angles, each little bead at their heads a different color. Occasionally the seamster would nudge or kick it with his foot, no idea it was even there. It had been set aside and forgotten like everything else in this room, used when needed or not at all. It felt like a metaphor for the villages clustering around this castle. Or maybe our kingdom as a whole.

This was my second stop on the measuring train. Before this, I had been in a very neat and orderly work room on the third floor, overlooking the Forbidden Wood. In that room, each piece of fabric was crisply folded and stowed in its place. Each thimble had a home. Each measurement was carefully measured and promptly recorded. It had been quick and efficient, and I didn't see the point in this second visit. But apparently the seamstress, a plump older woman with a pleasant disposition and easy smile, excelled at humdrum work clothes, and the eccentric seamster did up fashionable attire. Leala and Hadriel thought I needed both, though I had no idea where they thought I would be wearing the fashionable attire. There was no way I was going to parade it around the demons at night. That was a lot of drama I did not need.

The seamster had been measuring me for what seemed like hours. He hemmed and hawed and did the same measurements two or more times each. Apparently, he envisioned the various garments as he worked, and each garment needed its own set of measurements. No wonder he was still alive.

At one point, Hadriel offered to write my measurements down for him. That was when I got the full weight of his personality.

"This is my process, you sour-faced cur. Leave me to it!"

There was a reason he was not well liked, that was clear.

Given Hadriel chuckled to himself, I didn't bother kneeing the seamster in the face.

"I'll need to dry the everlass this evening," I said as I let my mind roam. "Someone needs to remind Nyfain."

The seamster, Cecil, sucked in a startled breath. "How dare a lowborn hagbag like you call the master by his given name? You shouldn't be messing around with his prized everlass at all!"

"Call me a hagbag again and I'll punch you in your beanbag," I replied.

He looked up at me slowly, met my gaze, and just as slowly looked back down. Message delivered, message clearly received. He stopped protesting.

Then: "I have new inspiration!" he cried. "I must start again. I was doing it all wrong!"

He worked faster the second time around, thankfully, but it was still another hour before we got out of there.

"I've never seen him work so quickly," Hadriel said

as we headed outside. The next order of business was finding me a garden to redo. "I mean, he certainly wasted a lot of time in the beginning, but he really seemed to find his way after you threatened him."

"And now we know what it takes to hurry him up," I said.

"You shouldn't have to go back for measurements. Once he has direction, he usually starts churning things out. Sometimes it just takes forever for that direction to come to him. Right, okay, where's this garden you had in mind?"

It took me roaming the outside grounds, sadly burned and browned without a team of people to look after them, to find it. I thought about asking after the gardening team, but I had a pretty good idea of what had happened to them. If they could make use of a pitchfork, they probably hadn't lasted long.

I caught sight of my tower room and cut that way. "It's just over here."

Except it wasn't. A brick wall rose in front of us, covered in a mess of vines.

"Oh no, you can't choose this one." Hadriel shook his head as I met the wall of the castle.

I started around the other way, finding the same thing. A glance up confirmed that I was in the right place. I just hadn't noticed the garden was walled because I'd been looking down. It must've been hidden within the overgrowth, which meant the overgrowth was extreme.

"See?" Hadriel said. "There's no way in. You—What are you doing?"

I found a part of the wall free of the thorny vines and jumped, hooking my fingers around the edge. I pulled myself up and threw my leg over, rewarded with a bite of pain in my calf from the thorns of an out-of-control blackberry bush. Sucking air through my teeth, I adjusted and sat, confronted with a swell of plant life.

"Holy crap, this place is in a state." I looked up at the tower window, accessing my memory of the layout from looking down. "If I fall in, Hadriel...tell someone."

"You shouldn't be up there. That garden is off-limits!"

"Nyfain didn't mention any gardens being off-limits."

"This is not something that has to be mentioned!"

Well, that just made it more attractive.

I stood, taking a moment to find my balance, and walked the top of the brick wall. There was a mess of roses to my left, and a thicket of thorny vines beyond them. I had no idea what those vines were, but I planned to cut them all down.

"I'll need some gardening tools, Hadriel," I called.

He nearly hopped along the ground beside me, incredibly anxious. This garden had probably belonged to royalty at one time—their private grounds. I'd read about that in the history books. But guess what? The royals were all dead, and the king had sucked. I wouldn't at all feel bad about taking over.

At the side near the castle wall, the massive overgrowth turned into tall and brittle weeds. They crowded within and atop rows that must've been used for growing herbs or produce of some kind. I wondered how the dirt was. I turned and lowered myself down.

"Come back out," Hadriel called. "Seriously, come out. This is a terrible idea."

"It's just a garden, Hadriel."

"It's the queen's garden!" he replied. "The queen's own garden."

"She'd probably want me to return it to its former glory, then." I meandered through the space, taking stock of any plants I could identify, weeds or otherwise. I'd need to check the library for anything I didn't recognize.

"The king forbade it. He forbade anyone to touch any part of the grounds except for the everlass. He said that was the queen's role—the management of the grounds—and without a queen, there could be no grounds."

"And look at the fix he's gotten us all in with his terrible decision-making. Besides, he's dead, Hadriel. His royal decrees or whatever don't mean squat anymore."

I bent and dug my hands through the dirt. Something scraped my finger, and I grimaced, pulling it out to look. A drop of blood welled up, and I smiled. I fed the blood back into the ground.

"You see?" I held up my finger even though he was still on the other side of the wall. "It drew first blood. It has chosen me. Now all I need to give it is sweat and tears, and we'll be all set."

"Since when do you talk like a warrior? They are plants, Finley. Come out of there this minute!"

"Nah." I continued sizing up the space, working out in my head what I'd need to do first, and what tools I'd need to accomplish it. I wondered if anyone could be spared to help.

"Okay, but listen here, Finley." Hadriel sounded like he was pressed against the wall. "The king passed that law because he wanted the prince to settle in with a noblewoman of dragon blood and make her queen. Or at least a queen in waiting."

"And when he couldn't get his way, he made a deal with the demons, and here we are. I know."

He kept talking, but I wasn't really listening. Although there was no door to the rest of the grounds, there was a lovely patio I hadn't noticed from my tower room. It led to a pair of large glass doors in the side of the castle. Darkness waited beyond.

Royalty had lived through there.

In awe, I stepped up onto the patio.

"No, but... The king blamed the queen's death on the prince. When the prince tried to marry for love, it broke the queen's heart, and she died. That's what was said. The funeral brought back the prince and the demons, and the king trapped him here."

The queen herself had come out through those doors and onto this patio. She'd used these—now rotting—wooden chairs to look out at her or her gardener's handiwork. She'd maybe breakfasted or taken lunch out here on fine days, soaking in the beauty. Maybe before the king had gone mad, they loved each other and celebrated that out here.

No, probably not. Royalty didn't find love.

Well, maybe she had enjoyed some self-love, thinking about a hot gardener or something.

I approached the glass, shielding my eyes from the glare.

"She and the prince had a really tight bond," Hadriel called, his voice distant as I tried to peer in the room.

Despite all the times I'd played make-believe as a

kid, pretending to be in the royal court, I'd never believed it would actually happen. And now, after the world had gone to shit, here I was standing on the queen's private patio. This was blowing my mind.

I couldn't see anything through the glass, but curiosity was burning a hole through me. I tried the doors, figuring they'd be locked. Could I find my way through the castle to check the other side? Nyfain had a skeleton key—if there were ever a reason to seduce someone...

I pulled on the handle. Nothing happened. A push had the same result. I dragged my hand as I stepped away, and the glass pulled away from the other side.

I froze. Sliding glass. I'd never seen such a thing! But then, I'd also never seen a single pane of glass as big as these doors. Money made miracles.

I slid it open farther.

"Finley?" Hadriel called. "Finley, did you fall in? What's happening?"

"I'm fine," I called, a bit hushed, pulling the door open.

"Don't nose around in there. The master blames himself for what happened, and that garden is the remnants of something she loved. He won't want it disturbed."

His words flowed around me as I ventured into the dark space beyond, and although I could hear him, I wasn't *listening.*

Two fabric chairs teamed with a couch sat around a little table by the door. A place for tea, probably. Not a speck of dust marred the shiny surface, as though this room was still routinely cleaned. The floor was plastered with an enormous rug, nearly large enough to cover my entire house. A little desk waited off to my right, cleared of any parchment, and a large mirror was stationed on the other side. Other furniture took up residence, but I crept toward the oddest thing in the room. A rosebush somehow—obviously magically—grew out of the actual floor! As though the floor were dirt. It looked almost fake but for the differences in the browns and yellows of the leaves and the way it curled as it died. The branches were brittle and roses deep brown and wilted except for a few. It was in terrible shape.

For some reason, it moved me. I wanted to roll up my sleeves and nurture it back to life. But there was something uncanny about it, beside it growing in the wood floor, so I left it alone lest I break some sort of magic remembrance spell or something.

Instead, I continued onward, absolutely delighting in the saturated tones and bold decorating choices. She even had a decorative sword and shield tacked up on the wall. A woman after my own heart.

An open doorway led to a room with a bed and another small chamber that appeared to be the bathing room. The bed stood against the far wall, a huge, canopied affair decorated in gold and ivory. The wardrobe in here had been dusted, too, everything clean and in its proper place.

Imagine living in this kind of finery, in rooms such as these. It was beyond belief for someone of my upbringing and social status, but I would definitely be dreaming my life away after seeing it. My make-believe audience was about to turn into a bunch of make-believe servants and adoring ladies-in-waiting, hanging on my every word. No more jester thoughts for this girl.

Making my way back out, I heard the metal tinkle. Like a key in the lock!

My heart sped up, and I hurried toward the glass door. Before I could get far, the door swung open. Nyfain filled the doorway, seeing me immediately. Suspicion and rage filled that golden gaze.

Everything Hadriel had said finally took root.

*The funeral brought back the prince, and the demons and the king trapped him here.*

*She and the prince had a really tight bond.*

*The master blames himself…*

"Oh, holy goddess, no fucking way. You're the prince," I said in a hasty release of breath, so many emotions warring through me that I didn't know what to do with any of them. Excitement, sorrow, disbelief—I didn't know where to land.

On the other side of that emotional storm sat the knowledge that this made complete sense. *Of course* he was the prince. The mad king had doomed us all to keep his son here. The demon king couldn't kill him with the curse locking him in. Still. Nyfain didn't heal the same, so it'd be easier for someone or something else to kill him. Only that hadn't happened yet. So the demons were trying to break him.

How could I have missed this?

The prince.

The fucking prince!

Why hadn't I known his name? But I hadn't. And I didn't even know the queen's name. All of that had fallen through the cracks in my memory. It just wasn't relevant. Still, he must've thought I was a simpleton. An ignorant, lowborn commoner.

I ran the back of my hand across my face.

Memories shoved into my brain. That majestic dragon cutting through the sapphire sky. The glittering gold scales catching and throwing the buttery-yellow sun.

"But your dragon is dull black, not golden—"

He rushed at me. I should've turned and sprinted

for an exit, or maybe curled into the fetal position, or at least taken out my knife and tried to stab him, but I was too busy freezing in place. The past warred with the here and now. My memories of him in the sky warred with this scarred man in front of me. I'd daydreamed about him as a kid. Wanted to be best friends. Then I grew up, and even though we all believed he was gone, I'd fantasized about slipping into his bed. I hadn't known what he looked like as a man, but I hadn't cared. That roar. That dragon. That effortless glide through the sky. He'd been the pride of the kingdom. Fierce and powerful. He would take the throne and elevate us all— that was what the elders in my village had said.

"What are you doing in here?" he snarled, stopping beside the rosebush. "Getting a look at my father's fallen kingdom?"

I frowned at the plant. "I think you're getting a little extreme in your metaphors…"

He laughed sardonically, pinning me to my place with a hard stare. "That's right, you are about as ignorant as they come. No idea about your animal, shifters, the dragon court…"

Pain pricked my spine. Even as a beast prowling his failing lands, he hadn't paid attention to our village. We'd been nothing to him. I was nothing now.

But he wasn't finished. He hovered his hand over

the rosebush. "My mother's favorite plant was the rosebush. She felt like it embodied her. When allowed to flourish in the wild, she was fierce and beautiful, sweet to smell but with a sharp bite. Then she was brought here, and the king treated her like he would a rosebush. She was pruned back. Shaped. Cultivated. Wild at heart, violent even, but unable to express it."

He drummed his fingers against the glass. His gaze sparked violence. I took a step back, suddenly unsure.

"My father wanted to remind me of my part in killing her," he said, and I could hear the pain twisting his words. "This rosebush was enchanted by the demons and sunk into the floor. It's connected to the kingdom. Each year I see a little more of it wilt and die. Eventually we will all die with it. There's nothing we can do but make the passing as easy as possible. I thought maybe bringing you here would help. I knew your village was using the everlass for something, and your rate of death was slower than everywhere else. Your branch has roses still in bloom. The only one that looks even reasonably healthy. I've been watching from afar. I just had no idea how you were managing it."

"What?" I blurted. "But you said—"

"I lied. How many times must I remind you that I am not a nice man?" He stalked toward me slowly, a hunter sizing up his prey. "Your scent is burned into my brain. That first night you ran into the Royal Wood, the young, plucky thing with more courage than a grown dragon, I committed it to memory. You didn't escape me, Finley. I allowed you to leave. You were too young to kill. I smelled the everlass on you and wanted to know what you were doing with it. After you left, I visited the field and scented your path through it. I realized you'd pruned as you went. You harvested just one leaf from each plant, taking your time to keep the plants healthy. Even though you came to steal, you were looking after that field."

He wound closer, one slow step at a time, his big shoulders swaying, his size dwarfing mine. His presence was imposing.

I swallowed. "Everyone knows to harvest like that."

He shook his head. "You know they don't. Especially not plucky little—what, fourteen? Fifteen?"

"Fourteen," I whispered.

"Yes. Before the first shift was possible. I didn't scent your animal, or feel it when I chased you out. The magic surrounding the wood was too strong for me to cross at the time, but I didn't need to. You returned to the wood before I could investigate you further. You've never entered without my knowing, but I could never catch you. Not until I had that birch enchanted. You're a sly little thing."

"I was just trying to keep my family alive."

He stopped in front of me. "The last time, when you left your knife, I felt you. I felt your animal. It called to us. I'd suspected, but only then did I know what was in you. Your power." He pushed in close, taking all the space. Trapping me in. "Tell me, when your animal first awakened, what did you feel?"

"Exhilarated. Scared."

"And?"

He put a hand to each side of my face. His heat soaked through my skin, turning me liquid. My body was fifty percent heartbeat.

"Turned on," I whispered.

His power coursed through me, caught by my animal and held for a moment before she fed it back, like we had done to save Hadriel. He was the brawn; I was the finesse. Together we'd literally pulled someone away from the brink of death. This time, though, pounding arousal came with our connection.

I panted, my breasts rising and falling with each breath. His gaze traveled down my front as though caressing my naked flesh. My animal pumped fire into me. The power between us turned molten.

A desperate, tortured moan parted my lips. He leaned in a little, almost imperceptibly, as though he couldn't help it. Like he was struggling against the desire. The air between us snapped taut and the room fell away. All I knew was him and me and this never-ending thirst for his body to fill mine. For his muscles to push me down onto the mattress and his cock to fill my world.

He inhaled, taking me in. "Goddess strike me down, Finley, I want to fuck you so hard you forget your name. I want to own that sweet pussy and destroy you with pleasure."

I couldn't seem to get enough air. Wetness gushed between my thighs.

"But if I do that," he went on, "that will be the end of you. I've explained why. I do not share. Not in my past life, and not now. Once I take you, I will not allow anyone else to touch you. Your life will be forfeit. To me."

His words crawled across my skin, making me shiver. His eyes hypnotized me, and a large part of me wanted him to do as he said. I wanted him to make good on his word and brand me with his desire.

But seriously, had I lost my mind? Had I gone completely insane?

He was a damned prince. What would I become, his side piece? Because no way was I the heroine of this story. I was a nobody from nowhere. I was a lure to his ruin. An end to his celibacy. And if I gave in? I'd land myself with the world's biggest cockblock.

Not to mention that he had imprisoned me here. He'd lied to me on multiple occasions. He'd brought me here and forced me into danger. Me and no one else. He could've met me in the wood like the others. There was no reason for him to drag me into this. Now he was messing with my head and my future. With my *life*.

I was a fool for letting him get under my skin. For allowing myself to forget how I'd ended up here.

He wanted me to stay away from him. So I would. I had a home, and the demons there didn't give two shits about me. He could meet me in the Forbidden Wood like he did his other informants, get the recipe for the elixir, and go about his life. The demons didn't want me. They wanted *him*.

The man could save himself. I had other shit to do.

With the last shred of sense I had, I ducked under his arms and darted toward the door. I hoped this area of the castle wasn't a maze, and I could find my way in case he chased me.

# CHAPTER 13

"**B**UTTERFUCKING CUNTCYCLES," HADRIEL exclaimed when he finally met me in the tower. Leala had been here when I got back, folding some panties and stowing them in the wardrobe. That had been awkward, watching her fold lacy undergarments. I'd quickly run her off and forced her to leave the key behind.

"Did you run and tell him that I was in that room?" I demanded, looking through the wardrobe for the clothes I'd worn here. There was no way I was staying in his clothes. I'd leave how I'd arrived, except this time it would be of my own free will.

"No! I only tried to find him when you wouldn't answer me anymore. I feared you'd fallen into...whatever the fuck was in there to kill you. By then, he'd already found you. Are you fucking insane, going into the queen's chambers?"

"Yes. I'm fucking insane for a lot of things. Like staying in this horrible castle for as long as I have. Like developing a soft spot for him. Like not staying stronger and keeping my head around him."

"What are you…"

I found the outfit I'd arrived in and changed quickly, then grabbed my knife and the little knapsack I'd found and stuffed with candles and a stick that would hopefully burn. At least I'd had the foresight early to create a panic bag for when I needed to run and check on my family. That was before the trip to the everlass field. Before getting to know him better.

Goddess help me, I was so incredibly stupid.

I lunged for the door.

"Where are you… Oh goddess, you evil vixen, what is happening now?"

I pulled the door shut and locked it. I felt a little bad, but I couldn't risk him running and telling Nyfain where I'd gone. In an hour or so, Nyfain would come to get me to tend to the everlass. At that time, he could free Hadriel and I'd be long gone.

"What are you doing?" Hadriel called through the door. "Fine, take the garden! Clearly the master didn't kill you when he found you earlier, so maybe he doesn't care. I'll even…"

His voice faded away as I hurried down the steps. At the next landing, I saw a woman with an apron and rosy cheeks. She gave me a pleasant smile. I waved like an idiot and kept going. At the first floor, all was quiet. People were probably fiddling with their hobbies or getting ready for whatever party would be happening that night. The staff in this place was sparse at best. That was clearly what happened after years of the demons offing anyone who gave a shit.

Anger curled through me, but I ignored it and let myself out the front door. This wasn't my problem, what was happening here. Nyfain was the prince; he could sort it out. My task lay in healing, not wrestling demons.

Without delay, I ran down the steps and across the front lawn, long since turned to dirt and weeds. As soon as I reached the Forbidden Wood, I let my animal rush to the surface.

*What did you do?* she demanded as I threaded my way through the trees.

*What I had to. Did you know he was a prince?*

*He's an alpha.*

*Yeah. An alpha prince. He's a fucking prince!*

*Slow your tits. You're going to have a coronary.*

I stopped for a moment and closed my eyes. Even in the jaws of a beast and scared out of my mind, I'd paid attention to the path Nyfain took that first night. I'd learned a bit more from our mad dash to save Hadriel. For me, it was enough to go by. I'd always been able to find my way in this place.

*Where are we going?* my animal asked.

*Do you have a name?*

*Finley, we're the same person.*

*I know. But do you have a name?*

*Finley.*

I waited for a moment. *What?*

*My name is Finley, you bum trinket. We're in the same fucking body, so we have the same fucking name. Where are we going?*

*I didn't think it was possible to be saltier than me, but you are proving me wrong.* I veered right until a pond got in my way. It gurgled and bubbled, smelling like compost, week-old fish, and farts. A grayish sort of steam rose from its middle. *We're going home. I'm not the sort of person who hooks up with a prince.*

*But you are absolutely the sort of person who hooks up with an alpha. I know this because I want to hook up with that alpha, and he was all for it.*

*You don't understand social hierarchy.*

*You don't understand that the real pecking order is based on power and prowess.*

I jogged east until I found a trail to go around the pond and took that, working south. I'd need to grab some more everlass leaves on my way out. I didn't have a great place to keep them, but they'd have to make do. If Nyfain was pissed, he could go blow a goat.

*That alpha wasn't interested,* I thought, stopping at a cliff face twice my height. The rock was sheer and glossy. There was no way I could climb it without rope. I didn't remember Nyfain working around that. I was clearly a touch off course.

The cliff face ducked behind some trees away left, and I headed in that direction.

*I just told you he was,* she replied.

*Fine, the man behind the alpha wasn't interested. He warned me away. Repeatedly. Like…every time we were in each other's presence, he warned me to piss off.*

*Because he is trying to protect you. That's what alphas do. It's up to you to tell him that you'll do what you want. And what you want is to fuck the living brains out of him. Then make babies and repopulate this kingdom.*

*Great goddess, that's a bit much.*

I wondered when the land was going to even out again. The shadows had started to lengthen. Twilight came earlier in the wood because of all the trees. I'd hoped to make it a little farther by now. Maybe I should've waited a day and started earlier.

But at least I knew the beast didn't intend on killing me. That took a lot of the pressure off. If he recovered me, there would be another chance to get away. I knew there would.

*When a man tells you he'll ruin you, it's best to listen and fuck right off*, I thought as I finally worked around the rise and got back on track. *It took a second, but this is me finally listening. I have plenty of other opportunities to ruin myself, I don't need his help.*

*He could only ruin you if you allowed it. We're stronger than that.* I'm *stronger than that. If you feel weak, I will make you strong. That is the power of shifters: two souls working in tandem. In any perfectly synced mating, there are four. Not even the demon king could tear down such a powerful pair.*

The demon king had torn down an entire kingdom. He held this place in the palm of his hand. But I didn't feel like arguing. I just felt like getting home.

Minutes multiplied to become an hour. The sun had officially lowered from the sky, leaving behind dense, black night. I'd fashioned the stick into a sort of torch that streaked through the darkness and spat embers in its wake. The trail of smoke burned my eyes. Undaunted, I continued jogging along the animal trails and listening for sounds of movement. I didn't know what time the creatures tended to come out at night in these woods, but I knew I didn't want to tangle with them. The beast wouldn't kill me, but I wouldn't put it past the mockingbird of terror to try, and it wasn't alone. I might have to fight my way out of this place. Thanks to Nyfain, though, I had help: Finley number two would fill me with strength and power or just take over when things got dire.

*The name of the game will be to always maintain contact now that we're away from Nyfain,* I thought, seeing a fork in the path. A looming tree stood sentinel to a field beyond it. Unable to help myself, I jogged that way quickly. Everlass, overgrown and wild.

So Nyfain didn't tend to them all. He probably couldn't. It made sense, then, why he'd chosen those near the castle—as was his duty, I imagined—but why had he paid any mind to the one close to our village, nearly at the edge of his kingdom?

"You've never entered without my knowing, but I could never catch you," he'd said.

Was that why he kept that field tended? Had he done it to help me?

Suddenly it was hard to breathe.

I turned in the direction of home, and my animal bled energy into me. I nearly asked why she had her own stores of energy and power, but I wasn't in the mood. There were a great many things about her, about me, that probably wouldn't make any sense until I could shift. For now, I'd just take the help and continue on.

A blanket of weak, twinkling lights dotted the black overhead, the only star of substance being the Southern Light, something I often used to guide my way. I used it now, moving as fast as I could while avoiding reaching roots and vines.

A snarl caught my attention, away left. Fear trickled into my blood. That wasn't Nyfain's sound. The creatures of the Forbidden Wood were out.

I racked my brain. Had anyone at the castle said anything about other shifters retaining their ability to shift? If Nyfain could transform, then he probably wasn't the only one. Maybe the wood really wasn't dangerous at all. Maybe it was just a bunch of guardians securing their ancestral lands.

Except Nyfain had attacked the mockingbird of terror.

Then again, it had been coming after me. Maybe it had been a pissed-off villager?

No, I couldn't discount all of the scars cut into Nyfain's robust, muscular frame. They spoke of years of constant battle. If the creatures of the wood could do that to his beast form, what chance did I have without shifting?

So much for watering down the fear pumping

through my blood.

*Okay, folks, we're just going to quiet down now. Let's slow those feet and step carefully. But what will we do about this spotlight on us?*

*What the fuck are you talking about?* my animal asked.

How did one explain their idiosyncrasies when very afraid?

A screech caught my attention, reverberating through the trees. It seemed like it had come from everywhere and nowhere. A roar turned into a distorted sort of howl, like it came from some sort of zombie wolf.

I'd always heard zombies weren't real. That they were a story made up to scare children around campfires. Then again, I'd also heard no one could shift and that the beast was a creature of the night instead of the broken prince with a curse hanging around his neck. I no longer had much faith in my peers.

A root caught my shoe, and I dove headfirst into a brittle fern. My knees scraped the ground, and my light tumbled into a cluster of dried grass.

"Shitballs," I bit out, up as fast as I could and trying to stomp on the quickly catching blaze. It zipped across the ground and spread, licking up a tree. I stomped through it, feeling the press of eyes on me. I'd created a beacon for the creatures of the night to find me.

*Run,* my animal said.

I didn't need to be told twice.

Before I could even turn, the blaze dimmed and then winked out, as though the wood were fire-resistant.

*Enchantment?* I asked, not hanging around.

*This place isn't right.*

*No shit, huh? What other incredibly obvious observations do you have for me?*

*You could use a thesaurus.*

*Shut up,* I inwardly growled, seeing familiarities all around me now. That tall and thin bush with the frayed top, the willow with the bald spot at the top—I was close to home. *Not far now.*

A humanlike scream froze my blood. It ended in a sort of wheezing groan, much too loud for my liking.

*Zombies better not be real, folks, or I'm going to have nightmares for the rest of my life.*

*I'm getting concerned about who you think you are talking to,* my animal thought, pumping power through me. *I'm going to see how much of this pairing I can take over before the need to change claws at me. Hang on tight.*

*Hang on tight to what?*

*Fucking hell, the simplemindedness of that castle is wearing off on you. It's an expression. One I know because you learned it.*

Her presence pushed against me, shoving me aside, and then she was taking over my limbs. The complexities of scent overloaded me until I slunk farther back, letting her handle them. Our speed dramatically increased. She kept going, taking more control. Trying to work with a body she didn't know well—I could feel the confusion creeping in. I felt the itching along our skin and the pumping of power ready to turn into an explosion. My hair started to tingle, and my back felt like knives were being stuck through me. The darkness receded, though.

Shapes loomed around us, mostly blacks, whites, and yellows.

*That's...about...as far as I can push it,* she thought, and I could feel her struggling.

Wasting no time, she picked up the pace, light of step and agile, even if she would have preferred to be on four feet. She jumped over roots that I might've stumbled on and avoided brittle bushes or crackling twigs that would have given us away.

My hand reached into my pocket and extracted the pocketknife. She opened the blade as a drumbeat of adrenaline pounded through us. Something was coming.

"Ha-ha-ha!" It sounded like a man's voice—after one hundred years of cigarettes and choking on swamp slime. "Ha-ha-ha!"

It wasn't laughing. The being was literally saying those words as though attempting to fool someone into thinking it was both human and having a jolly time.

*Here we go.*

A distinctly human shape stepped out from behind a tree up ahead. It wore worn clothing pocked with holes, and part of its scalp had rotted off. Jutting teeth filled its mouth, and the jaw looked unhinged.

*There's your zombie,* my animal said, slowing just a bit as she approached. *I wish I had four feet and claws. This would be so much easier. You might have to help drive.*

The darkness rushed in a bit, the shapes around us going fuzzy.

*It's a dybbuk, I bet,* I said, images of demonic creatures running through my head. *They are supposedly demons in the bodies of sinners. One wandered into our village when I was about fifteen. It was clumsy. I can handle this.*

*I apologize for making fun of your well-read-ness. This makes up for it.*

I ran at it, knife in hand. He swiped when I got

close, and I ducked under his arm, exhilarated by the strength and speed with which I could now move. I stabbed him in the stomach. He barely noticed. I'd expected that, though. These buggers couldn't feel pain in the way a human could. Their bodies could still die, though.

If only I had my dagger…

I swiped his leg, quickly following up with a stab to the kidney, and then used both hands to drive the blade into the base of his skull. That would disable him until it bled out, which would happen quickly.

A snarl sounded from the right before a large dog-like creature lunged. Over half my size, it had momentum and muscle behind it. I dropped to the ground, waited for it to sail over my prone body, and popped up like I had springs. I could get used to this animal-inside-me situation, salty attitude aside. The dog creature landed and stumbled a little, not having expected me to move. A ribbed fin rose from its back like a wave, each rib topped with a spike. Its eyes glowed green, and saliva dripped from its huge canines. A badly bred hellhound? I hadn't seen this sucker in any of the books I'd read.

*I need four feet and claws!* my animal thought-yelled, frustration swirling through us.

Yeah, we both did, because I couldn't handle this

thing with a stupid pocketknife.

I darted around a tree and jumped onto a low branch. It groaned under my weight but held. The creature snarled, launching after me again. Heart rampaging, I pulled myself up another branch and took our life in my hands as I jumped across to a thick branch on the neighboring tree. I wrapped my arms around it, but my legs swung into the open space below.

The creature jumped up and snapped at my dangling boot. I yanked it out of the way and heaved myself up, shimmying to the trunk.

*Now what?* my animal asked.

*Now you pretend to understand my little peccadilloes as I figure this out.*

With that, I launched into my usual internal dialogue.

*This is a harrowing feat, folks. I can't wait to see what happens next,* I thought, sizing up the area. There was a mostly clear and decently wide trail leading away from here. It should intersect with the trail I often took into the wood.

An owl hooted distantly, my old friend Chatty Kathy. Something else clearly prowled the wood. Part of me hoped it was Nyfain. Most of me realized it was probably some other horrible thing the demons had unleashed in this wood. I needed to get out of here. But that dog thing could surely run like the wind. I couldn't beat it, so I'd have to kill it.

It waited just under me, still looking up like it was thinking of learning how to climb a tree. I had the drop on it.

*Fantastic, it seems like she has had an outstanding idea. Thank you, horrible wild boar, for giving her the practice to make this precarious move possible.*

*This is really tough to bear.* My animal sounded pained.

*It's my process,* I said as I stepped onto another branch and moved around the trunk. I lowered to the branch below. The creature moved with me, saliva dripping from a jaw made for crushing bones. A low groan reverberated through its muscled chest.

I perched above the creature, full of determination, my knife clutched in a slightly shaking hand. I needed to jump down onto it and drive my knife through a vulnerable point. I've done it before with other animals, but that fin would make it difficult. I'd have to aim near its head, and that end had teeth. Still, I didn't have any other ideas. Waiting here was not an option. The creature was alerting everyone to my presence, and if a more dexterous monster came along, it could come up here and get me. Escape wasn't an option, either. If I dropped down now, the creature would just step out of the way and then maul me.

*Fuck, this sucks,* I thought, and bent so that my face leaned down toward it. It braced itself, its growl getting louder. I swung down my knifed hand. It trembled as it waited, ready to jump up at any moment.

"C'mon, you bastard, come and get me," I said, lowering a bit more.

My foot slipped, and I fell against the branch, my leg dangling over and my stomach touching down. I scrabbled to get back up as the creature jumped.

*Now or never, folks!*

*No, no, no, no, no!* my animal replied.

Too late. I waited until those jaws snapped a foot from my face and then rolled off, falling toward it. The creature hit the ground but couldn't move in time. I tumbled down on top of its head, two hands on the knife hilt and thrusting downward. I jammed the blade at the base of its fin, between its shoulder blades.

It howled and snapped, catching my arm. Blistering pain shot through me, but I didn't let go. I used the knife to drag the thing down with me. It snapped at my face, its strength starting to dwindle. I dodged the bite and yanked out the knife, punching into the thing's throat and pushing upward. It scraped my legs with its front claws, and I wished I'd worn Nyfain's leathers after all. Blood showered me, but I kept at it. It floundered and then crashed down, really fucking heavy.

I climbed out from under it, breathing hard. My arm throbbed in agony, and my legs felt like they'd been seared, but it wasn't anything Hannon hadn't healed up before. I just had to make it to him.

Pulling my animal back to center, I let her take the lead. Her power doused the pain a little, and we hobble-jogged along the path. A sigh of relief eased out of me as familiar landmarks came into view. We were close to home.

I took a quick detour, backtracking just a bit, and hurried to the everlass field. Hannon surely had some left from my last harvest, but I didn't want to take it all. Goddess knew I'd need some for these bites and gashes.

The birch rose ahead of me, and I actually smiled at the sight—until I remembered its propensity to jig.

"Oh crap—"

Too late. It shook and waved, its branches groaning and its leaves shaking. Might as well summon all the curious creatures in this wood.

I packed the everlass leaves into my knapsack, as many as I could reasonably fit. They'd be annoyed by the material anyway, so I might as well really piss them off by shoving in more than normal.

Ignoring the birch's sashaying, I jogged back around it and out of the area. Pain throbbed in my legs and fingers, and blood dripped from the wounds. Some demonic creatures fed off blood, but not from the vein like a tidy vampire. No, they liked to rip into flesh and lap at their victims' bodies. If they were in this wood, I was essentially calling them.

*I've never heard of so many creatures wandering in the wood,* I thought as I made my way, gritting my teeth against the pain. *I've never encountered this many.*

My animal didn't say anything, just assumed most of the control again and kept our feet going, one in front of the other.

Halfway there, a strange smell caught my attention. A little musky, like a demon, but with strong overtones of sulfur. First it came from the right, then the left.

*Is the smell hovering or what?* I thought as my animal picked up speed. I knew she'd be cataloging a lot more complexities than I could comprehend.

*No.*

I waited for her to elaborate, but she slowed instead.

*What are we doing?* I asked.

*They're surrounding us. I'm trying to decide— without talking to a bunch of folks—what to do. I can't tell their speed or agility yet.*

We continued along, slower now, and the smell kept getting stronger. From the right. From the left. A whiff from behind. Then one of them emerged onto the path in front of me. It was ugly as sin, and one glance was enough to tell me it had never made an appearance in any of my books.

Its face was like a parody of a human skeleton, with large, grayed-out hollows for eyes, a hole for a nose, and a wide, lipless grin. Its stringy yellow mane reached down to a large hunch in its back, formed because its front legs were longer than the back ones, and a little tail in the back. It was nearly as big as the dog creature but spindlier. Its front legs had an opposable thumb, however. It could probably grab.

More of them pushed out from between the trees and foliage all around me, surrounding me as my animal had warned they would. Five in all. As I watched, black sludge dripped from their pointed teeth. The one in front swiped its fingertips through it.

*That's probably not good,* I thought with a sick feeling in my gut. *That is probably some chemical designed to disarm an opponent, like poison.*

*I take it back. I don't like how much you read.*

*Just go ahead and talk to my invisible audience. They are always excited during times of trial. It helps with the fear.*

*If only we could pick our human partner...*

I took deep breaths, leading now. My animal and I seemed to be getting better about who took the reins when. Still, I kinda wished she'd picked this moment.

More deep breaths, sending much-needed oxygen into my blood. I had my animal's power, lending strength and speed. Dulling the pain a little. Not enough, though. This was going to be hairy.

"Do you speak?" I asked, because it was a great stalling technique. "Take me to your leader."

The one in front gnashed its teeth and made a *nack-nack-nack* sound. It was a little better than the "ha-ha-ha" from the other guy, but not much. Sludge oozed down its chin.

"Right, okay," I said softly, testing their limits. I walked forward slowly. The configuration of the creatures immediately changed, moving with me, continuing to box me in. I'd just encouraged them to tighten the circle.

Nothing for it, then.

I charged, sprinting at the one on the side. Surprisingly, it pulled back, creating space between us. The ones that used to be front and back rushed in, flanking me. I changed direction immediately, slashing right with a knife that was much too small for the situation. The blade sailed through empty air. The creature dashed in and swiped at me. I staggered back but turned as I did, sticking out my knife. The blade sank into the ribs of the one that had planned to score its claws across my back.

"Suck it, fucker," I said, grabbing its bony shoulder and pulling it forward. It stomped, off balance. I slipped behind and stabbed three times quickly and in any old area, watching the others reconfigure.

*How smart are these bastards, do you reckon?* I thought.

*They are pack animals, obviously, and they are clearly good at hunting prey. They also clearly underestimated you.*

*Yeah. That's what I was thinking. Balls.*

Breathing heavily, I intended to use the dying one as a shield, but its legs gave out. It flopped to the ground, not dead but not willing to serve as my super-handy shield.

They tried to skitter around me to cage me in, but I back-pedaled, keeping them in front. I caught more whiffs from behind.

*Don't tell me—*

*There are three behind us,* my animal said. *They are a good predator.*

And I was turning into serious prey.

I tried to switch direction, but they switched with me. I turned and ran, but one jumped out of the trees to stop me. The ones behind closed in.

I kept going anyway, charging the one in front.

Nearly to it, I turned around and struck the one I could feel dashing up behind me. I knew how they worked, and my sense of danger was on it, not to mention Finley Number Two. The creatures on the side pushed in. I spun to get in a jab at the one that was now behind me, only to spin back around to take another stab at the first. They were one step behind me, which was great, except they weren't going down from just one jab with the knife. I wasn't thinning the numbers.

My breath came out in ragged puffs, and my injured right hand wouldn't hold the knife anymore. I wasn't as good with my left.

Once again, I faced them down, looking for an alternative. Trying to figure out a way. Knowing I likely wouldn't. Leaving the castle like that had clearly been the last mistake of my life.

# CHAPTER 14

I WAS READYING myself to strike again when something yanked on my middle, like someone plucking a bowstring. Power thrummed through me, caught and held by my animal.

*Stay alive,* she said. *The alpha is coming.*

Excitement and relief and hope boiled within me. I sucked in air and steadied myself. The pulse of fresh power blocked out some of my pain, so I transferred my knife to my stronger right hand. The balmy smell of pine and lilac with a hint of honeysuckle reached me, Nyfain treading silently closer. Aiming to surprise my attackers.

The creature on my right moved forward slowly, warily. I stood my ground. If I went to it, the one on the opposite side would close in. The other way, and the rest would tighten up.

Its progress slowed. Then slowed further. I sensed fast movement from behind and rushed forward to stab the one directly in front of me. I turned as the one on the right moved in. Its blackened fingertips elongated into claws at the last second, heading for my arm.

Nyfain's massive beast exploded through the trees. He reduced down into a man while on the run, reaching me right as the fingers finished their swipe through the air. He grabbed me in his strong arms and turned, showing the creature his back. I heard his intake of breath, felt him tense, as the blow landed.

"No, Nyfain—!"

He bodily tossed me, throwing me up and over the tightening circle of creatures. I fell on my side and rolled, my wounds crying out and new bruises springing up all over my body. The creatures rushed in as he increased in size back to his beast. Another swipe scraped harmlessly across the scales of his mighty foot. He stomped on one, flattening it. Then another, all the creatures conveniently close together and easy for him to take out. They quickly figured that out, though, and increased their circumference.

He turned and knocked one with his tail. That creature slammed against a tree trunk and slid to the ground. He turned again and got two more before kicking out with his hind foot and raking his claws up the face of the last.

It was over in moments, all the creatures smooshed, knocked against trees, or missing faces and half their chests.

He reduced down and ran at me, falling to his knees at my side.

"Finley, are you okay? Oh goddess, Finley." It sounded like he was begging.

He laid me out flat and ran his hands across my chest, looking for the source of the most blood.

"No, it's fine." I waved my good arm at him. "Just some scratches and bites. It's fine. Hannon will patch me right up—"

"Their bite is poisonous. We have to get you—"

I flinched as he handled my arm. "It wasn't from them. It was from some hellhound thing with a fin. But one of them scratched you. How poisonous?"

"It's fine, don't worry about me." He ripped into my pants so he could see the scratches on my legs.

"*How poisonous?*" I demanded, pushing through the pain to sit up.

He glanced at me and then did a double take. His look conveyed all I needed to know.

"Hurry," I said, shoving him away and struggling to stand.

He threaded one arm under my legs and another

A RUIN OF ROSES

around my back then stood and cradled me against his chest. "I'll walk you there as far as I can. When the poison takes hold, you'll have to make it the rest of the way on your own. There is everlass and bandages—"

I yanked up my animal and owned the power she'd taken from Nyfain's dragon. With every ounce of fear and urgency I possessed, all of my will, I said, "Take me to my village, *now!*"

His animal roared to the surface. Power rode his response, pushing back on someone telling him what to do. My animal was there to meet him, iron and fire and salt and stubbornness.

"Do it," we said. "*Now!*"

His muscles popped as he fought it, and then he turned. I didn't know who was in control, my animal or me, and I didn't much care. I just needed him to get to safety.

"Let me walk. You don't need to carry me," I told him, tapping his shoulder.

"Don't push it," he growled.

Right. Pick my battles.

"Are there any more creatures to worry about?" I asked as he started to jog.

"No. The wood is mostly clear. I would've reached you sooner, but creatures kept crossing my path, as though they were purposely preventing me from getting to you."

"Are there always this many?"

"There is a portal from the demon kingdom to ours, powered by the curse's magic. On the first day after a full moon, when my power dips, they let in more creatures than normal. He is trying to kill me, of course. The consolation prize is my disfigurement. I collect scars as children collect stones. But finally...he might have managed it."

"He didn't manage anything. I can fix you. Did you know that in many kingdoms, children collect shells because they aren't landlocked by wood like we are? Wouldn't that be nice?"

"Instead of collecting nature's bounty, they collect the houses of dead sea creatures?"

I blinked a few times. "Those houses are really pretty, though. And the sea creatures aren't using them anymore, so..."

"Your distraction techniques need work."

"So, if you're not distracted, I might as well ask...how badly does it hurt?"

"Like a motherfucker, actually. But not as badly as it would hurt if it had been you."

I was suddenly choked up, not knowing what to say. Not knowing why he would say that. Not knowing if it was true.

He stalled by the edge of the wood. "I need some power."

"Sure, yeah, let me just…ask Saltier Finley…"

*Need more power.*

So it wasn't technically a question.

"Do you still suppress her?" he asked as a wave of power washed through me and into him, carrying a bit of me and my animal with it. I sighed at the sensation of the stronger connection between us. A dangerous feeling to enjoy. Did I never learn my lesson?

"No, but…she handles the power supply because she seems to understand the mechanics of it, and I do not."

He stepped through the barrier, and I felt him tense again. "It's easier to cross with you."

He continued at a quick pace, walking between the wood and the houses backing up to it. I noticed he took a roundabout path, clearly being careful not to pass the area where demons habitually strolled or lounged or got/gave blowjobs. The houses we passed belonged to humans who didn't mess with demons on the regular, and most had dark windows. This path spoke of familiarity and practice.

"You were lying again," I said as he wound closer, "about coming to check on me instead of waiting for me to go into the wood."

"Omitting more than lying, but yes. Since you turned eighteen, I have visited from time to time, more often in the last few years."

"How could I not know? How come I've never heard about a strange man stalking this village?"

"Because it was dark, and demons come and go. What would they care about another face they don't know? I was careful not to be seen, though."

"Why did you come?"

"Curiosity. I wondered about the everlass and then the conundrum of your village's declining death rate, but I wasn't smart enough to make the connection. It seemed impossible that someone could devise an elixir to help. I wondered if maybe your numbers had dwindled to a red line."

"But if you've been around, how come my animal just recently pushed forward?"

"Shifters hit their max power at twenty-five. You are…twenty-three, correct? You're still building."

"How old are you?"

He finally reached my lane, sticking to the shadows as he worked his way up. "Time froze for me at twenty-five. All experiences but voyeurism and nightly ground-bound battles stopped. I've had no experiences of note, nothing new to learn, and no new society to invigorate me or help me mature. I'm a budding shifter adult trapped like a fly in honey."

Something stirred inside of me, and I said, "I feel old and young at the same time. My childhood turned quickly to panic, disease, and strife. Danger forced me to mature too quickly. I feel like I've lived two lifetimes in just sixteen years."

"It's strange, the way it happened. Time stopping in the castle while it marches on in the villages."

He stopped at the door to my family home, setting me down gently. His balance tipped, and he stumbled into the doorframe. He braced his hand against the wood and straightened up.

"I don't think you'll see me again, Finley," he said, his eyes taking in my face. "You're an incredible woman. You have a bright future. This curse prepared you for a life of survival." He paused, swallowed, and then added, "The demon king loves beauty. He collects it, like trophies. With people, he likes them to loiter around his court and carry golden trays of food and wine for his guests. Make a deal and get your family out of here. Just hide that fierce determination. Hide your power and ability to lead. Hide everything that makes you great. It's within your power."

"Stop talking crazy." I rapped on the door before grabbing his big shoulder and turning him. He leaned his forearm against the frame this time, bowing.

"Normally I wouldn't let you see my back," he murmured, slurring a bit.

"How long do I have?" There wasn't enough light for me to see the wound clearly.

"I honestly don't know. I've never felt their poison. We have some antiserum, but it is decades old. I doubt it still works. There's nothing to cure me, Finley. Just let me go. Please, just let me finally go."

I rapped on the door again before spinning him around. I slapped him across the face. His eyes sparked fire. Good. Anger was good.

"I will fix this, do you hear me? Our library has a book on poisons. Well, it's mostly about trees, but it also talks about a bunch of natural poisons. There is this—"

The door swung open, the light from inside making me squint. Hannon stood there with wide, disbelieving eyes.

I stepped forward and slapped him across the face, too. Just so he knew I wasn't a ghost.

"This guy got hurt saving my life. I need to work on him, and then you need to work on me."

Hannon yanked me forward into a tight hug, shaking.

"We don't have time, Hannon," I wheezed.

He pushed me away before quickly assessing my

wounds. "How bad?"

"Me? Not terrible. I can wait."

He nodded and looked behind me. His eyes widened, and I followed his gaze. I sucked in a startled breath at the sight of Nyfain's back. The claw marks were pure black, the skin around them torn and puffy, and black lines streaked from the wound.

My gaze shot to another injury—rough scars ran down each side, starting at his shoulder blades and running down to the middle of his back. These injuries were old, the skin almost waxy and lighter than his tanned back. Sixteen years old, I'd bet. They looked like the kind of scars one might get after their wings were shorn. That was clearly why he didn't want to show me his back. He was embarrassed about what the curse had done to his animal. To him.

My heart constricted. Tears washed over my eyes. I barely knew my animal, and I would hate for her to be hurt like that. It would be like someone cutting off both of my arms.

One thing at a time, though. I couldn't heal that. I could heal what was happening to him from the poison.

Hopefully.

"Hurry," Hannon said, pushing me out of the way and reaching for Nyfain. "It's going to be fine. Take it easy now."

"Put him in my bed," I told Hannon as we labored Nyfain down the hall. His movements were sluggish, and his shoulders stooped. "I need to break into the library and try to figure out what kind of poison that is—"

"The poison of a Fah Rahlen," Nyfain said as Dash and Sable ran out of their rooms with wide eyes.

"Finley!" they said at the same time, rushing forward to hug me and, in so doing, hug Nyfain.

"It's a creature the demon king creates from the souls of the twisted, and a special blend of his magic," he said. "The poison is not well known."

"You didn't think anyone knew how to work with everlass, either. And yet..." We struggled with him through the door as coughing sounded from Father's bedroom. "One thing at a time," I told myself, remembering to breathe. "Help one person at a time."

"Poor Finley," Nyfain said, slurring. "The world on your shoulders."

"I need to break into the library," I repeated to Hannon as we settled Nyfain on his stomach.

"Hmm, it smells like you," Nyfain murmured. "I'd know that smell anywhere."

"Who is this guy, Finley?" Sable asked.

"Long story—"

"You're looking for that book on trees that you had

before the beast—" Hannon's words cut off in a rush of emotion. I met his eyes over Nyfain. He shrugged. "I heard you talking outside. I needed to make sure it was you before I opened the door. We've been worried the beast might come for us."

"Yes, of course. And yes, that book."

He shrugged again. "I didn't have the heart to take it back. I was hoping you'd show up and do that for me."

I put my hand on his shoulder. "Bless you, Hannon. Where is it?"

"Where you left it. On the table by the door."

I'd clearly missed it, not that I'd been looking.

"Here!" Dash ran into the room holding three thick volumes, struggling under the weight. "Hannon, Sable, and I have been researching. The other ones won't help you, but these might. They're about the different kingdoms, and there is one about the demon kingdom. Hannon didn't see any blood, and he saw tracks of the beast, so we thought that maybe he was taking you back to the demon king. We were going to save you."

Hannon gave me a helpless look. "We couldn't not try to help in some way."

"True grit," Nyfain mumbled into my pillow.

"Yes, of course." I scowled at Hannon. "Give me that, Dash. Let me refresh my memory. It's been a while since I read it. And here. I have some everlass leaves.

Can you go set them out? I'll need them."

I pulled out all the leaves and grabbed the volume with information about the demon kingdom, huddling near the candle to read. It took me no time at all to find the section on demonic creatures. I remembered being mildly interested in those a few years ago. As I suspected, though, the book didn't mention this particular breed of nasty.

"The type of poison…" I flipped through the tree book, knowing that the information on poisons was interspersed with facts about trees. The idea was to give the illusion that it was an innocuous book. I'd actually checked it out to read up on the birch, but whatever.

Returning to Nyfain's sickbed, I sat near his head. Hannon was working on cleaning his back, and the kids, Dash fresh in from outside, looked on.

"Tell me about the poison," I said as I refamiliarized myself with the contents of the book. If only I'd chosen to leaf through this one the night I was taken, and actually stayed awake long enough to learn something, I would have had a head start. "Every detail you can remember. I already have the color."

Nyfain gave me what he could, but it wasn't much. As he listed what he knew, his words became more and more slurred.

Hannon reached over and peeled his lids open.

"Eyes are clear, not bloodshot." He put the back of his hand to Nyfain's forehead. "High fever. Dash, go outside and get some cold water from the bucket. Sable, get some bandages."

Dash ran down the hall, his feet light as a feather. That kid would make an excellent spy. Or thief.

"He can't die," I said as I hurried through the pages of the tree-slash-poison book, already knowing I wouldn't find any answers. "Hannon, he cannot die."

"You like him, then? Where'd you meet him? Where have you been?"

He applied cream to the claw marks. Nyfain jerked, his eyes snapping open and finding me immediately. After a moment, they closed again.

"I don't like him. Or at least…it's complicated. Just… He cannot die. Our future depends on it."

Hannon studied me for a moment before going back to it. Dash showed up with the bucket, and Sable sat at Nyfain's head. She dipped the cloth in and delicately applied it to his forehead.

"Your family is extremely competent, princess," Nyfain mumbled.

"Is he mocking you?" Sable took the cloth away, scowling.

"Sable, when you are with a patient, it is not for you to judge him," Hannon said in a level voice. "Only the goddess may do that."

"Go ahead and judge me, Sable," Nyfain said. "Your sister does."

I blocked them out, poring over the poisons. Nothing perfectly matched the characteristics of the Fah Rahlen poison, though that wasn't much of a surprise. The book chronicled natural poisons.

"Those creatures were created," I said softly. "Sable, let Dash do that. Come over here and get ready to write things down."

"What do you have?" Hannon asked.

"Those creatures were created. They are a mix of…evil and garbage, I don't know. Their poison doesn't come from nature. It's not one thing, it is a collection of multiple things, and therefore I need to mix up various components to get the right antidote." I waved my hand at Hannon. "It makes sense, I promise. I just need to start working it out. It's risky…but if I get it wrong, he was going to die anyway."

"That's the spirit," Nyfain murmured, running his hands up to clutch the pillow.

A crooked grin worked up Sable's face. "I like him, Finley," she whispered.

"You're the only one," he said. "It's not burning. It feels like it is digging down into my back. Like it is sizzling against my spine."

I nodded and got to work.

FIFTEEN MINUTES LATER, and with a few more details about Nyfain's incredible pain, I was outside with Sable. She held the parchment, ready to read off the ingredients for my makeshift healing potion, but I didn't need the list. I *felt* what was needed.

I found the crowded everlass exactly as I had left it. I'd never actually used it before. I stared at it for a moment.

"But Finley—"

"I know, Dash. I know. It's just that…"

I couldn't explain it. I couldn't put to words the rightness of this feeling. It was crazy, this idea. Risky. But something about it felt right.

This plant could act as a poison because it was so potent. It attacked the body. But what if that only happened when it didn't have a strong enough ailment to fight? What would it do if introduced to the system of someone who'd been dosed with a poison that ate through flesh and blood?

Everlass's main goal was to heal. Sometimes it wasn't enough, so someone had figured out a way to make it more potent. The unfortunate side effects of using too much crowded everlass, or not using it on a big enough job, was…death.

This was as big of a job as they came.

"Goddess help me." I closed my eyes and brushed my hands over the plant. "I need help here. He's one of your own. How much do I use?"

I ran my fingertips across its leaves. Then under, by the stem. A soft feeling drifted through me. Peaceful, almost.

I remembered the song that Nyfain had sung.

Without a moment to spare, I ran into the house and crouched by his head. He was shaking and covered with perspiration. Hannon looked grim. That was a very bad sign.

"Nyfain." I rested my hand on his bare shoulder, covered in scars.

He jolted. "Finley," he breathed.

"I need you to sing that song. The everlass song, remember? When we were harvesting? I need you to sing that song for me."

His lips barely moved. His voice came out wobbly at first, but it grew stronger as it rose and fell in that beautiful symphony.

"How bad?" I asked Hannon. "How close to death?"

He shook his head slowly. Hannon didn't quite know, but it was not looking good.

"How aggressive is that poison?" I asked.

"Incredibly," Nyfain mumbled. "It was made to kill quickly and gruesomely."

I bent over him, getting right in front of his face. "Do you know how much of a crowded everlass plant to use with a gruesome and aggressive poison? Did your mother ever mention it?"

His lips stretched into a sublime smile, so full and soft. I remembered the feel of them. The rush of his kiss.

His voice rumbled even though it wasn't much more than a whisper. I could feel it in my chest, as though it were tethered there. "You just figured that out on your own, didn't you?"

"I'm right, then." I blew out a breath. Then pointed at Sable. "Go sing that song to the crowded everlass plant."

"You are such a clever girl, Finley," Nyfain went on, reaching out his hand. I took it—too warm to the touch. His fever was raging. "I half suspected all this time that someone had been feeding you our family secrets on the sly. Preposterous notion, but all the same…"

"He's headed into delirium with the fever," Hannon warned. "If you are going to do something, do it now."

"But here I am, watching you figure out the cure to save me. I wasn't going to tell you. Mostly because I don't actually know the details, but also because my mother passed the secret down to me, and I swore only to tell my family line if they were dragons. Unbelievable. You'll do things with everlass the faeries have only dreamed of."

I shook his hand. "How many leaves?"

"For this, probably two. But start with one in case you have a very pissy plant."

I squeezed his hand and returned it, belatedly realizing that he hadn't opened his eyes once through our whole exchange.

Back outside, Sable was singing to the plant in pitch-perfect soprano. She was unconsciously playing with the leaves as she did so, and I couldn't help a grin at the thought that she was doing something Nyfain's mother once had. I wished I could've known his mother. Or her people.

I'd think about the absurdity of knowing a queen another time.

"Thanks." I ducked down beside her and then paused. I hadn't asked whether they should be dried first. Then again, I didn't have time to dry them anyway.

I plucked one of the healthier ones because I knew the withering leaves were even more unpredictable. If I didn't use enough, I could always add more. Too much, and I'd need to reach for a shovel.

"Here goes nothing," I said, working the everlass like I might for any ailment, only now adding dashes of other herbs. I worked outside in the fresh air, keeping focus.

"He's bad, Finley," Dash said, at the back door. I hadn't heard his approach. "Hannon says you have very little time."

"Cuntcycles," I muttered. I'd been working over an open flame. This was going to be hot. I grabbed a tea mug and scooped up the contents.

Back in my room, Nyfain was groaning with his hands splayed off the sides of the bed, the backs of his fingers resting against the floor. The black of the poison had crawled nearly across his back and was working on his shoulders. His head felt like a furnace.

"Slap on some bandages; he needs to turn over onto his back and sit up." I put the antidote (hopefully) on the table and hurried over to help Hannon with the bandages. Once we had Nyfain's wounds covered up, I moved his legs to the ground and then pulled on the strength of my animal to help Hannon gently lift him.

"Since when are you so strong?" Hannon asked.

"There've been a lot of developments. Now is not the time. Also, did you know that people in the castle put on animal costumes and—Never mind. Now is definitely not the time."

My arm ached and my legs burned, but I ignored the pain. We got Nyfain on his back, but he wouldn't wake to sit up. His eyes fluttered, and he moaned.

"Okay, it's going to be fine. Here we go." I sat him up and then swung my leg over the bed behind him. I leaned against the headboard and had a startled Hannon help lean him back against me. I held out my hand, and Sable gave me the mug.

"It's still too hot," I murmured, then took a second to blow on it.

Nyfain groaned, and his hand came up toward my arm holding the mug.

"No, no. Someone grab his arm!"

Hannon reached over and took it, holding it down. Nyfain's other hand came up, searching. Just barely, I heard, "Finley."

"Okay, it's been enough time." I leaned closer to his ear. "You have to drink this, Nyfain." I infused the command with the strength of my animal, who was doing the mental equivalent of wringing her hands. "Drink this, Nyfain."

"His eyes are fluttering," Sable said, sitting on her bed and leaning over to look.

His head lifted just a little. Hannon bent to make sure he had both hands captured. I peered around Nyfain's face to line up the cup and tilt just a little.

"Dribble," Hannon said. "Sable, wipe it up quickly."

"Keep this mixture far away from your mouths," I said, the power of my animal still threading my voice. All my siblings froze. "Sorry. I'll explain later. Come on, Nyfain, you need more."

I fed him the elixir little by little, making sure he got most of it down. Then I waited for a moment.

"Most antidotes are a small amount of fluid," I said, going over what I knew and what I'd just read. "A vial's worth. But this cure isn't concentrated. I also might not have used enough."

"If it has any hope of working at all, it's bound to do something," Hannon said. "The everlass elixir you make only takes hours to work on Dad."

"I know, I know." I heaved a sigh and brushed Nyfain's hair back from his face. "I guess now we wait and see what our lives will become."

# CHAPTER 15

TWO HOURS LATER, I sat on Sable's bed covered in bandages, looking at Nyfain as he squirmed and thrashed. His fists clenched and unclenched. His head turned from one side to the other. He groaned, his forehead and back slicked with sweat.

I'd told my family the whole story, from the second I left the house to the second I returned, omitting only a few things. They'd gleaned that Nyfain was important, but they didn't know he was a prince. They thought he was a noble who had survived and had the fate of the kingdom resting on his shoulders. I hoped they were as gullible as I had been. And while they knew about the castle of nightmares, I obviously hadn't gone into detail about the nature of those nightmares. The kids were present, after all. But they got the general picture. I was sure Hannon connected the dots, given his knowledge of the demons that infested our village.

When I was finished, Sable asked, "But why he is covered in pain?"

The question took me aback. "Because he thinks he killed his mother and failed in protecting his kingdom."

"No." She screwed up her face. "That thing with his mother is just silly. Women don't die of broken hearts. That's just something people say to hide the neglect and mistreatment the women *actually* died of. But you said his momma thought of herself as a rosebush. Well, rosebushes don't give in to anybody. You can cut the hell out of them, think you killed them, and they grow a new shoot and come back from the dead. Rosebushes die from being stifled and cut off from the things they love, like water and sunshine. I bet it's the dad's fault. The dad killed her to bring the son back and then trap him. You tell me I'm wrong."

"You've been reading too many mysteries," Hannon murmured.

"Better than Dash's stupid picture novels," she said, and Dash threw a pillow at her. "*Anyway*, no, I wasn't talking about what his father did to him. That's obvious. I meant, why does he have all the scrapes and stuff all over his body? Is that what warriors always look like?"

More time passed as I watched Nyfain, moving as slowly as cold honey, Sable sleeping on the couch and just him and me in the room. More stirring from the bed. He lay facedown again, and I found myself looking at those thick indents running down his back. At the zigzags slicing through his flesh.

"Why do you really patrol the Forbidden Wood?" I said softly, leaning over to trace one of those wide scars. He shivered and moaned a little, stilling.

I got onto my knees beside the bed, tracing to the bottom of the scar and starting at the top again. He breathed deeply and turned his face my way, his eyes fluttering. It seemed to soothe him for some reason.

"It's because you're protecting all of us, isn't it? That's your duty." I surveyed the black lines from the poison, receding from his skin. The crowded everlass was working. If those lines weren't nearly gone in another hour and a half, I'd give him a tiny bit more of the elixir.

I thought back over the years. Back then, we'd had visitors more violent than the incubi. Those creatures had terrorized the town and killed anyone they could. I remembered the fear and panic. My parents had made us hide under the bed until the threat was gone, just in case they busted into the house. We'd been religious about locking the doors and closing the shutters.

Over time, that threat had diminished, though. I couldn't remember the last time it had happened.

Now I realized it was because of Nyfain. He'd clearly gone through a steep learning curve, and now he patrolled the wood every night, killing the violent creatures before they could reach the villages.

"The demon king is playing a game with you, right?" I asked, smoothing his tousled hair from his high forehead. "He made it so you couldn't go into the villages but his creations could. At the start, at least. The game is that you need to find and kill them before they make it into the villages and prey on the people. Your people."

What a slimy snake. No, calling the demon king a snake was a disservice to snakes.

"I wish I could help you." I traced his strong jaw and then down the scar along the edge of his full, shapely lips. "I wish I could shift and help you. I know my animal would be all for it."

His eyes fluttered open. Hooded and drowsy but open.

A rush of excitement ran through me. I moved a little closer to his head.

"Hey," I whispered, tears stinging the backs of my eyes. "How are you feeling?"

He opened his hand closest to me and moved it a little in my direction. I took it, stroking the back with my thumb.

"Will a pain reducer mess with the everlass?" I asked, putting my other hand on his head now and gently stroking his forehead. "I might be able to figure some stuff out, but the rest is trial and error. I'd rather not try with you right now and mess up."

"Please." His voice was barely more than a whisper. Scratchier than normal.

"Water, right? Do you need water?" I moved to get up, but his hand held me firm, still incredibly strong.

"Stay with me," he rasped.

I cupped his hand. "Of course I will. I'm watching you to see if you need more of the draught. We'll get you out of this, okay? You will live to fight another day."

"Please. Keep talking. It helps me know that...I am still part of this world. The other side is sucking at me. I long to give in. But for you, I would have already. The last sixteen years...have been misery. Each day has been worse than the last. I am so tired, Finley. I am so tired of this nightmare."

Fear pierced my heart. I squeezed his hand between mine.

"More everlass, then? Do you need more now? I know you promised your mother not to voice the family secret, and we will absolutely fight about that when you are well, but you need to help me help you right now, okay? She wouldn't want you to die so young. I know you think you're responsible for her death, but Sable said something, and I've been thinking about it. Your mother loved you. She would've wanted you to be happy. She missed her home"—I was assuming that part from the things he'd said—"and she wouldn't begrudge you for leaving. She ended up in a loveless marriage with a mad husband and wasn't even allowed to speak her ancestral language. Why the hell would she want that for you? I mean, look at me. I am not like the other women in this village. I'm wild, and I hunt, and I take risks, and I come home a bloody mess. I don't care about pretty dresses with ruffles or whether the town hunk wants to marry me…"

His hand squeezed mine, and his body tensed. I blew out a slow breath, checking over those lines on his back again. They were still receding. Maybe there were just a few jolts of pain as they did so.

I kept talking.

"I've been this way since I was a kid. People used to tell my mom that she shouldn't allow me to hang out with Hannon so much. That I was a bad influence on him because he's gentle and kind and lovely. But she could be as stubborn as a rock. She ruled this house. She would not allow anyone to cow me. She let me wear whatever I wanted. She let me do as I pleased, so long as

I was respectful. She trusted me to make the right choices. That's what mothers do—they guide. They strengthen. They support, and they never stop loving their children. Never. I doubt a rosebush would begrudge her son his wild spirit."

Tears filled my eyes. "I miss her so much," I confessed, leaning forward and laying my cheek against the pillow by his head. "I couldn't save her. The recipe for the nulling elixir wasn't as good back then. I ran out of time. But you know what? I have to remember that it ultimately wasn't my fault. The curse and the sickness killed her. I couldn't beat it at that time, but I will beat it in time for Father. I will. I will not lose another."

I stroked his cheek, my other hand still around his.

"You know, they were right about Hannon being nicer than me. My mom always argued I'd be a lost cause without him. He hates hunting and fishing and drinking pints in the pub with the lads. He thinks they are all thickheaded apes. He's right, obviously. He'd actually like the whole hobby situation at the castle. He could probably make a really pretty watercolor. He's super good at sewing and needlepoint. And you've seen how he can nurse people. He and I are as opposite as opposites could be. It's why we make an excellent team. I'm good at all the things he hates, and he's good at all the things I hate."

"He needs a strong mate," Nyfain rasped.

I startled. Then blushed in embarrassment. He'd said to keep talking, true, but I hadn't realized he'd sift through each word.

"Yeah. But there are none in this village. I mean, that's not true. I'm sure there are strong women; they just won't go against the grain. No one has approached me, for example, to learn how to hunt. Except Sable. I was teaching her about traps and small game before meeting you. But she also likes frilly dresses and looking pretty, so she can hide her weirdness a little better than I could."

"I like your weirdness."

"I didn't think you liked anything of mine."

"Water, please."

"Right. Yes, of course." I pushed back to get up, but one of my legs had fallen asleep. It gave out, and I dropped like a stone, hitting the edge of Sable's bed and clattering to the floor. "Dang it."

He jerked and then groaned, his eyes peeling open to peer over the bed.

"I'm good." I gave him a thumbs-up as I crawled onto the bed. "All good."

The bedroom door opened, and Hannon stuck in his bleary face. "What happened?"

"I need water for him. My leg fell asleep, and I fell

on my head."

He rolled his eyes and moved across the room to the water pitcher. He picked it up and filled a tin cup. As he bent to give it to Nyfain, I lifted back onto the bed and started to pound the feeling back into my leg.

"Can you sit up, or should we help you?" Hannon asked.

Nyfain tried to lift himself, but his arms gave out, and he fell back down to the mattress. "This bed is as hard as rocks."

"Same denseness as your head, then," I said without meaning to.

He grinned as Hannon moved to the other side and waited for me.

"You will go sit at the right hand of the goddess when you die, Hannon," Nyfain said as I got up to help. Invisible pins and needles stabbed my leg. "You deserve the highest honor in death for dealing with a sister like that all your life."

"Apparently you're feeling better," I grumbled as Hannon and I turned him over and propped him up.

"How do you feel?" Hannon asked, turning nurse again. "Has the pain receded?"

"A bit. It is biting deep into my bones, but it is no longer throbbing. Small miracles."

"Do you need more elixir?" I asked, taking the cup

from Hannon. Nyfain's clumsy hand came up to take it, and I batted it away. "You'll end up spilling it. You're an invalid—act that way."

His lips tweaked upward. "Yes, ma'am."

He drank the contents, spilling the last bit out the corner of his mouth.

"That's enough for now," Hannon said softly.

I put the cup on the ground, and we turned Nyfain back over. He let out a ragged cough and gripped the pillow, but settled down, his face still angled to look at me.

"I'm in the next room if you need me," Hannon said, holding out his hand.

I deposited the cup into his waiting palm. He nodded and made his way out the door.

"What will he do with it?" Nyfain asked, coughing a little more and then groaning.

"With what, the cup?" I got a weak nod. "Wash it. There's another up there. When that one is clean, he'll bring back the first. He's really big on cleanliness when it comes to nursing people."

"As he should. You two do make a good team."

"Yeah. We were raised in hard times, with very few people to lean on."

"No, no more elixir for now. I could use some of your power, though."

I prodded my animal, and a wave of power washed through me and into Nyfain. When it washed back, we caught it in confusion, and it diffused through my middle and sank down deep. I sucked in a startled breath. It felt like I was still connected to Nyfain through the power, or maybe magic. Or maybe just our animals, I didn't know. And while I couldn't specifically feel him, I could feel his essence. His imposing presence taking root deep inside of me. It was something I should probably be annoyed about, or worried about maybe, but right now I just wanted him whole again. The kingdom needed him. I'd deal with the repercussions when he was well.

I sighed and slunk down next to him.

"You should get a haircut," I said, laying my head on my arm this time as I twirled his hair with my fingers.

"I haven't cared about my appearance in a really long time. There has been no one to impress. No one I *wanted* to impress, at any rate."

"Well, thank you very little." I laughed softly. "I had a boyfriend once, and a couple of times I tried to dress up. I wanted to feel sexy and turn him on."

"What happened?"

"He got really weird about it. He said he didn't want to take me out around people looking *like that*. I wasn't exposed or anything. I didn't understand his problem. He came clean when he dumped me. He apparently thought that I'd flaunted my appearance to make him look *lesser*. Like he didn't deserve me. I guess he wanted me to kneel so he could stand taller. I was heartbroken at the time, so I didn't punch him for that as I ought to have…"

"Why would he look lesser for dating someone more attractive than him? I'd think other men would be clapping him on the back in congratulations."

"I don't know. I can only assume it had something to do with Jedrek, this dickface in the village. He wants to mate me mostly because of my appearance, I think. He's likely been thinking about this for a while. I bet he spread rumors or picked on my ex. Men's egos are so fragile. No offense."

"I wouldn't have gotten far if I took offense every time someone spoke the truth."

I laughed, trailing my fingers down his cheek. "That whole 'pretty' thing annoys me. Everyone's one and only compliment to me has always been about my appearance. It's all I get to be."

"What does that mean?"

"I'm so much more than my appearance. We all are. I'm as well read as I can be in this village. I'm smart and strong and good at problem solving. I have courage—

mostly. I've created various healing remedies people use, not to mention the one that keeps their family members alive. But I only get praise for being pretty. It feels like, in this village, if you're beautiful, you've reached the highest level of achievement for a woman— something none of us can control. Something given to me and that I didn't work for or have any choice in. And if you aren't perceived as beautiful, or if you don't play up your beauty, you're constantly told ways to fix yourself to look better—hair, makeup, clothes, whatever. As if we somehow need fixing because someone else doesn't like us the way we are. As if we should care what others think over what we think of ourselves. It's bullshit."

He didn't respond. I heaved out a sigh.

"I want to be known for what I *do*, not how I look. I want to be praised for my achievements. But in this village, I feel like all I am is pretty and full of flaws. I just... I just want something more, I guess."

"You will have it," he whispered, and I could tell his strength was failing him. He needed sleep. "You were meant for great things, Finley. Things this kingdom cannot provide you. One day you will see a crack in your cage, and you will fly."

# CHAPTER 16

I BLINKED MY eyes open and took a moment to get my bearings. The sun highlighted dust motes swimming lazily through the air of my room. I breathed in the familiar smells, happy to be home again. Happy to have gotten to see my family.

It took me a moment to realize Nyfain's eyes were open and staring at me.

A shock of panic made me suck in a breath and jerk, thinking it was a sightless gaze. Thinking he'd died between the time I crawled into Sable's bed in the early morning and now. He blinked, though, and resumed his stare.

I eased back to relax on my side, facing him.

"How do you feel?" I asked, bone-weary and my limbs aching. I'd needed stitches, salves, bandages, and rest, and I'd gotten everything but the last.

"How do *you* feel?"

"Great. I didn't almost die, though. Mostly because you saved me."

"I was the reason you ran away in the first place. The reason you even had to run away. The reason you are trapped in this kingdom—need I go on? I didn't save anything."

"Your surliness is back. You must be feeling better." I yawned and stretched, flopping to my back.

"How many of those creatures did you kill before I got there?"

I thought back. "I think only one. The rest I just stabbed with a pocketknife. It didn't seem to slow them down much."

"And you were hurt at the time?"

"Yeah. The hellhound with the fin got me. That wasn't pleasant. I think I'd rather take on boars. You can at least drop down on boars without worrying about being stabbed with a fin."

"Before that?"

"A dybbuk. He was nothing."

I turned my head to the side, meeting that beautiful gaze. The lighter gold streaks were highlighted by the sunlight filtering into the room. His wild hair and loose curls made his sharp cheekbones stand out.

"Did the curse change the color of your dragon's

scales?" I asked.

"Yes."

"Were your eyes always gold?"

"No. Close, though. Hazel. But something about forcing the shift burned my irises. Or maybe it is something baked into the curse, forcing me to remember what was lost. I need only look in a mirror."

I nodded and then pushed to sitting. I stretched again for good measure.

"You should get more sleep," he said. "You look terrible."

I swung my legs over the edge and stood, my pajama bottoms—which I'd put on fresh after patching myself up yesterday—falling to my ankles. I bent over him, running my fingers over his back. The black of the poison was all but gone. I pulled up some of the bandages covering the claw marks. Only a few blackened threads wove through the puffy pink-red wound.

"Normal everlass doesn't do much about poison," I said, biting my lip. "We might need to chance a little more of the crowded plant later. Maybe half a leaf or a quarter. I'll see in a few hours. You'll need to rest anyway."

"I need to get back to the castle." He made a move to get up.

I braced my palm between his shoulder blades,

keeping him put. "Yeah, because it's a *fantastic* idea to let the demons see you like this. You'd be easy to finish off, Nyfain. This kingdom can't have that. You will rest for a day or two, and then we can see. How's the pain?"

"I don't need to be coddled, princess. I can take care of myself."

I stepped back so he could see me from his prone position on the bed. I held up my hands. "Who are you talking to right now?" I looked around for show. "Are you under the impression someone in this room will believe your bullshit?"

His lips tweaked up in a small smile. "I guess just one person."

"Who?"

His smile spread wider. Him.

"Thought so." I smoothed his bandage back down and sat on the slice of bed near the edge. "I will try again, and let's try to cooperate this time, shall we? I know your weakness."

"Everyone knows my weakness—pushy, stubborn women."

I flattened my lips in a "you're lame" expression, even though he couldn't see it. "Not quite."

I put my finger to the top of one of his wing scars and lightly trailed down. He shivered, and goosebumps rolled over his flesh. He gripped the pillow in two fists and turned his face downward. A soft groan rumbled deep in his chest.

His muffled voice came from the pillow. "No, princess."

I felt a wicked grin cross my face. "How's the pain?" I asked, repositioning my finger at the top again and lightly pressing down.

The muscles along his back tightened. His bottom half moved, pushing his pelvis down into the mattress.

Was that simple touch enough to get him hard?

My core tightened. That thought right there was enough to make me wet.

I glanced back to make sure the door was closed. I knew I should back off. He needed to rest.

But the guy was sexy as hell, scars and all, and he'd been tormenting me for days. He deserved a little payback. The poison was under control for now, and the bandages would catch any blood that spilled if his gashes were irritated. Plus, he had all day to rest.

I couldn't help it. *He* couldn't help it, even with his bad attitude and surly demeanor. At least my animal would be proud, though I didn't reach for her because I didn't want her hijacking the scene.

I pushed the covers down, exposing that muscular butt.

"Do dragons have wings when they are in human

form?" I stroked a little. He groaned, and I could tell it was half pleasure, half pain as his shoulders and butt flexed, thrusting into my sheets. "I've never read that."

"No, they don't," he growled. "They have strips of scales, though, where wings might go. They were ripped out of my body when his wings were ripped off his back."

I flattened my palm next to the scar, above the bandages. "And that strip of scales…"

"Is incredibly erotic and forbidden."

"Why is it forbidden?" My voice was husky. I slid my hand up and grazed the top of the scar with my thumb.

He shivered again. "It's reserved for mates."

My lips curled a little higher. "What else is forbidden to princes that you have absolutely done?"

"No one has ever touched those scales."

"Oops. That's the second question you didn't answer. On purpose? I think so." I ran my thumb across it again. Then down, feather soft, barely touching.

"Oh goddess—Finley, please…you shouldn't—"

He wasn't fooling anyone.

A memory of his thumb tracing along my asshole made a few things click together very quickly.

"The demon king has the incubi and succubi in the castle—and villages—because a lot of that kinky sexual stuff was forbidden, right?"

I stroked up the scar. He breathed in deeply, his spine bowing and his pelvis pushing forward, grinding his hard cock into my bed.

"No anal, no orgies, no…flogging, certainly, right? No one tied up? I must admit, I have always been wary of being tied up—control issues—but when you had my hands pinned the other night, I was into it. I would let you tie me up, and blindfold me, and have me." His hips jerked forward, clearly at the image. "What about the salons? Ever visited one of those? Did you try any of that before the curse? I don't reckon the king could thoroughly regulate the whole kingdom, but he could certainly restrict the castle. Or at least try. Did the dutiful, honor-bound son follow the laws of the land?"

When he didn't answer, I returned the favor from the other night and ran a finger up his crack. "My ex used to like a little ass tickle and sometimes a poke when he was getting a blowjob. Did you ever try it? There's a very sensitive spot I know how to hit—"

"Do not talk to me about other men," he growled, and heat slithered down my spine. I felt my animal arch and purr within me. She did like when he went alpha.

"Have you ever tried it?" I asked in a husky voice as I traced a finger up along that scar again, still feather-light.

"No..." He pumped his hips forward. "Finley, please."

"Hmm, you're begging, Nyfain. I'm sure Mr. Big Bad Alpha was never supposed to beg."

On impulse, I leaned forward and licked the top of the scar.

His hips bucked. He let out a long, tortured moan. "When I am better, I am going to slam you against a wall and make you pay for all this. I will fuck you so hard you can't remember your name. You will never want another man so long as you live."

This was a dangerous game we were playing. His dragon wanted to claim me, after all. If I lost, I'd lose big.

Sometimes you just had to take the gamble.

"Big words, for an invalid." I licked again, then kissed softly, reaching over and rubbing his other scar.

"Finley," he sighed, his hips jerking now, humping my mattress. "Spread your legs in front of me. Let me taste you."

"Nah. I'll just finger myself while you get off on my bed."

"I'm pretending it's your pussy I'm rutting."

"Pretend all you want, but when we're done, you'll always think back on the way that common girl made you come for her in the most awkward way imaginable."

His groan was pleasure and torture again, and I laughed as I dipped my free hand below my waist. I felt along my slick wetness before dipping a finger in. I licked along his skin, rubbing softly with the other hand.

"Hmm," he said, then turned his head, looking at my arm dipped below his field of vision.

Rising, I knelt one knee on the edge of the bed and pushed my fingers into myself, my arm jumping with each thrust. I pulled them out and offered them to him. He sucked greedily.

I did want to position myself in front of him, to let him at my pussy like a starving man. But that would be a bit too much moving and tearing for his wounds, and besides, he hadn't let me have access to him in the past, and I'd intended to make him pay.

I jammed my hand back into my pants and bent to his back again, licking and sucking, rubbing his other scar. He lifted his ass and tried to reach down, shaking with the effort. I slapped his hand away.

"I need to get my cock right so I can defile your sheets."

I grinned wickedly, reached down under his body, and grabbed hold of that huge, beautiful cock. I salivated with the desire to suck it in, take it farther than I could comfortably go and then force it down even more. But not this time.

I stroked it twice in a firm grip, making him moan, before arranging it to point toward his chest. He lowered back down, thrusting immediately. I took a quick break to lock the door, then came back and pushed down my bottoms. What could I say? I'd never been great at self-control. I resumed my position, rubbing two fingers between my slick folds before dipping them into my pussy.

"Fucking hell, Finley."

I picked up our conversation, reminding him of where we were.

"Have you tried this before, Nyfain?" I ran a finger a little more firmly down his scar. "Have you ever watched a woman get herself off?"

"No," he wheezed, watching my fingers work, thrusting against my bed. "I need to fuck you, Finley. I need to fuck you so bad."

"Have you ever sunk your cock deep into a woman's ass?"

"Fuck—" He squeezed his eyes shut, pure pleasure soaking through his expression. He humped like he was rabid—big, strong movements that caught my eyes and trapped them. His body, even in pain, moved with graceful fluidity. He was quite the specimen. Powerful.

Raw. So fucking hot it shouldn't be allowed.

I stroked that fevered skin. Pounded my fingers into myself. Wished I had another hand so I could manipulate a nipple.

"Have you dreamed of me, Nyfain?" I asked, almost at an out-of-body experience. For some reason, it was so erotic holding the control right now. Taunting him. Playing with him. I knew the role reversal was driving him crazy with need. I knew he wanted to rise and steal that control back. To throw me under him and plunge deep into my wet depths. Dominate me until we were both spent and sanguine.

"Have you dreamed of fucking me?" I whispered, licking him again.

"Dreamed at night, daydreamed, fucked my hand raw replaying you arching into me, trying to force your breast a little deeper into my mouth. Or pumping against my fingers while I held you to the tree. Begging for my cock."

His ass released and then tightened. The bed shook with the power of it. My body wound up, and I plunged in time with his thrusts as he watched, his golden gaze glued to my fingers, shining with my wetness.

I bent again and sucked in a bit of skin, massaging with my tongue.

"No... I can't... It's... Fuck *me*!" He spasmed

against the bed, the whole thing shaking.

I worked a little faster, rising and closing my eyes as pleasure amplified. I took my hand away from him and ran it under my shirt, over my breast. I tweaked a nipple, and my orgasm stole over me. I moaned softly, shivering with pleasure.

When I was done, I was breathing heavily. Sweat coated my forehead.

I fluttered my eyes open, seeing that he'd risen onto his forearms, regardless of whatever pain it must have caused, so he could watch me finish.

I smiled and grabbed some clothes. I put those on before I flipped the top sheets over his bottom half.

"And now you will lie there in that wet spot until I have breakfast and come back to check on you. Take this as payback for the bouts of lady blue balls you've given me. Or, hell, for being a dick all those times."

I bent to grab my pajama bottoms off the floor, and he reached out and grabbed my shirt. He yanked me to him and claimed my lips. I opened my mouth in surprise, and he filled it with his tongue in a rush, swiping it through before plunging. His taste drove me wild. The electricity of our touch sizzled along my skin. My pulse fluttered.

He released me, and I staggered back, my lips tingling and swollen. My body starting to tighten already even though I'd just climaxed.

He must've seen the startled look on my face, because he smiled smugly before lying back down. "If you want my come soaking into your bed, princess, who am I to say boo? I'll need a wash later. I will look forward to you giving me a sponge bath. And no, I haven't done many things, including visiting one of those salons, though I've seen them in my travels. Yes, I've always wanted to. Yes, when you give me a commoner's rendition of it, I *will* want a happy ending."

"Dream on, Sir Alpha."

He chuckled darkly. "We'll see."

AFTER BREAKFAST, I checked on my father, only to find his situation deteriorating. Hannon met me by his bedside, his face grim.

"It's just been a couple days," I said. "Did you mix the elixir correctly?"

"Dash did it exactly the same way you always do. You know that he does it right."

I nodded, because he did. I ran my hand down my face, feeling sadness well up in me. "I have to get more creative. I have to think of something."

"You're not a miracle worker, Finley," he said sadly.

"You can't save everyone."

I was damn sure going to try.

I placed a chair next to the everlass plants and let my mind wander, thinking about the demons' magic. Thinking about the creatures I'd run into in the wood. Thinking about the poison in Nyfain.

Using a crowded everlass plant had killed the lady's husband down the lane, but maybe her elixir had been too strong. Or maybe the recipe itself needed to be tweaked to accommodate for the stronger healing agent.

It wasn't until I heard my name that I realized someone was in the yard with me. Also that tears were rolling down my face.

Unless something changed, quickly, I was about to lose another parent.

Nyfain had his arm around Hannon's shoulders, and Hannon's arm was looped around his waist, supporting him. Nyfain wore sweats that were too short and no shirt, showing off that muscled physique.

I wiped the wetness from my face and stood. "What's up?"

"Have a look at his wounds. He needs to be stitched up, but first we need to make sure the poison is gone."

I stepped around the chair and patted its back so Hannon would walk him over and sit him down. Nyfain's eyes stayed rooted to me as the guys moved closer, only pulling away when he had to sit. He bent forward, the bandages having already been taken off. No threads of black wove through the exposed pink flesh. Hannon had done his usual good job of cleaning it, too. No dirt, no dried blood.

"Yeah, he's good." I put my hand on Nyfain's shoulder. His muscles smoothed a little under my palm, as though he were relaxing. "We're getting to this in plenty of time, so they shouldn't scar."

"Let me guess, you've somehow managed to speed up healing or smooth out scars with your plants," Nyfain drawled.

"Both, yeah. You haven't noticed any scars on me, have you?"

"One at the top of your right breast. Another on your left butt cheek—"

"Right, yes, okay. Enough," I said.

Hannon's eyebrows shot up, and my face heated. Those scrapes hadn't been bad enough for me to suffer the embarrassment of Hannon doctoring it. Clearly Nyfain had been paying attention.

"Well...right." I dug my fingers into Nyfain's skin. "Except for the places I didn't have Hannon stitch up, obviously."

"Let's get him to the bucket, and you can wash him down," Hannon said, stepping to the side of Nyfain. "I'll stitch him up after that. Then he needs rest."

"I can't rest here. I need to get back to the castle. I'll be—"

"You'll rest here because it's much too far to crawl," I said, my tone infused with power and brooking no argument.

I could see the vein in the side of his jaw dance in irritation. He didn't comment, which meant he'd do as I said.

"Also, I am not going to clean him. You're the nurse, Hannon. You do it. I need to figure out something for Father."

"Finley, may I speak with you?" Hannon gestured me away from Nyfain.

"What's up?" I asked when we were a small distance away, around the corner of the house and in the side yard.

He spoke softly, his eyes assessing. "I would normally be happy to clean up a patient, as you know, to make sure it is done properly. But he asked earlier that you do it, and now you're trying to get out of it. It's clear you two are playing games with each other, and I do not plan to get in the way."

"But—"

He held up his hand. "I think you need to see this through, wherever it may lead."

"It could lead to death, Hannon."

"More than half of your ventures out of doors could always lead to death. You've never shied away from those."

"This is different."

He studied me for a moment. "Good. You need something new in your life. Now, remember to do a good and thorough job on him." Shivers coated my skin at the thought of what Nyfain had said about the salon. "Gashes from dirty claws infused with poison are a prime source of infection. It seems like he needs to get better in a hurry. Whatever games you're playing, you need to concentrate on what's important. His health. Put that first."

I breathed out slowly and nodded, nothing more than an annoyed jerk of my head.

Hannon took a beat and then asked, "Will you go back to the castle with him when he goes?"

*No* was on the tip of my tongue. It was sitting there, ready to be cast out into the world. But…the truth was…I didn't know. There were many reasons to stay in the village, and there were a few reasons to get to the castle, mostly to do with the gardening resources available to me there. That could really help my efforts to find a cure for the sickness, especially considering the crowded plant might be the missing link, and I didn't have much of that.

There was only one reason I was waffling, though—that big stack of muscle sitting in my backyard, covered in scars and ink, needing help protecting his kingdom. I wanted to provide that help, but I didn't know if I'd be able to resist giving him the rest of me as well.

# CHAPTER 17

HANNON AND I got Nyfain into the little wooden washing shed on the side of the house, an outdoor facility close to the water pump. Within, a smoldering fire heated a cast-iron pot—we called it "the bucket"—filled with water. The floor was made of wooden slats set over gravel, providing some drainage. We rallied the fire in the morning, took turns washing up, and then let the coals die until the next morning. At this point in the day, they were glowing embers, and the water wouldn't be more than warmish.

We stopped in the doorway, and I paused for Nyfain to make a disgusted sound or comment. Despite the kingdom's fall from grace, he was still a prince. He lived in a castle with indoor facilities. Even my lonely tower had a washroom with a nice tub.

Instead, he put his hand against the frame and said,

"I'll need that chair."

"Of course." Hannon ducked away, leaving us standing there in silence for a moment.

"I know you're used to finer things," I started lamely. "This is what we use, though."

"A kingdom is only as good as the poorest person," he murmured. "My mother used to tell me that. I'd never understood the gravity of it until now."

I stiffened defensively. "We don't have much, but we have enough. Before the curse, I remember happiness and smiles. Neighbors helping each other and monthly communal dinners. We didn't have bad lives— we just didn't have fancy tubs or towers to put our sidepiece abductees in. Even now, we all pull together as much as we can. Some people are the worst, but they help out. We don't let anyone go hungry. Your kingdom could do a lot worse than to be fashioned after our community."

"You're exactly right. I apologize for how that came across. I meant no disrespect, but I think your village was neglected by the crown. Your people were left to their own devices while still having to pay the tax. You didn't get your coppers' worth. Failure to properly take care of one's people creates a black mark on the kingdom, that's all. You should've had more."

"Here you go." Hannon wedged himself in with the

chair and set it on the wooden slats. He ducked down to work the fire, but I waved him away.

"I think our guest would benefit more from a cold bath."

Hannon stoked the fire anyway before testing the water. To Nyfain, he said, "It's warm enough. If you'd rather wait for me to build up the fire—"

"Not at all," Nyfain interjected. "Finley thinks this is fine, and so it must be fine."

The flat look Hannon gave me said he knew this was a continuation of our game, and he was not amused. He did not like any hint of tomfoolery where healing was concerned. Still, he excused himself and shut the door behind us. Nyfain "locked" the door with the little wooden peg that fit into intersecting round circles.

I rolled my eyes. "Like I said, dream on, *your highness.*"

"You haven't told Hannon who I am." He grimaced as I struggled to help him into the chair. "Why?"

"What would a prince be doing in a place like this?"

"Resting. Healing. Allowing a fiery little tart to save his life."

"Tart, is it?" I dipped my fingertips in the water before splashing it in his face.

His grin dissolved into chuckles.

"It would make them uncomfortable having the actual prince in our home."

The smile slipped off his face. "They'd be uncomfortable with what I've become."

I huffed out a joyless laugh before grabbing the waist of his sweats and tugging. He labored to lift so I could drag them off his legs. His semihard cock twitched against his leg, and I ignored my sudden urge to wrap my fingers around its girth.

"How could they have any opinion about what you've become when they have zero idea of what you used to be?" I said, draping the sweats over the rack against the wall by the door. "All nobles could be inked up and full of scars for all they know. Battle-hardened, basically. But as you yourself have frequently reminded me, there are very clear social differences between someone of your station and someone of ours. I just…I just don't want to hear how lucky I am to feel the condescending glow of the prince's attentions. To hear how lucky we are to have been graced with your presence. Not to mention one of the kids might tell someone, and we don't need the village knowing."

He watched me silently as I grabbed a sponge and some antiseptic serum that stung like a motherfucker. Could I have used a milder kind? Probably. Would I go easy on him? Absolutely not.

"I don't think rank means much anymore," Nyfain said quietly as I dipped the sponge into the lukewarm water. I then rubbed it on the soap stone and stalled at Nyfain's back. Now that the poison was gone, so was the evidence of danger. I was squeamish to rub soap over his pink-red, ragged skin. That seemed super gross for some reason.

I stepped to his side instead, deciding to start with his shoulder and work up to the back.

"Quite a change of heart from mockingly calling me princess and constantly pointing out that I'm a commoner."

"We all have to face reality eventually."

"That isn't reality, *highness*." I rubbed over his shoulder, picking up his arm and scrubbing down. "When this curse is over, things will go back to the way they were."

"If the curse is torn down, we'll be thrown into war. The demon king will try to take the territory." He gave me a significant look. "I'll be killed quickly, as will anyone who tries to stand beside me."

"There is always hope."

"So you say."

"You'd do well to believe it." I braced his hand on my shoulder as I dipped the sponge in the water and then rubbed it against the stone again. I washed down his side this time.

"I was incredibly impressed with your flight through the wood last night, by the way," he said. "The creatures you killed have taken the lives of many battle-hardened men. You killed and wounded several of the Fah Rahlen. With a *pocketknife*. That's unheard of."

"Except for you."

"I was in my beast form."

"Speaking of that." I dropped his arm with a rush of anger that wasn't wholly expected. His body dipped, but he caught himself, grimacing.

"I'm as weak as a day-old kitten," he grumbled.

That was the poison. His body would rally soon. I didn't bother explaining it, though. It wouldn't prevent him from groaning about it.

"What were you thinking, changing into a man to take a blow that you knew would be poisoned? Were you trying to find a way out of this life and your duty?"

"You'd rather I let *you* take the blow and surely die? As I said, we have an antiserum at the castle, but it was made before the curse. I had very little hope that it would still work, and less hope that I could mix the plants in the right way to cure you. You would've died."

"What I mean is, why didn't you stay in your dragon form, since the scales would thwart the attack?"

I took the clay pitcher from the shelf and poured

water on the soapy part of his side before moving to the other side. I wasn't ready for the front of him any more than the wounds on his back.

"Dragons aren't incredibly dexterous on the ground, and I had almost no time. With how tightly they were gathered around you and the angle I was coming in, I would've either stomped on you accidentally or the Fah Rahlen's blow would've landed before I could intercede. Shielding you was the only thing I could think of."

"Except you were putting the kingdom in peril to save one commoner."

"And I would do it again in a heartbeat."

My heart constricted. I struggled to hold on to my anger as I soaped up his side and moved for the pitcher. "I don't know why you came for me at all. You're trying to stay away from me. You want me to stay away from you. And yet you follow me instead of just letting me be free."

"I was worried about your safety. It was the worst night of the month to travel that wood. And also…"

He waited as I poured water over his soaped-up skin. He breathed out through his nose as though suddenly frustrated about something.

"I think we can help each other, Finley," he finally said.

I soaped up the sponge and hesitated. Gross wound or beguiling golden eyes, delicious, kissable lips, one hell of a torso, and a cock that was slowly gaining momentum in its quest to be the biggest thing in this room.

I stepped around to his back.

"I can supply you with knowledge about working with everlass that you probably don't already have. For example, the crowded plants do have more uses than what you know."

"Ah yes, the crowded everlass. We still need to talk about how you refused to give me that info so I could help save your life. We'll get to that, but I want you to be healthy first so I can give you a solid thumping."

"I look forward to it." I could hear the mischievousness in his voice. "Maybe we can devise something together that will help people like your dad."

"We can do that with me living here instead of the castle, though."

His shoulders hunched, and I couldn't tell if it was because I'd scrubbed across the claw marks or something else. I kept scrubbing regardless. It had to be done.

"Yes. We can. And maybe we should. You'll be safer here, I think. I can meet you and escort you to the everlass field in the Royal Wood. You can take all you require and come back here. I'll guarantee your safety."

"If I use the crowded plant, I might not need to go at night."

"And then you can stop seeing me entirely."

I swallowed the sudden lump in my throat, not sure what to say. That had been the plan when I left, right? To get away. To get some freedom. So why did I suddenly feel panicky and nervous about that idea?

My animal rolled through my chest, trying to force her way to the surface. Given Nyfain's sudden tenseness, I had a feeling he was fighting his animal as well. Forcing him back down.

I wanted to ask if everyone's animals acted liked sex-starved lunatics around alphas. Under different circumstances, would he have all the lady animals fighting for his attention?

But if things were normal, he wouldn't be here now. He wouldn't lower himself to bathing in a shed or sleeping in a crowded room. He wouldn't give me the time of day, that was for sure. He'd have a lot more options than a rogue chick running around in boys' clothing in the Forbidden Wood. So I didn't bother asking. I didn't want him to lie to placate me, and I definitely didn't want the truth.

"Your dad isn't well," Nyfain said into the silence.

I cleaned his back and waist before reaching for the

pitcher. "No. He's taken a turn for the worse. He doesn't have long. This will hurt." After washing off the wounds, I rubbed in the salve that would help him heal and greatly reduce the chances of scarring. He sucked a breath through his teeth, and his muscles rippled.

"Is that why you were crying?" he asked in a growl, clearly fighting off the pain.

"Yes. I was thinking through options for changing up the elixir. That was a side effect."

"I will help you as much as I can," he said softly as I continued to apply the salve.

"When it isn't your life in the balance, you'll be more forthcoming, is that it?"

It was meant as a joke, but it came out an accusation.

I took a deep breath, readied the sponge, and moved to his front. His cock had softened, likely a result of the pain. That helped a little. But those beautiful sunburst eyes, filled with sympathy and support, were almost my undoing. He knew exactly what I was going through, and he was trying to ease the blow.

"With regards to last night, I underestimated you," he said.

I washed his neck and down to his pecs, my movements slowing, my eyes feasting on all that glorious muscle. I didn't care about the scarring anymore. It didn't detract. The swirls of ink, some of which looked like ancient scrawls, I rather liked.

I stepped a little closer, my breathing shallower. His palms found the outsides of my legs.

"I don't know how to work with everlass like you do. I don't have the touch that my mother had. That you have. I only know the basics. I have never worked with a crowded everlass plant because it would likely mean death to whoever drank the concoction. As such, I couldn't really tell you about the antiserum recipe, could I? And if I told you it could work, you might've created something too powerful and killed me. That would've left a mark on you, I knew it would've. And now I have proof, seeing how your father's failing health torments you even though it is not even remotely your fault. I didn't want my death on your conscience. There was simply no need for it. So I didn't mention it."

"So that thing about your mother…"

"I lied. You're very gullible."

"But you underestimated me."

"Obviously. I could've mentioned it and cautioned you and saved you ten minutes of thought." He laughed, mostly to himself, it seemed like. "You're sharper with the plants than anyone I've ever known. And I've known the best. Your ability to not only reason out the answers, but to *feel* out the answers is remarkable. In the old days, it wouldn't have mattered where you came from—with that skill, you would've stood out. You would've elevated the standing of your entire family."

"In the old days, there would've been no reason for me to reason out the best elixirs. So no, I wouldn't have stood out."

He looked up as I poured water over his chest. He dipped his hands under my shirt and slid against the skin on my sides.

"You would stand out anywhere."

I let my gaze dip over the planes and angles of his face. The severity of his handsomeness was softened by his sparkling eyes and soft smile. I barely saw the scars now, looking instead at the man within. I couldn't hide the truth from myself any longer—the more I knew of him, the more I liked him, rough edges and all. I liked his growly personality, his bad moods, and his bursts of passion. I liked his thoughtfulness and protectiveness. Even his possessiveness fanned the blaze within me.

My animal within purred at that last thought because she liked it when he dominated us. When he held us captive and pleasured us until we begged for more.

It wasn't meant to be, though. I knew that. I knew this could never work.

But that didn't mean I couldn't give him a happy ending to this bath. I'd said I wouldn't, sure, but thankfully, he didn't seem like the type to gloat.

I wet the sponge again and slowly took care of his right leg, bathing the outside first and then the inside. I made slow circles, higher and higher, until I was nearly touching his balls. His breathing grew deeper, heavier. I poured the water, splashing myself in the process, turning my white shirt see-through. I did the same with the next leg, tantalizing him with my slow ministrations. I poured the water, rinsing off the soap, before softly kissing his inner thigh. Then I shifted to the other, trailing my tongue before sucking in his skin.

He sucked in a breath. I reached up and wet my hands before rubbing the soap stone, getting my palms sudsy. I caught his gaze, his eyes hooded and on fire, then ran my hands up the sides of his cock and down, scooping up his balls.

He groaned as I massaged, reaching down and tangling his fingers in my hair. I felt a soft tug, and my animal about surged to the surface. I forced her back down. She'd push us to go too far. I wasn't going to bang him with my cunt. No, I'd do it with my mouth instead. I'd get it hard, and get it deep, and I'd get myself off on holding the power between my teeth. It was as far as we would go.

I wrapped the fingers of one hand around his shaft and continued to massage his balls with the other. I pumped my hand and massaged, delighting in the feather-soft skin. I ran my finger over his tip, where precum had beaded. I worked the suds back down, pumping faster now, seeing his hips tilt and retreat. His fingers in my hair turned into a fist. He held me firm, and I moaned within that hold.

His breathing came fast. Mine was faster. My sex swelled, so wet, so desperate for him.

I couldn't wait. I couldn't do this slow. It was killing me.

I upended the pitcher over him, washing off the soap, and attacked his cock with my mouth. I licked the tip before sucking him down, taking him as deeply as I could go. I pushed up higher on my knees, shimmied closer. I pumped my hand and followed with my mouth, taking in more of his big cock with each bob of my head. He let me, his fist in my hair for show.

I didn't want a show. I wanted a hard face-fucking.

Opening a crack, I let the fire of my animal fill me. She slipped through as much as she was able, her power pulsing, but I was still in control.

Even still, a heady wave of Nyfain's dragon answered, power filling me. I popped my mouth off Nyfain's cock and closed my eyes as I soaked in that thick rush of blistering bliss. It tethered us—spicy, sweet, and sexy as hell.

"Yes, Nyfain," I groaned, still pumping him with my hand. Wanting to climb on top of him and sink down onto that cock.

He gripped my head harder and forced it down. My animal growled in ecstasy as he shoved up with his hips and parted my lips with the head of his cock. I softly scraped his shaft with my teeth. He growled in desire and flooded me with another rush of power. Then he yanked my hair, plunging in deep. My eyes watered, and I gripped his balls with one hand, tighter than a lover's caress. My fingernails of the other hand dug into his thigh.

*This is not quite right,* my animal cried in frustration, spurring me on nonetheless. I bobbed on his cock with reckless abandon, taking everything he had to give and begging for more. I reached down and ran my fingers through my wet pussy before massaging my clit.

*He needs to be in our cunt, not our face. We should fight, force him to dominate us to prove his worth and mate us with a passion he would show no other. Does the man not know where a cock is supposed to go? His dragon can help.*

*Shh.*

His movements got jerkier. Harder. His cock ravaged my throat. My chin banged against his balls. It was fierce and rough and brutal, and I was so fucking here for it. It was exactly what I'd wanted.

My finger kept going on my clit, winding up my body, and my spit bathed his cock and pooled around his balls. His thighs tightened, and his hand yanked my hair, and then he was groaning and filling my mouth. His release slid down my throat, and I backed off so I could swallow it all. Usually I didn't, but with him...I just fucking wanted to. None of this was thought out. I'd probably have reeled away if someone asked me two days ago whether I wanted to be roughly throat-fucked and get a mouthful of a man's climax, but here, in the moment... *Fuck yes.*

He pulled my hair so I'd have to stand, and I winced. He smashed his mouth to mine, apparently not at all concerned about tasting his saltiness on my lips, then yanked my pants down and slipped his fingers into my panties. My slick wetness made him groan.

"Come for me, baby girl," he growled softly, plunging in two fingers and working my clit with his thumb. "Come for me."

He kissed me, and I clutched his big shoulders and lost myself in his lips. In the expert movement of his hands. I groaned into his mouth as he pumped those fingers faster. He wrapped his other hand around my nape, deepening our kiss as he sucked my tongue into his mouth and rolled it with his. His kiss was deep and passionate and delicious, and before I knew it, I slammed into the ceiling with a toe-curling orgasm.

I cried out into his mouth, trying to pull away. He wouldn't let me, finishing me up as he nibbled my bottom lip. I melted against him, my knees buckling. He caught me before I bonelessly slid between his spread knees and guided my butt onto his thigh. His hold relaxed and his kiss changed, sweet now. Lingering, like he didn't want me to leave just yet.

*I liked the ending, but I still think he's doing it wrong,* my animal muttered grumpily.

I smiled and shoved her down. An echo of Nyfain's dragon vibrated within me until the feeling receded. He seemed just as annoyed.

"Can you feel my animal?" I asked Nyfain, pulling my arms from around him. "I mean…more than just her presence. Can you feel her mood?"

He constricted his arms around me, trying to keep me put.

"Let me up," I whispered, then snagged one more kiss. Feeling my heart ooze just a little.

My eyes snapped open, and I staggered out of his embrace. No, no to the heart-oozing thing. Admitting to liking the guy was one thing, but oozing hearts and what that might mean was entirely another. He was not someone I would be developing deep feelings for. I couldn't afford to lose my heart to him any more than I could let myself be claimed by him.

His gaze tracked me like a predator. He leaned back against the chair with a wince.

"You don't have the energy for...any of that. I shouldn't have..." I grabbed the pitcher and filled it with water, walking around to his back.

"Given me the best blowjob I've ever had?" he asked lightly. Shivers coated my skin, and I gritted my teeth against the pride warming my middle. "Shown me that no sex salon in any of the kingdoms could compare to you?"

"I don't need flattery. That's not happening again."

"I love when you make promises. The challenge to help you break them makes it all the sweeter."

So he was a gloater. Damn it.

I poured water over the claw gashes, only a small smear of blood running down his back. He hadn't overdone it. I added more salve to make sure they'd heal quickly.

"As for your animal, I can feel her better than you can feel mine, clearly. I can only feel traces of your—her moods, though. Only when your emotions are heightened in some way. That ability has probably been subdued by the curse."

"So it was normal back in the day?"

"To a degree," he said vaguely.

I put everything away and brought over a drying cloth. "What does that mean, to a degree? To what degree? How does it relate to us?"

He stood, using the back of the chair for a brace while I dried him. "All these questions." He sounded annoyed. "Aren't you well read? There are books about it."

"There are books on the history of shifters, on animal types and their rarity—things like that. That was all before the curse, though. Those authors assumed people knew the fundamentals of being a shifter. There aren't any books about that."

"In my library, perhaps."

"Right. Well. *Someone* hasn't granted me entrance to their library."

"Yes. Because *someone* ran away before I could give her a rundown."

"Fine. Well, when you come to escort me to the everlass fields, will you bring a book that explains it so I don't need to trouble you with my questions?"

"And how do you assume I'll carry it? They don't sew knapsacks for ground-bound dragons."

"Carry it in your mouth."

"And risk getting it soaked through with my spit? If you want to check out a book, you'll need to move back to the castle."

I huffed in annoyance and braved a hand on my hip. Instead of forcing me to come back, he was trying to lure me. And then, once I got there, he'd be back to telling me in one breath he wanted to lick my pussy and in the next he wanted to lock me in my room.

I rolled my eyes and went for the door. "Get yourself into the house. Better yet, crawl back to the castle like you planned to do earlier. Maybe a lesson on being humble will be good for you."

"I've had plenty of lessons on being humble. I certainly don't need one from you, *princess*. And if you don't help me back—"

I slammed the door behind me before he could deliver the threat. He was impossible. *Impossible!* He was like two opposites sharing a skin—come here, go away. Although maybe that was a natural result of sharing his skin with a dragon.

I wished he'd just say that, though. Or try to explain himself. This couldn't be the way of all shifters. It just couldn't. If it were, the orgies would have been worse than the ones hosted by the demons, and I was fairly sure those hadn't been a thing back in the day. I was definitely missing something here.

I wondered if Hadriel would tell me. Or if there was, indeed, a book about it.

Of course, I'd have to go back to the castle if I wanted to seek out either form of confirmation, and once I went back, that was probably it. I wouldn't be able to escape again.

# CHAPTER 18

THE NEXT MORNING, I woke up facing the window, and was surprised to feel a strange sense of melancholy. There was no reason for it. It had actually been a really great evening after Hannon rescued Nyfain from the wash-up shed.

Nyfain had watched me while I made some elixir for Father and then some healing elixir for him and myself, since my arm and legs still had some healing to do. Then Hannon made stew for dinner, and we'd all crowded around the little table to eat as a family, Nyfain not seeming anxious or out of sorts at all. He'd seemed quite comfortable, actually. After dinner, Nyfain and Sable had found a song they both knew and harmonized like two masters, serenading us all.

Bedtime had been…

I let my eyes flutter shut for a moment, a smile curling my lips.

Bedtime had been completely mundane, and I'd loved it. I'd honestly needed it. No sexual confusion or pushing of boundaries. No worrying about fighting my animal or holding the line. It was just...natural. Normal.

We'd all sat in the living room for a nightcap, sipping tea that Nyfain had been kind enough to make us to compensate for not helping with dinner or cleaning up. I would've refused, but Hannon said that Nyfain should move around some to keep his body limber. Making tea was an innocuous task. The flavors had been a bit odd, but what could you expect from a guy who'd had servants his whole life?

Feeling supremely relaxed, we'd all headed to bed. Sable slept on the couch, and I helped Nyfain settle into my bed on his back, the bandages still on. That done, I crossed the room to change into my own pajamas.

"Do you want me to close my eyes?" he asked, his voice low and soft.

The candlelight flickered against those sharp cheekbones, throwing shadow across his eyes. I shrugged, because it honestly didn't bother me to think of him watching, and started to change like I might've with Sable in the room. Even though I couldn't see his eyes, I could feel him tracking each movement, watching me put things away and pad over to Sable's bed.

After I settled, he lay with his face pointed toward me.

"Are you in pain?" I asked into the hush.

"Not at all," he murmured. "Your remedies put mine to shame. I'm nearly at one hundred percent."

"Not hardly. You can barely walk in a straight line. That poison did a number on your system. You're out of danger at least, though. You'll heal. You just need rest."

"I know." He paused for a moment as I got into bed, fluffing the pillow and tucking myself under the blankets. I lay on my side, facing him.

"Can I tell you something without you getting mad?" he asked.

"Probably not," I said honestly, chuckling.

He nodded but said what was on his mind anyway.

"You are incredibly beautiful to me, and I do not just mean your appearance or your body. Down to your soul, you are beautiful. You are so honest about who you are. So free with your thoughts and emotions. Growing up, everyone around me was guarded. So closed off. But you...you have this divine light about you. This pure honesty and goodness. It shows when you work the everlass, and it shines through in your healing gifts. Your thoughtful expressions are so lovely because I can practically see the wheels in that big brain of yours turning. You're so smart and capable, Finley. So tough and unyielding in your ability to survive. I am in awe of you. But most of all, I love your fire and your passion. I love that you refuse to let others dictate who you are. I love that you dig in and push back when I try to dominate you, challenging me to be better, stronger. It's arousing but also… It's just… You're perfect. I wish I were a poet so I could express it properly. When others look at you, they might see your surface beauty. I wanted you to know that when I look at you, I see the beauty of your soul, and I am in rapture. I see you, Finley. That is what I wanted to say. I see all of you, and you are beautiful."

A tear escaped my eye. I didn't know what to say. No one had ever said something like that to me before. Nyfain was genuine, too—I could hear it in his tone, and feel it in his words.

My lids tugged at me, the result of a stressful few days, no doubt, and the comfort of being safe at home.

I'd dreamed of him. Of a sweet kiss on my lips, and then battles, and war cries, and the golden dragon saving the kingdom. It had been very exciting, especially since it concluded with him between my thighs. Of all the dreams I'd had, that was one of the best.

The man had a firm grip on my heart, though. That

was definitely not good. I had to start distancing myself. Soon he'd be leaving, and I would let him. I had to. We were almost at the point of no return, and I could sense myself teetering on the verge of a very big mistake.

I blinked my eyes open and let the light wake me up. I felt a little hollow for some reason. I felt like something was missing. Maybe because I knew Nyfain would leave?

My animal rolled in my chest, trying to scratch her way to the surface. Her panic bled through.

Frowning, still bleary-eyed for some reason despite having slept through the night, I rolled onto my back. A soft cough came from next door, then another. Father was still hanging on.

I glanced at Nyfain as I sat up and stretched, careful not to make any noise. Then froze.

My animal scrabbled at me wildly. I shoved her down as a sick feeling curled in my gut. He was gone, the bed neatly made. There was no note. Maybe he'd just woken up before me and hadn't wanted to disturb me.

Down the hall, I found Hannon at the kitchen table, wiping his bloodshot eyes as he held his steaming mug with a death grip. He sagged, looking as tired as I felt.

"Hey," I said, catching Sable yawning on the couch. That was odd. Usually she was the first one up. "Have you guys seen Nyfain?"

"No. But I found his efforts from last night." Hannon's voice was flat, his eyes brimming with something I rarely saw in him—anger. "He wasn't subtle."

I shook my head. "He wasn't subtle about what?"

"I didn't clean up his ingredients. You'll know what they mean." He glanced beyond me to the kitchen and then held up the parchment. "And then there is this."

I grabbed the piece of parchment. The message, written in a delicate scrawl, read: *Someday you'll forgive me. Don't come after me; there'll be no point. This is where our acquaintance ends. This is for the best.*

There was a blank stretch of parchment, as if he'd struggled for what to write next.

*Remember, no cage can keep you for long. Find a way out, Finley, any way you can. You deserve to be free. Hopefully I'll meet you in the next life when there isn't so much standing between us. -N*

That sick feeling churned in my gut. My animal roiled. It didn't take a genius to know something was badly wrong. He'd clearly done something I wouldn't like.

*I'm not a nice guy.* He'd said it once. He'd meant it a dozen times.

Breathing deeply, I padded to the kitchen to see what Hannon was talking about. The ingredients were out on the counter, clear as day. Valerian root, chamomile, and a few herbs I had in my garden that promoted deep sleep. I gave them to my father in a different recipe when the coughing got too bad.

Nyfain had effectively drugged us, and I hadn't been the wiser because he'd chosen a collection of flavors designed to muddle the taste.

My animal kept pushing, desperate to be heard. I finally relented, opening a crack so we could communicate.

*He's gone,* she said, and her panic infused me. *I can't feel his magic connecting us anymore. He cut us off.*

"Finley, are your eyes glowing?" Sable said as her mouth dropped open. "Hannon, are her—"

I pushed Sable's words to the back of my mind, focusing instead on a strange, dark hole deep inside of us.

*He went back to the castle last night,* I said. *Obviously we wouldn't be able to feel his power from here.*

*You don't understand. Since that time we helped Hadriel, I've always had his dragon's presence with me. I thought that meant we were working toward mating and just waiting for you idiots to get your shit together. It got stronger when he was here. And now it's gone. He's ripped it away. He's broken the connection.*

*Why didn't I know about the connection?*

*Because you're dense? I don't know. He basically blasted us with it. I accepted, and there we were.*

That must've been what I'd thought was Nyfain's power washing through me, sometimes held by my animal, sometimes pushed back. They'd been playing footsie for days, but I hadn't realized it was anything permanent.

Except...she was saying it was no longer there. He'd severed it. He'd cut me out.

No, his dragon had. His dragon had apparently heard the things he'd said to me and chosen to walk away. Except animals didn't care about social stuff. They didn't care about kings and commoners. At least, mine didn't.

Maybe the dragon of a prince understood things a little better.

"He's gone," I said flatly, not sure how to feel.

Memories flooded me. How many times had Nyfain told me what would happen if the curse was broken? Hadriel had hinted at it, too.

The demon king had killed the defenders of the kingdom. He'd killed anyone capable, for goddess's sake. Anyone who could hold a sword or even just do their job well. Once the curse was broken, the demon king could kill Nyfain and move in. Nothing would stop him.

But that had always been the case, and Nyfain had done his duty anyway.

I remembered what he'd said the other night when the poison was taking hold.

*"The last sixteen years have been misery. Each day has been worse than the last. I am so tired, Finley. I am so tired of this nightmare that never seems to end."*

Fear lodged in my middle, blotting out reason.

He'd left here half healed. He'd ventured into the wood in a weak state at night, when the demons would be prowling. He hadn't a hope of defeating all of them in the state he was in.

But that hadn't mattered to him. He was a man of duty, late to the game, maybe, but now the only fierce defender of the kingdom. He'd try to clear the wood even in the state he was in. I knew he'd go out and die fighting, if that was his fate, and the curse would die with him. When it did, he'd expect me to make a deal with the demon king for my family and village. For my kingdom, if possible.

Didn't he know that was madness? I would never have let him put himself in jeopardy like this without trying to help—

And that was why he'd drugged me. Because he knew that I'd follow and try to help him. We'd always had our differences, and half the time he'd annoyed the shit out of me, but that didn't matter when it came to helping people. He knew I would go down with him if it came to it. And he clearly would not suffer putting me in harm's way.

Well, fuck that. I was not some delicate flower, and this time he'd gone too far.

I ran into my room, changed, grabbed my trusty pocketknife, an older dagger that would have to do, and ran out the front door. If he wanted me to play hero, I would.

And I'd make him my damsel.

## THE END

# About the Author

K.F. Breene is a Wall Street Journal, USA Today, Washington Post, Amazon Most Sold Charts and #1 Kindle Store bestselling author of paranormal romance, urban fantasy and fantasy novels. With over four million books sold, when she's not penning stories about magic and what goes bump in the night, she's sipping wine and planning shenanigans. She lives in Northern California with her husband, two children, and out of work treadmill.

Sign up for her newsletter to hear about the latest news and receive free bonus content.

www.kfbreene.com